ABOUT FACE

ABOUT FACE

CAROLE HOWARD

GLENMERE PRESS
WARWICK, NEW YORK

ISBN: 978-0-98529-485-4

Printed in the United States of America.

For Geoffrey, forever
and for Lisa, Jason, Nina, and Ezra

Acknowledgments

WRITING A NOVEL is a long process, and so many people helped me along the way, either with feedback on drafts, technical support, and/or encouragement. I thank them all: Laura, Polly, Fran, Lou, Juli, Glenn, Jim, Richard, Marilyn, Peggy, Tony, Anne, Joby, Elizabeth, Anita, Gretchen, Gini. Much gratitude and appreciation goes to my always-supportive, honest, and generous Writers' Group.

A special category of thanks to my center of gravity, my family: Geoffrey and Lisa—and now Jason, Nina, and Ezra too—who did it all.

PART I

1

Under the Table

RUTH TALBOT LOOKED DOWN AND WINCED. She couldn't believe today, of all days, she'd forgotten to change out of her commuter's red high-top sneakers into the pumps that would complete her corporate camouflage. From the knees up, she fit right in at the big meeting with the new CEO in the ultra-elegant conference room with small oil paintings in ornate frames. But her feet belonged in the playground.

"I want that list of criteria to go out to all our vendors right away. Right away. So they'll know exactly how Mimosa Inc. will decide whether they're in or out," Jeremy said.

The guy from Purchasing—was his name Ralph?—answered, his voice dissolving around the edges like a milk-dunked Oreo. "We use quite a lot of vendors, actually. We always have. And some of the criteria we use for them are difficult to quantify. They're intangible, really. We've always—"

"Intangible won't do. No, no. Won't do at all. We need to know exactly, *precisely*, how to decide who we'll do business with. Right away. Criteria on my desk by close-of-business tomorrow. Then out to the vendors next week."

Poor Purchasing-Guy. "Intangible" turned out to be a poor word choice.

"Next, the splashy launch of 'Lipsticks & Scarves,'" Jeremy said as he looked at Ruth with raised brows. "The results are … shall we say … very disappointing."

Disappointing? What's he talking about? Ruth cleared her throat and spoke a little louder than was necessary. "These results are well within our standard for pilot programs. We can make them better, yes, you're right about that. But that's why we pilot, so we can tinker with the variables. Price, size, packaging. Meanwhile, they're quite decent."

"Decent? Dee-cent, you say?"

Uh oh, she thought. Looks like "decent" goes in the garbage heap with "intangible."

"Maybe they are what you call … decent … but no more than that. Maybe under previous management, that was good enough." He looked around, making eye contact with everyone at the table, one by one, as if they didn't already know he was the new management. "But not now. There's a new sheriff in town, and now we need better than decent. We need a grand slam."

"I agree, that's the goal, a grand slam, but pilots are almost never grand slams. They're usually singles. This one, I think, was even a double."

I'm using baseball metaphors? How low can I go? Her disappointment in herself triggered the day's first hot flash, a bit earlier than usual. The fire started somewhere in her chest and galloped through her neck, up to her head, while also traveling south. She felt every thread of her clothing against the sweat-sheen on her skin. To her amazement, people had said they didn't notice anything, even when she thought she was ablaze.

"I was referring to a grand slam in *bridge*. All the tricks. Doubled and re-doubled. Lots and lots of points." Jeremy smiled a quick, minimal smile, managing to move only the muscles at the edge of his lips but not engage his cheeks or eyes. With his dry skin, sharp nose, and darting tongue, he looked like a snake. Or maybe he just needed moisturizer.

"What do you plan to do about this, Ruth?"

Rather than walking around as she spoke and revealing her

feet of canvas, she stood in place and grabbed the edge of the table. Richly grained walnut, highly polished, the color of dark rye toast with honey, it was the centerpiece of this room of beauty and good taste. Being here stimulated and calmed her senses at the same time, like walking along the beach.

The first few times at the table, she'd thought she could only say very important things. Now she knew the setting itself made anything sound very important. She concentrated on the rare pleasure of towering over people as she reviewed the figures that backed up their decision to launch the innovative packaging of lipsticks with matching scarves.

"The data told us loud and clear this was an idea worth pursuing. And the data were right, of course, based on our preliminary results. People didn't mind buying a lipstick to match one scarf if the set was appealing and the price was right." She looked over at Jeremy.

Disappointing? Don't be ridiculous.

"Just out of cur-i-o-s-it-y…," Jeremy dragged out each syllable with a deep, slow cadence to his voice, and Ruth could almost hear mournful cello music as accompaniment, "… who came up with this idea? Marketing? R&D? Perhaps even … even Dean himself?"

After forty years at the helm, Dean had sold Mimosa to B&D, a conglomerate looking to "feminize their offerings," as it said in the press releases. Jeremy had been B&D's Senior VP of Operations and was chosen to transform Mimosa from a small touchy-feely family-owned business to a rootin'-tootin' buttoned-down operation.

"You know, I honestly don't remember," Ruth said, catching a glimpse of Judy staring down at the table to avoid giving away her authorship. "Anyway, we work as a team, so it doesn't really matter."

She shuffled her papers for a second. "But you're right, we can make our results better. Why don't we turn our attention to how to do that."

Disappointing, indeed.

The rest of the meeting was no more boring than usual, and

they did come up with a plan to redesign the Lipsticks & Scarves campaign. Ruth hoped she and her sneakers could be the last to leave.

Ordinarily, she wouldn't have cared so much—she *was* senior management, after all, and had been at Mimosa for twenty-five years, so people paid more attention to her track record than her track shoes. But Jeremy had gotten rid of a bunch of people soon after he took over, quietly, no muss no fuss. Certainly, sneakers were not grounds for dismissal, but she didn't want to get off on the wrong foot. So to speak.

She took as long as she could to put her papers together and enter notes into her organizer/planner. Red for meetings, green for phone calls, blue for To-Do List entries. Pat Givens, Ruth's Assistant Product Specialist, made nice to Jeremy on her way out. Did she actually say she enjoyed the meeting?

But Jeremy out-waited Ruth. "I'll see you at the benefit tonight," he said to her.

Facing Jeremy in his perfectly-tailored suit, conservative tie, and bookish horn-rimmed glasses, she was glad she'd dressed the part for today's meeting, invoking her standard rationalization for eschewing her normal less-than-formal garb: "It's not phony, it's effective packaging, as if I'm one of our products, sitting on the shelf to be seen and evaluated."

She knew she undercut the gray suit and pearls by gelling a few spikes—the kind of spikes usually seen on twenty-year-olds with multiple pierces—in her short, dark hair. Oh well, her whole life was a mixed message anyway. There was the normal middle-aged middle-class corporate executive who lived in the suburbs, and then there was the overgrown hippy. Trying to integrate the two parts of her identity felt like juggling three live chickens. On an inclined plane. In high heels.

"I'm glad you'll be there," she said. "It's clear we disagree about the status of the Lipsticks & Scarves results, but I'm sure we'll agree about raising lots of money for a worthy cause. I think we'll set a record tonight. And we'll get great publicity in the process."

"I love opera. Turandot is one of my favorites."

Then Jeremy told Ruth he wanted to follow the re-design of the Lipsticks & Scarves campaign very closely. It was his way of delving into the actual work at Mimosa. He was in high guy-talk mode as he said he wanted to penetrate, wanted to get his hands dirty. Especially the Marketing Department, which he called the heart and soul of any company. He told her to let him know about everything connected to the campaign. Everything.

This is not good, she thought. Yes, the Marketing Department is important. Yes, he needs to understand the work of the company. No, looking over her shoulder is not the way to do it. She wasn't some entry-level newbie who needed close supervision. That second "everything" put her on alert.

"How about if I—"

"Just send me the relevant material as it comes up." He looked at the antique clock on the wall, then at the expensive watch on his slim wrist. "I've got to go." He looked down at her feet. "And I guess you've got to jog back to your office."

On the way back to her own little piece of Mimosa real estate on the other side of the eighteenth floor, Ruth thought it was going to be hard to break in this new CEO. It was clear he wasn't going to be the "I want to be your friend" type of boss. More like the "Me Tarzan, You Jane" kind. Or maybe "Control Freak." Two control-freaks battling it out, she thought. Not a pretty sight.

And someone was going to have to teach him the value of intangibles. She hoped it wouldn't have to be her.

Once, as a Peace Corps volunteer, she'd tried to convince a villager to incorporate vegetables into the traditional fish-and-rice diet because of good things called vitamins. The woman shifted the baby on her back, reached into her basket for a lumpy whitish tuberous yam, and held it close to her eyes.

"You can't see them, they're very small," Ruth had said. "But they're there."

Thankfully, she was more successful than Purchasing-Guy had just been. She wondered what that twenty-three-year-old version of herself would have thought of this fifty-three-year-old version, the Marketing Director of a cosmetics company. Actually, she didn't really wonder, she knew.

Back then, she lived in a hut with one orange crate for clothes and one for books. She was saving the world, or at least making a difference to the people in her village. Every moment of every day was, if not giddy—she did experience homesickness and doubt, not to mention diarrhea—at least related to every other moment, directed either at her worthy goals or physical needs. The individual cells in her body felt more than just alive, they fairly vibrated. A far cry from talking about selling cosmetics.

Had it been thirty years or thirty light-years? Why can't her past and present finally learn to shake hands and play nice?

Rather than explaining to her imaginary younger self that the compromises she'd made in her life were justified—"I had to earn enough to send Josh to college; besides it's not just makeup, it's skin care, too"—she strong-armed the thought from her consciousness with an audible "Oh well."

Her staff had gotten to her office before she did. When she joined them, they were ready to pounce. "Lordie, lordie, Ruth, that was … well … it wasn't great, you know? Don't you agree? I mean…." Judy somehow managed to wring her hands and bite her thumbnail at the same time.

"It was abundantly clear that Jeremy didn't like our results," Pat said. "But I wouldn't disagree with his priorities. Profits are the name of the game." Her deep voice, always surprising from such a small body, made crankiness and anxiety difficult to distinguish.

"Profits certainly are important, Trish," Ruth said. Pat flinched and start to tap the toe of one tasteful navy-blue pump like a metronome. Ruth knew that using Pat's childhood nickname was a low blow. But so was disloyalty.

Tom interrupted his choppy, disconnected gait. "What did you think of the meeting?"

"It was the first launch under Jeremy's watch, so let's assume he's being a little defensive. He did pretty well at B&D, so he must know something. And he clearly has his own style," she said with as straight a face as she could muster, "but that's the way it goes. He's the boss. We have to get used to it."

No need to worry them yet.

Turning to the Lipsticks & Scarves redesign, they constructed an action plan and divided the tasks to be done, from manufacture to packaging to advertising. Later, when their work started to bear fruit, she'd think about "keeping Jeremy informed," whatever that meant.

For the moment, though, the few last-minute details for tonight's benefit were numero uno on her prioritized To-Do list. She'd take care of them and then, she hoped, be able to leave early. It probably didn't even pay to change out of her sneakers.

2
David's Bombshell

SHE STARTED SHEDDING HER WORK CLOTHES the instant she was inside her house. David, a teacher at the local high school, had gotten home even earlier than she and started an early dinner by inspecting the fridge contents and giving his creativity free rein. Tonight's palette had consisted of chicken thighs, left-over Brussels sprouts, peas, rice, and beets. Had it been her turn to cook, she'd have looked for a recipe.

Over dinner, she filled David in on Jeremy's interpretation of the Lipsticks & Scarves campaign and his "I want to get my hands dirty" speech.

"Dirty hands are bad?"

"No one needed to look over my shoulder on 'Glamorous Glimmer.' A big success. Same with 'Red, Red, More Red.' Hundreds of others. I'm good at this stuff, I have a great record."

"Maybe he's not doing it to check up on you, but, like he said, to get to know the business. It doesn't seem—"

"It may not seem so bad to you. Believe me, you had to be there."

She speculated that maybe Jeremy wasn't happy about being sent from a mega-corporation to a little bitty company. But then why micro-manage? Maybe he just didn't like her because she wasn't cut out with the standard corporate cookie-cutter. Didn't worship at the altar of buzz-words, didn't like professional associations, didn't dress like a store dummy. He'd probably even call her a "women's libber." Maybe he was planning to put a B&D guy, a Big Daddy, in her job. Then why hadn't he done it yet?

"It feels like he's marking his territory, pissing on the hydrant."

"Why don't you think about—"

"There's got to be more to him than meets the eye. Because, really, not much meets the eye. Judy said she has a friend who used to work for the Big Daddies so maybe she can get some gossip."

David had cooked, so she insisted on cleaning up, even though it was the night of the benefit. "Fair's fair. I have time."

Just before leaving the kitchen and switching off the light, she adjusted a plate in the dishrack. It was the one they'd had made from Josh's drawing, years ago, with a face whose eyes were V-shaped blue birds and the big smiling mouth was a series of red flowers. When the face was right-side-up, she smiled back at it.

"I can't put it off any longer." She walked over to David and stood between him and the TV. "Time to get dressed up."

He picked up the newspaper. "It's still early. I only need fifteen minutes to put on my tuxedo, and, really, seven of those minutes are spent putting on my tuxedo frame-of-mind." He peeked over the top of the newspaper.

"Yes, but I need your help. As usual." She pulled him out of his chair.

He saluted and started towards the bedroom. She took the paper from the chair, folded it and put it on the side table.

They headed down the corridor, plushly-carpeted in forest green, past walls that could barely contain the jumble of photos. Ruth thought she must be the only person she knew whose favorite room in her own house wasn't a room at all, but a hallway.

Pictures of Josh dominated, sprinkled throughout the display: Josh being breast-fed by a tousle-haired Ruth, Josh in his SpiderMan Halloween costume at the day care center, David and Josh in orange life vests on a canoe trip, Josh doing magic tricks in middle school, Josh being comforted by his parents after a disastrous performance with the high school debating team, Josh and his deer-in-the-headlights prom date, Josh being suave on the college tennis team, Josh graduating from college.

Interspersed among the Josh-growing-up series were vacation shots of them with friends from one part of their life or another: on a barge trip through France, in a rented house in Italy, at a health spa, and assorted skiing, biking, hiking, and beach trips. There were family pictures, too: Ruth and her sister Marge, Ruth and her diminutive mother just a year before she died, David and his blond Midwestern parents. A wedding picture had all the family members from both sides looking as if they actually came from the same friendly planet.

At the far end of the corridor, closest to the bedroom, were three shots, side by side. There was one of each of them in front of the huts they lived in as Peace Corps volunteers—young, filthy, happy. And there was one of a six-year old Josh in Ruth's village, surrounded by village kids, when they'd all gone back for a visit.

Looking at a picture or two when she passed through the hallway was her version of stopping to smell the flowers. The pleasure was mingled with the recognition that the moment captured in each photo was over. This photo gallery was the place where happiness and sadness intersected, leading her to observe, on one of her many trips through it, that she thought the hallway could be her obituary.

In the bedroom, she started ruffling through the hangers in the "dress-up outfits" section of her closet. "Tonight's event is something Jeremy would probably call a 'do-gooder kind of thing,' so part of me wants to stick it to him with something outrageous."

David made a move towards his favorite, the cherry-red dress with the deep-V neckline that made her blush the first twenty minutes she wore it.

"Wait. I'm thinking maybe I'd do better to look powerful, especially after today's meeting. Maybe tonight I need to look like 'one of them.' A real corporate suck-up. With an outfit that says," and she placed both hands on her hips and dropped her voice, "'Jeremy, what in the world are you thinking, I'm a bottom line girl, a powerful bottom line girl.'"

"This is a lot of message for one outfit." David's eyes were unblinking, his mouth horizontally neutral, but she was fluent in his body language and knew he was struggling to stay on topic.

"Yeah, yeah, I know. And there's actually one more thing. There's Pat. Young Pat, thin Pat, cranky Pat who's sprinting to get on Jeremy's good side."

"I can't believe you haven't won her over or gotten rid of her."

"She's too good at what she does to get rid of. And I'm too good at relationships to give up on her. Soon she'll realize I'm not the enemy. And I'm not her mother. Meanwhile, I want to look like a middle-aged knockout."

"Sounds like a night for..." He reached into the closet and pulled out, with a flourish, a sparkling black sequined top. "... sequins."

"Sequins. I could wear that top with the long swishy skirt, which hides my tummy bulge nicely. Or maybe the plum dress"—she reached into the closet to pull it out—which shows off my legs, but it's a little tight right here in the danger area." She put her hand across her abdomen. "What do you think? And then I'll let you go."

"I think the skirt and top are beautiful and dignified, but the dress is beautiful and powerful and says 'Watch out, Pat.'"

"What about the tummy?"

"Ruth, I swear, it seems to be all you can see, but the rest of us don't notice it. Especially with those legs. And I think I officially can't take any more of this."

As they finished dressing, Ruth provided an overview of tonight's likely cast of characters, including those who needed buttering up and those who could use some therapeutic snubbing. They took a final side-by-side look in the full-length mirror near the front door.

David's graying hair and white neatly-trimmed beard framed sensual features he'd once feared were effeminate. He looked like he was born to wear a tuxedo with matching purple and green bow tie and cummerbund decorated with math formulas. At six feet tall, he didn't overpower Ruth, but created the perfect counterpoint for her slight frame, especially when he put his arm around her shoulder. She fit right in. And she didn't look too bad, either.

"Not bad," he said. "If only Mrs. Sills could see me now. Back in third grade, she never thought I'd amount to anything."

They headed for the door. Ruth asked about David's day. "Wasn't today that last-minute hush-hush faculty meeting?"

"Yep."

"So? What gives? Is the principal resigning? Did they finally find out about all that special help, that very-special help, he gave the social studies teacher, what's-her-name?"

"Gloria. No, not that. Not quite so juicy. But it was pretty... pretty intriguing."

"Well? What? Tell me."

Ruth slid in on her side of the car, her movements deliberate so she wouldn't snag her pantyhose or dress. David hesitated for a second before he folded his body into his seat, buckled up, and started the engine. He turned to face Ruth and told her the meeting had been about saving money, especially on salaries, because of the recent defeat of the school budget.

He faced forward and eased the car into traffic.

"You weren't laid off, were you? Even they wouldn't lay you off to hire a younger teacher for less money. Would they? I mean, you're their best math teacher. And besides, you've got more tenure than God." Ruth's alarm was not so much about job security as concern for David's emotional well-being.

David adjusted the heating controls, then the position of the side view mirrors, then the radio. "No, nothing like that."

"Well?"

He explained the one-time only, take-it-or-leave-it early-retirement deal proposed by the district with buy-in from the state:

teachers between fifty-two and fifty-six could choose to retire at the end of this school year or next. They didn't have to wait until they were fifty-eight and they didn't have to have the requisite thirty years on the job. In terms of their pension, they'd not only get credit for the years they'd worked, they'd also get a bit of a boost.

"It's really a...." His voice trailed off.

"It sounds to me like it's really a scheme to replace the older teachers with ones they can get cheap. Honestly, don't they care about the quality of the education they're paying for?"

Traffic was heavy, but moving. David looked in his rear-view mirror and adjusted its position. He looked over his shoulder at his blind spot as he slipped into the left lane for an upcoming turn.

Ruth tried to console David for what she thought was troubling him, that some of his friends would retire. She was sure he'd still enjoy being there, being the best geometry teacher they ever saw.

At a red light, David stopped, more suddenly than necessary, and turned his whole body to face Ruth again.

It was starting to rain, and Ruth worried about getting from the car to the concert hall without getting wet. Or did they still keep that umbrella in the car?

"Ruthie, you're not hearing what I'm saying."

She looked over at him. The streetlight shone behind him, so his face was largely in shadow, but he looked funny. His mouth dropped off a little bit on the left. And his brows were furrowed. That wasn't like him at all. He was turning his wedding ring around. Uh oh, a bad sign.

She folded her hands like a school-girl. "So spell it out."

The light turned green. He faced forward and drove more smoothly as he told her about the details of the one-time offer. He needed to let them know in the next thirty days or else he'd wind up working until he was fifty-eight.

"And I want to take it. And—"

"You want to retire? You can't be serious. Retire?"

"Retiring at fifty-four is not outlandish. Besides, you knew I'd be retiring in four years anyway."

"What would you do? Another job? What kind?"

"No new jobs. Actually, I thought maybe … maybe we could both retire. Especially with your new boss being such a pain. And then we could play all day. It'd be fun. Don't you think?"

"You want me to retire?" Ruth looked out the side window, the front window, over at David, then back out the side window again, her eyes bouncing like pinballs. It was really raining now. Little puddles accumulated on the roadway, though not on the streets. She noticed the reflections in the puddles, of the street lamps, the tops of the buildings and even their car. But it went by in a blur, too fast to catch a good glimpse. She didn't like that blurriness and would have liked David to slow the car down so she could see her own reflection in her own car in one of the puddles.

"Why didn't you tell me this before instead of springing it on me now?"

David didn't answer for two blocks.

"I didn't spring it on you. We were busy talking about other things. Anyway, I did try. But…. And then you asked. It was…." He shook his head.

"David, we're not old enough to retire. It's too soon. Isn't it? Retire? Oh God, I didn't know you were thinking of retiring."

"I have thirty days to tell them if I'm taking the offer. But that's what I want to do. And it would be more fun if you did it too."

For the next twenty minutes, David pretended to be concentrating on his driving and Ruth pretended to be calm. He's crazy, she thought. We're not really old enough to retire. Isn't that for old people? Older than us, for sure. Let's see, when my mother was fifty-four, where was I? In the Peace Corps with Vivian. We certainly did think our parents were old back then, older than we'd ever be.

Ruth insisted she couldn't retire. She had too much to do at work. And she had to leave on a high, without looking like she was being forced out. "You wouldn't retire without me, would you? Jeez, David, we haven't talked about retirement at all. I like working. I don't want to wear plaid shorts and play golf."

"Can we be serious?"

"You're right. You don't wear plaid shorts. Sorry."

"And how can you say you like working? You complain a lot. You're tired all the time. And you're always agonizing about being so corporate and so involved with make-up, you talk about not being who you used to be. Maybe it's time to—"

"Oh, sure, I complain, but I really like the challenges and the problem-solving, I like the people. Enough of them anyway."

She felt the vertical crease between her eyebrows starting to deepen into the Grand Canyon of the Forehead as the antagonists in her familiar internal battle started warming up: Why had she stayed at this job? Because she liked it. Why did she like it? For the creativity and the validation of her talent. Was that enough, and was it time to leave? Yes, and don't be ridiculous.

David started a sentence he chose not to finish. It wasn't distraction, she could tell, it was a self-stifle. "Go ahead," she urged.

"I think what you like is being good at what you do, even if you don't exactly like what you do. You're addicted to competence, you're an achievement junkie. You could do volunteer work, maybe, and then be competent at something you believe in."

He looked over at her. "C'mon, don't be mad."

"I'm not mad. Not exactly, anyway. If you were thinking about this, why didn't you tell me? I feel kind of betrayed. You were clearly open to this idea, and I had no inkling."

"Ruthie, you want me to tell you everything I might conceivably be open to thinking about? That's nuts. *Even I* don't know that. And even if I did…." his voice dropped off.

"I'm just trying to figure out and explain how I feel."

"I don't actually need precision about the ingredients and proportions of your various emotions," David said. "I get it. Enough of it, anyway."

"I just wanted to be clear. So you'd understand."

"It's time you knew. Your need to be clear is much greater than it is for your audience."

"But it is a need for me, David. Maybe it's because I felt so misunderstood growing up. Or because I'm short, so I feel like—"

"Ruthie!"

"What?"

"You're doing it again."

"Oh. Okay. Let me just calm down, okay?"

"Good idea." After a few minutes, they pulled up to the concert hall, into the designated "Big Shot" parking spaces. It had stopped raining. Ruth took a deep breath and looked at her watch.

Hoping David would come to his senses in a day or two, she said, "I need for us to talk about this later. I don't like it at all, but I'll think about it. Later. But right now, more than anything else, I need to glow. Okay? Glow now, think later."

"If that's what you need, you glow, girl. I'll be right beside you."

3

Face-to-Face in the Women's Room

RUTH GRABBED DAVID'S HAND AS THEY ENTERED the concert hall. They strode directly to the far right corner of the dazzling glass-and-brass lobby, to the Adams Room, where Mimosa was hosting a pre-concert party for employees who'd bought one of the specially-priced tickets that included a charitable contribution.

The Adams Room boasted fragile antiques upholstered in navy blue velvet, heavy curtains, and huge ornately-framed oil paintings of white men. When she entered this room with the pre-concert champagne and elegant dessert nibbles designed to entice donations to the Foundation for Children with Scleroderma, she felt as if she were leaving the twentieth and nineteenth centuries behind.

Pat had volunteered to come early to help set up and greet people as they arrived. Ruth was surprised but glad to be shed of it, and also thought it would be good career-development for Pat. That is, if Pat's long-range career plan included anything resembling charity benefits.

Ruth immediately set to work as hostess, making people feel included and appreciated, glad they'd come, and motivated to do it again.

First she approached the Keatings, tall and standing stiffly as if posing for a picture. His white hair and her white dress, combined with their height, made them hard to overlook.

"I'm so glad you could come. Jay, I never see you at work, so it's great to get a glimpse of you here. And Charlotte, how have you been? Last time I saw you, you were quite eloquent about the horrors of parenting an adolescent. Have things improved?"

Charlotte vented about her daughter's independent spirit and bragged about her PSAT scores.

Ruth moved on to a thin woman in a black suit looking around for someone to talk to while trying not to look desperate. "Hi Clarissa, how's it going?"

"Ruth you're such a genius. And it's so good of you," said with hand over heart, "to raise all this money for these poor children."

"It's a terrible disease. Imagine what it must be like to have your own immune system attack you. To count yourself lucky if it's only your skin that's affected and not your organs.

"Their friends are probably worried about acne, and these kids would give anything to have acne be their worst skin problem.

"And the most heart-breaking part is that these kids have no idea why this is happening to them. No one does, really. All they know is that their skin gets thick and stiff. That's why it's so important for us to raise money for research and treatment. Thanks, Clarissa, for being part of it."

Next was diminutive Rita, with the huge eyeglasses and even huger earrings, who wondered aloud if the corporate benefits were cost-effective while her eyes ceaselessly roamed the crowd like a lighthouse beam.

"Come on, Rita, you have plenty of time at work to arm-wrestle with me about the bottom line. Tonight, let's just be music lovers, okay? Who knows, tomorrow I might actually agree with you."

Cameron's son was considering the Peace Corps, which made it a convenient topic whenever they needed one.

"So there I was, running a health dispensary at the tender age of twenty-two, seeing people with diseases ranging from polio to elephantiasis to scleroderma. And also meeting David, the volunteer in the next village. Little did I know he was my future better half."

Charm on command was exhausting, she thought. It was necessary social lubrication, she knew, and, even though David, the natural-born storyteller, had helped her learn to do it, she still preferred one-on-one intimacy. No one could tell she was a recovering introvert whose shyness had sometimes been mistaken for snobbery. And she'd even managed to stop worrying about how she looked in her dress.

Flickering lights signaled Turandot would start in five minutes.

As people ended their small talk and drifted out to the Mimosa block of seats in the first mezzanine, Ruth started towards Pat to tell her what a fine job she'd done. But Pat was busy talking to Jeremy. From her body language, she might easily have been talking about how big a fish she'd caught. She really shouldn't suck up so soon and so obviously, Ruth thought. You just never know. Office Politics 101.

Ruth tended to three others who needed herding into the theatre, then found David's waiting arm.

"How's it going so far?"

She commented on the gratifying mix of "regular" people mixed in with the rich folks. "I'm not sure, but I think we'll set a record. Lots of people paid at the door. Which means they paid a lot. I can't wait to see the figures tomorrow. Plus, Mark Bloom pulled me over. Remember him? He used to be CFO at our place, and everyone thought he'd be our new CEO but now he's being groomed for some top Big Daddy job. He went on and on about how great my charity benefits are, so he's okay in my book."

Seated, Ruth quickly did an inventory of who was sitting with whom just as the lights dimmed and the overture welcomed her to the spectacle.

To avoid her usual operatic head-flopping, she'd read the English translation of the libretto and listened to the music before coming. And she was glad she had: knowing what was going on helped, even if what was going on was a fairy tale. Familiarity with the music made the arias more beautiful, too.

Maybe the plot isn't exactly twentieth-century realistic, she thought, but that's only if you take it literally. Longing for what you can't have is universal. And emotionally accessible.

Everyone wanted something they couldn't have. Or maybe they just don't want the right things. Some of them don't even know what they want. Like Turandot. The ice princess. And that poor slave girl, so faithful to her master while also obviously in love with his son.

Ruth was completely swept up by the music, the colors, the emotion. When the lights announced intermission, she was gratified to realize she'd done none of her usual mental flitting, had no negative fantasies about retirement or To-Do lists or Jeremy-the-enigma. All she'd done was wrap her attention around the opera.

However, like Pavlov's dog, her bladder responded to the break. She bolted for the women's room and her heart sank at the ten-person line. It was the cold, hard fact of restroom life: Women waited, men didn't.

"I'll bet the men don't have to wait," she groused.

"Do they have more stalls, do you think? Or are they just faster?"

"Wanna find out?"

"We need to level the peeing field."

Giggles all around. Then, as if they'd rehearsed, everyone got serious about waiting patiently. As she advanced from the anteroom to the main room, she counted: Four stalls, and I'm ninth on line. That's like being third on line for a single stall. Not too bad.

She turned to the long horizontal mirror to her right and multitasked. Hair, lips, cheeks, eyebrows. And check out the tummy. How could David say he didn't see it?

Finishing her personal mirror-work, her eyes brushed past the reflections of the women in line. She was struck—who wouldn't be?—by the wild head of light-brown frizzy hair on a woman near the end of the line. Thick, curly, with no attempt at good manners or any other form of restraint. It reminded her of kids at a swimming pool who yell to their parents, "Look at me, look at me. See what I can do. Look, watch me do a trick. Look at me." Beneath it all, the woman had one thick eyebrow.

Among all the black sequins, rhinestones, and silk, she wore a huge blue and green print creation, the kind of dress usually referred to as a flowing robe.

The hair may be different, she thought, but not the mono-brow. That's Vivian.

SHE'D FIRST SET EYES ON VIVIAN, her Peace Corps Volunteer hut-mate, after six dusty hours on a washboarded red-clay road in a crowded bush-taxi. Emerging from the closely-packed vehicle, her brain shaken like a malted from the bumpy ride and the fatigue, she saw the village where she'd be living for two years. The huts were various shapes and sizes, but were all the color of the ground. There was an occasional fromagier tree whose base looked like the rich folds of a wedding gown spread out at the bride's feet for the traditional picture.

A large white woman emerged from one of the mud brick structures. She wore a faded blue version of the standard wax-dyed cloth wrapped around her waist like a beach cover-up, a reddish version around her head, and, separating the two competing patterns, a tee-shirt that had once been white. Ruth thought it hadn't taken her Peace Corps hut-mate very long to go native. Vivian, as she later recounted, was awed by how clean Ruth was.

"RUTH, OHMYGOD, RUTH, IS THAT YOU? Is that really you? Here on the same bathroom line as me? Is it really you?" Vivian's eyes widened as her voice got louder and louder.

Everyone looked up.

Busted, thought Ruth. "Vivian? Vivian Denise Cassidy? Is that you? Geez, it must be … thirty years now? How are you?"

Plum-sequined Ruth and wild-haired Vivian tentatively stepped off the line, meeting half-way to talk. The women who had followed each of them in line kept their spaces empty as the line advanced. Everyone was rapt.

How lame, Ruth thought. What do I mean by 'How are you?' How are you now? Or how have you been for thirty years? Or what?

Vivian didn't seem to notice. "I'm good. I'm really good. Oh, it's so good to see you. You look exactly the same. Haven't you gotten any older in all this time? How are you? You look so good. All grown up and everything."

"I'm good too. And you look great. So beautiful, so exotic."

And then they were at the moment Ruth dreaded. Where to go from here? Again, Vivian seemed oblivious to the awkwardness Ruth felt.

"I was just saying to Carlos the other day—"

"You two stayed together all this time? That's so great."

"We knew it was true love or maybe no one else would have either of us but anyway here we are and we have a daughter too. She's in the orchestra here tonight, she plays the oboe, she's first oboe, actually, oh I can't believe I said that but I really am proud of her and that's why we're here. We've been living in New York for awhile now, and..."

She stopped for a second. "As you can see, I still talk too much. Tell me about you."

"Remember David from Sine Saloum, the one who was just a friend even though everyone wanted us to get together but we insisted that it was just platonic?"

"Remember him? Of course. I believe my exact words were 'Platonic, shmatonic.'"

"You were right. We've been married for about twenty-six years now … almost twenty-seven … and we have a son, Josh."

The silence during the ensuing pause was interrupted only by flushing toilets. And then they hugged.

Ruth was mentally wording a question about Vivian's work life in a way that adhered to the feminist principle that work inside or outside the home was valuable, when Vivian said, "So what do you guys do?"

"I work in Marketing, here in midtown. And David's a math teacher. What about you?"

"I'm at a woman's shelter and Carlos is with a foundation. We both—" She stopped, looking around in a panicky way, then concentrating very carefully on the paper towel dispenser. She turned red and started fanning herself furiously with the program as beads emerged on her forehead. "Just wait a second and I'll be back on planet earth again."

"You too? Believe me, I know just how you feel. Like you can feel your outline, the boundary between the hot and the normal."

"Yeah, that's it."

"Me too," chimed the woman who was saving Ruth's place on line. Her short, close-to-the-skull salt and pepper hair framed a beet-red face.

The fanners fanned, the toilets flushed.

A stall door opened and the woman in front of Ruth's empty space entered. Ruth said, "Vivian, I'm next and I'd let the woman behind me have my turn so we could keep talking, but, believe me, I can't. I've really gotta go and I can't hold it in a second longer. And then I have to get back to my seat because I'm baby-sitting some people from work. Can you hang out after the performance for awhile?"

"No, we can't, cause we promised Ida we'd come backstage immediately so she can introduce us around, before the lines form. But I would love to see you again."

"Me too. And I know David would, too. Can you two get together for lunch tomorrow? Or Sunday? Or next Saturday or Sunday?"

"Let me think." Ruth wondered if Vivian was trying to figure out how she'd sell Carlos on the idea of a date with the Talbots. He was so wild back then, so pure, so opinionated. Who knows what he's like now, she thought? Actually, who knows what Vivian's like?

"Next Sunday would be good."

"Are you in the phone book, Viv?"

"Yep. Brooklyn. Suarez. With a Z at the end. Just like always."

"I'll call you tomorrow."

She got back to her seat as the curtain was rising, and quickly told David about Vivian in the bathroom. Then, despite all her preparation for the opera, and all her involvement in the story, she never heard the second half. She never saw the slave girl kill herself, never saw the prince answer the riddles correctly, never saw Turandot realize her love. She never heard the piercing aria she'd been looking forward to, Nessun Dorma. She was back in Africa.

VIVIAN TOLD HER she could just dump her stuff anywhere while they went around to greet the members of the family compound, then the village chief himself. "It's a village. It's safe. Trust me."

They walked from one hut to another, trailed by the dust their feet kicked up, dust Ruth would eventually learn to live with almost constantly, except during the brief rainy season. A throng of children followed them wherever they went, chanting and laughing, dressed in a melange of African fabrics and such exotica as a Detroit Tigers tee shirt. One or another of the kids was occasionally emboldened to wipe a finger across Ruth's bare arm or leg, then look at the finger to see if her strange color had wiped off.

Each time Ruth entered a hut for the introduction, she'd take a minute to adjust to the dark, the coolness, and the lingering smell of thousands of cooking fires. The people inside looked up at her and smiled in an international nonverbal welcome even though they didn't know her and probably thought she might as well be a space alien. Then came the ritual greeting.

"Asalaam-malekum."
"Malekum-salaam," she said.
"Nanga def?"
"Mangi fi rekk," she said.
"Naka waa ker ge?"
"Nunga fe," she said.
"Naka sa baay?"
"Munga fe," she said.
"Jamm nge am?"
"Jamm rekk, alhamdulilay," she said.

Taken literally, she was answering questions about her parents and her house—she thought—but accepted the Peace Corps's wisdom that it was all ritual, like saying "Fine" when someone asks "How are you?" even when you're sick as a dog. And it was the only currency she had to respond to the warm welcome she was receiving.

By the time the introductions were over, Ruth had begun her own transition to dusty monochrome. They retrieved her belongings and Vivian delighted the proud *guardien* of the luggage with a reward of five francs CFA, worth about two cents. Vivian took her to the living quarters she'd built two months before, over by the dunes, while providing a non-stop commentary on the construction process.

"The walls and roof are made of crintin. I didn't actually make the crintin, some of the villagers made it for me. They were anxious to do anything they could for me, but I really think they mostly wanted an excuse to just stand around and look at me because I was such a curiosity to them. After all, they'd never seen a creature like me before. It was wild, really wild."

Ruth could see that the crintin consisted of the spines of palm fronds woven into a flexible mat, about five feet high and of any length desired. She didn't ask for any more details, fearing the length of the answer.

"See, I stuck these poles in the ground. Well, they're not poles exactly, they're saplings, but I had to look for saplings that were about eight feet tall and had a 'V' at the top, and I stood the crintin up to be the walls, and then I attached it to the poles so they stand up straight. Neat, huh? And then I put more saplings between the V's to be like rafters, and the rafters hold the crintin that goes horizontally, you know, for the roof, and then I tied the palm fronds on to the horizontal crintin to finish off the roof. It's different from everyone else in the village, but it was faster and easier to build. And anyway, we *are* different from everyone else in the village."

Ruth liked the look of the place. It was easy to understand: one room, with the "bathroom" over by the dunes. The crintin allowed in air and light, while clearly indicating the border between their space and the other members of the family compound. As Ruth had already experienced, they were a source of immense curiosity in the village, so borders were important. And the eighteen-inch gap between the top of the walls and the roof provided a perimeter of picture-window.

"Here's your cot," Vivian said. "I thought you'd like it in the east part of the hut, so you can watch the sunset in the west, over the ocean, like if you're having a beer and writing letters at the end of the day, but if you'd rather, we can move it over there, to the corner where the kerosene refrigerator is right now. I call the refrigerator Ada, you know, from refrigerADA. But if we moved the bed, Ada would have to go over there, by the door, and then, when we sweep the floor we'd have to go around Ada on the way to the door and that could be a pain, and we have to sweep the floor all the time, really, or the sand piles up like crazy, so why don't you just try it this way for a while and see how it feels?" Then she took a breath.

It took Vivian about a week to exhaust her pent-up need to communicate in English. Other than the few hours a day they spent at their "jobs"—Vivian working with villagers to plant a vegetable garden to provide the vitamins missing from the traditional diet of rice and dried fish, Ruth setting up a dispensary by sorting and labeling American-style medicines—and the time they slept, the remaining time was devoted to conversation. If Ruth had something to talk about, fine. If not, Vivian filled the gap, having no tolerance for silence when English was possible.

Ruth learned that Vivian was the oldest of three children, that her father owned a bar and, when his first child disappointed him by being a girl, and no other children appeared to be forthcoming, he resigned himself to teaching her the business, including training her to be tough as nails. When her two brothers followed, ten and fourteen years later, he not only dropped Vivian's training and withdrew his special attention, but also did a complete turnaround, suddenly expecting her to wear pink and bat her eyes.

"Lots of luck, Pop," Vivian said as she took a long drink of beer, then continued with the story of her parents' divorce. "They divided us up like so much property. I went with mom and my brothers went with dad. So I lost a parent and two brothers. I haven't seen them for about four years now. Or maybe it's five."

"Oh, Vivian, you poor thing, how terrible." Ruth secretly thought she could have done with a little estrangement from the suffocation of her own family.

"Yeah, well, that's the way it is. What about you?"

Vivian's interest turned out to be genuine, not just a step she had to go through until she'd get another turn in the spotlight. Ruth could gradually open up about her own family bones, not knowing if they qualified as skeletons or not.

There was her father, effusive and loving until things weren't perfect. "Then he just blows up. It's like he's just got all this rage inside and it's only a thin layer of skin holding it in. Meanwhile, Mom is flitting around, repeating her theme-song, "It's all right, he didn't mean anything by it."

"Sisters and brothers?" Vivian asked.

"Just one. My sister Marge."

"Older or younger?"

"Neither. She's a twin. Don't make a big deal about it. Please."

"Really? A twin? Is it like you hear in magazine articles? Like a double? Like you know what she's thinking and she knows what you're thinking? A twin, wow."

"No, not for us. We're fraternal, so we're no more alike than regular sisters. Except maybe, being the exact same age, it's a little different. I don't know. But we're definitely different from each other."

"Different how? Do you look different? Do you both like coffee or tea? Stuff like that?"

"We look like sisters, I guess. But the physical resemblance is stronger than any other kind. We're just different. It's like she's the evil twin. She yells, she throws tantrums. She actually stamps her feet if she doesn't get her way. It's one thing for her to be like that with me, but she actually goes up against our father. The two of them go at it, and there I am, on the sidelines, hoping it will go away. Miss Goody Two Shoes. Which I have to be, to keep the peace. So, that's how we're different. The evil twin and the good twin. One can stand up for herself, one can't. But she got first choice."

"Maybe it's the evil twin and the scared twin."

"Is there a difference?"

"I guess I'm more like your sister. When I'm mad at someone, it's like they have their hand in front of my face and I can't see anything else until I say something and get that hand away. I could do with a little of your restraint."

"Well, I pay a price. I wish I had a little of your balls."

"Balls aren't all they're cracked up to be. Speaking of which, what do you think about hum jobs?"

Ruth's head spun with the non sequitur, the raunchiness, and the nosiness. After a second or two, Vivian continued with another non sequitur, and Ruth realized that not all of Vivian's questions required an answer.

"So, let me tell you about the wild family stuff here in the village. People marry each other, but for only about five or six years. Then they switch partners. Really, I'm not kidding, they switch. But there's more. The village is divided into seven sections, and everyone tries to get a spouse from a different section from the last one they had. The idea is that, when they die, they want people from as many sections as possible dancing at their funeral. Neat, huh? Kind of like spinning as many tops as possible at the same time. Oh, and speaking of sex...."

Even their disagreements were stimulating, like the times they argued over Vivian's macho attitude toward the health precautions.

"Come on," Vivian said. "What are the odds that one tiny little microscopic amoeba will happen to wind up in the one ice cube made with unboiled water that I happen to have in my coke? And that the amoeba will be in the part of the ice cube that melts into my drink? Besides, the Africans have been drinking the water long before we got here with our superior knowledge, and they're not all sick and dying, are they? They're doing a whole lot better than some Americans I know."

"Be rational." Ruth tried to convey just the right degree of scientific objectivity. "Why take any chance of getting an amoeba in your system? The Africans have adapted their internal chemistries to their environment over generations and generations, but you don't have time for that." She dropped her voice a few tones when she added, "And besides, who wants to have to put their shit on a slide for the Peace Corps doc to look at under a microscope? Euuuuwww!"

Vivian did get sick. During the worse of it, she was weak and green, though the visiting PC doc dropped off meds and assured them it would pass. What little strength she had went for vomiting and diarrhea, then she'd rest up for the next bout. Their intimacy deepened as Ruth read to her, stroked her head with a wet rag, sang to her. She even killed a chicken and made chicken soup. Vivian's illness subsided and Ruth was torn between love and anger. "Vivvy sweetie, you are my best friend in the whole wide world and I'm so sorry you're having such a bad time, but I have to tell you in all honesty that it doesn't pay for you to get well, because as soon as you're out of bed, I AM GOING TO KILL YOU!" They laughed until they cried.

Sometimes they struggled, as many volunteers did, with the idea of the United States, with its affluence that came packaged with crime, materialism, and empty values, purporting to teach traditional cultures to emulate it.

"Really, Ruth, it's ridiculous to think that these villagers, who know nothing about suicide and very little about emotional illness of any kind, where everyone knows his purpose in life and has a whole villageful of love, might someday be able to watch TV and actually want to be like us. That's so crazy. No, *they* should be sending the Peace Corps to *us*."

"Right, like a reverse Peace Corps to teach us traditional values. Core Values. The CORE Corps."

"With a model of a traditional village set up in Times Square."

"And the villagers would show us how to care for people who need it the most."

"Without bitching about taxes."

"Right. And accepting everyone for who they are, without pushing everyone to be a doctor or lawyer."

"Right. Or asking them when they're going to get married and have kids and settle down in the suburbs."

They indulged in this or any kind of discussion they wanted, playful, serious, creative, impassioned, tearful, or a combination. They never needed to hurry back to a paper due the next day, never feared being pre-empted by a boy calling. The evening's only entertainment was a full discussion of the day's insights, with the guarantee of a willing listener, a hefty measure of understanding of both the words and the intentions behind the words, and acceptance.

The relaxed rhythm of their lives was as much a new experience as living in Africa. Their life together was intimate, but not sexual, though visiting volunteers—and they got more than their fair share because the ocean in their back yard made visiting them like a trip to the beach—spread whispers about the two girls who were … "you know … really *really* close."

When they were all talked out, they'd play Ray Charles on their battery powered record player and do the twist to "What'd I Say" on the sand in the moonlight, until they were giggly and sweaty. They'd collapse and listen to the waves.

LONG AFTERWARDS, when the dust had settled, Ruth realized it had been naïve to think their friendship would survive the transition from the hothouse of their close quarters, new experiences, and isolation to their lives back home. They didn't realize that, in the real world, they'd have to be satisfied with something less, and the diminution would be unacceptable.

When the rift came, though, they just thought they were arguing about the Viet Nam War. Vivian was counseling young draftable men on their limited options: try for Conscientious Objector status, aim for one of the few remaining deferments, flee to Canada, or fight. They were having dinner at Chuan Hong, a Chinese restaurant on the Upper West Side. It was Szechuan, a new kind for both of them, and they were enjoying its spiciness and novelty. Vivian tried to convince Ruth to join her in working for "Is Fighting the Only Option?"

Taking a bite of her Kung Po chicken, carefully avoiding the pepper pods, Ruth explained, "Look, Viv, I support what you're doing, really I do, but I'm just not an activist sort of person." She blew on her food. "I'm just not. I mean, it's sort of like—"

Vivian slammed her chopsticks down on the table, and one of them flew into the air, landing on the next table. "What do you mean, not an activist sort of person? Does that mean," she spoke in a singsong as she continued, "'I'm too busy starting my fancy New York career and going out to bars at night to do what I think needs to be done, so I'll just let others do it for me?' Is that what it means?"

"Don't give me that crap, Vivian. I just gave two years of my life for something I believe in. Save the radical speeches for people who deserve it."

"Bullshit. You did Peace Corps because your parents didn't want you to. You did it because it made you feel good, not because it helped people."

This traditional conundrum for Peace Corps Volunteers was like a Zen riddle: If you felt good about giving service, were you really being an altruist, or just doing what made you feel good? Who is the greater altruist, one who loves to give service or one who hates it but does it anyway? Still, it shocked Ruth to hear it thrown in her face.

She quietly put her chopsticks on her plate, took a sip of water and wiped her mouth with her napkin. She returned the napkin to her lap, carefully insuring it had no wrinkles, then said softly, "You know, Vivian, if I'm not radical enough to be your friend anymore, just tell me."

"You said it, not me." Vivian fished a five-dollar bill from her jeans and flung it on the table. As she stormed out, she called back, "Have a nice life."

4
Jeremy Rules

WHEN THE ELEVATOR SLOWED AND THE DOORS WHOOSHED open to the tune of the too-perky ding, Ruth hesitated for a second to let her eyes get used to her nine-to-five bleached landscape: white floors and desks, white-on-white artwork, framed in white, on white walls. The exuberant floral displays in matching vases supplied the only color, as if the walls were the canvas and the bouquets the paint. Breathing deeply, she detected "Moi, Moi, Moi," the scent of the week.

She marched with a determined stride, each step compensating for her measly five feet two inches by stretching a little further than was comfortable. An instructor in an Executive Presentations course had once referred to this stride as her "I may be little but I can lick any guy in the place" walk, and suggested she try more of a "fairy godmother" style. Yeah, right.

In the sanctuary of her office, the windows directed a gentle morning light on her collection. Soft black-and-white photos of faces dominated. Her favorites were the strong unsmiling profile of the Senegalese man in his village whom she knew to be gentle and loving, and the withered Indonesian woman hunched over her garden with an ancient tool.

Masks occupied the wall behind her desk, next to the window, all variations on the theme of camouflage and disguise. Most were African masks, brown wood with some accoutrements like shells and straw. The few Balinese masks with exaggerated facial gestures and wild colors were a stark contrast. There was even a papier maché mask Josh once made with garish polka dots resembling measles from outer space.

She allowed herself a few minutes vacation, basking in last night's glory. There were already lots of emails congratulating her, including one from the head of the Foundation for Children with Scleroderma. She spread the newspaper out on her desk and thought yes, we really did it this time.

Would Jeremy eat humble pie? Probably not. But maybe he'd be nice about it, only throwing in one or two snide remarks? She thought of Dean, the pre-Jeremy, or maybe the anti-Jeremy, and how glad she was that he'd let her start the Charitable Giving program when she made the switch from Human Resources to Marketing. Not only were the benefits fun, they helped even up her moral balance sheet. What a dream-boss he'd been.

Later today, she'd think about having glimpsed her retirement future—maybe David would change his mind—and her Peace Corps past in the space of a few hours. And she'd also figure out how she might use the success of the benefit to counter Jeremy's over-the-shoulder look at Lipsticks & Scarves.

Outside her window, the quickly-moving clouds against the gray-blue sky gave her the jump-start to confront today's To-Do list, including the leftovers from yesterday. She dove headlong into the corporate busywork of phone calls to return, memos to write, butts to kick, asses to kiss. Activity aimed at closure was her drug of choice. She loved nothing better than to cross things off her list, and some days yearned for an emptied list even more than a hot lavender-scented bath.

In her list-shortening orgy, she resolved three scheduling glitches. Two concerned product development, for which she preserved budget at the expense of schedule; one was about advertising, for which schedule got priority over budget. She composed the first draft of her weekly report, sticking to Jeremy's new prescribed format almost completely, leaving the section on the bottom-line results of the benefit temporarily blank. Then she rewarded herself by replying to some of the "Bravo on the benefit" emails, including a delicious one from Josh that she read about ten times.

"I know it's the mom who's supposed to be proud of the kid, but I just can't help it, ya know? If you don't want me to be proud of you, stop doing great stuff."

She left about fifteen more congratulatory messages in her e-inbox for later, when she'd have time and need a pat-on-the-back pick-me-up. It would probably be mid-afternoon, and it would be even better than caffeine.

While she was on the phone with one of the colleagues whose product development schedule was about to be tinkered with, Tom knocked on her open door. She waved him in and finished her call.

Tom looked younger than twenty-eight, with sandy-brown hair that fell straight down with the slightest movement of his head, leading him to reflexively finger-comb it back. His deep brown eyes were ringed by lush eyelashes ("They're wasted on a guy," was the take in the women's room) which drew attention from a large-nostrilled nose, too-skinny lips and crooked teeth.

Ruth liked Tom's idealism, his sincerity and eagerness to learn. "Hi Tom. What's up?"

"Wow, I love those pictures of when you were in the Peace Corps, out in the middle of nowhere."

"Proof that I was once young."

"I didn't mean…."

"Of course not. I know. Have a seat."

He asked Ruth how the benefit went, and she spent too much time telling him how successful it was. "Even Jeremy came."

"But that's good, you know, after yesterday's meeting and all."

"The meeting wasn't so bad. Not like when you were a teacher, I know. But you'll get used to it."

She asked if he'd finished his application to graduate school, knowing he hadn't or would already have mentioned it.

He'd been too busy.

That's what he said last time, she thought. She reminded him how valuable it would be to have the company pay his tuition. And that she'd write him a great recommendation. She jotted a note to herself in blue, to check once more, maybe in a month. But that would be the last time.

"So…?"

Tom was having trouble with the figures she'd wanted on the lavender bath oil and he didn't think he'd be able to get them to her by the afternoon. He showed her what he meant, then asked if Monday would be all right.

"Sorry, Monday's not okay. I need them for the report I'm doing for Jeremy over the weekend. Just do the best you can, but get me something."

"Um, okay. I'll have to drop everything else and concentrate on those figures."

"Good idea."

She stayed at her desk through lunch. Just as she was finishing her sandwich, Jeremy called. About time, she thought. He liked the concert. He hadn't seen the write-up in the paper. He wanted to talk to her, though. About the benefit. Could she please come up to his office? Now.

While she didn't like the way he commanded her to run upstairs, at least it was for the purpose of praising the success of the benefit. Also, she'd get her first look at his permanent office, the one the decorators had been preparing with whatever personal preferences he'd expressed.

She tried to imagine what the office would be like, but there'd been little gossip about Jeremy's tenure at B&D. Orderly and a micro-manager, yes, but nothing juicy. Maybe that's why he'd brought only a few Big Daddies over with him, because he was afraid they'd talk.

Somehow, she just couldn't believe he was interesting enough for that type of intrigue.

"Come in, Ruth. Have a seat." He was behind his desk, a massive chunk of dark grainless wood. Blank legal pads and variously-colored file folders in piles of differing heights looked like a LEGO® brick village. He used green B&D sticky notes instead of the ubiquitous pink ones from Mimosa. Frugal or passive-aggressive?

She looked at the practically-obligatory family photos. First, Jeremy and his attractive wife in their mid-twenties, maybe ten years ago. On a cruise ship, perhaps.

Next to it, a larger one of him and an older woman, in a silver frame, arm in arm, very happy. His mother?

Then a smaller shot of Jeremy and Mrs. Jeremy with their two freshly-scrubbed smiling sons, very close in age, hovering around seven or eight, dressed up and standing behind a formal dining table.

None of the photos showed a sailboat, a tennis racket, a tent, or anything denoting passion or even the willingness to sweat. There was something else odd about them.

"Beautiful boys," Ruth said.

He turned the photo around to look at it. Wait, that was it. The photos were facing the wrong way, and it was as odd as people standing the wrong way in an elevator. Guess he doesn't know he's supposed to look at them during the day and derive pleasure, Ruth thought.

"Thank you. They're good boys."

"You must be very proud."

"In fact I am."

"Are they twins?"

"No, just very close in age. Abraham's the elder, then Charles." Quick smile. "How do you like my new office?"

The carpet was off-white, called "ecru" above the twenty-first floor, meshing perfectly with the tan, brown and white geometric print of the couch and two arm chairs just inside the door. Three walls—the fourth being the high-status floor to ceiling window with drawn curtains—had sparse nondescript artwork that seemed to have been chosen only for color and size. One frame was blank. Other than the family photos, the only personal element in the room was a country club award for duplicate bridge. Jeremy must have given the decorators "bland" as his preference, and they'd done a good job.

"It's very nice. Do *you* like it?"

"It's a good, calm space. I know you took a different approach with yours," he continued. "A bit more … more eclectic … shall we say. But this one suits me just fine."

She nodded. "That's what it's all about."

He looked at his watch. "Let's get down to business. Down to business. I've been analyzing our charitable giving. We certainly raise a lot of money."

"And last night—"

"But we have to spend a lot to raise it. The salaries of the people who work on the events. The profits that those people—like you—would be generating if they spent all their time on something more, something more…more profitable. All the expenses. We have to balance the negatives against the positives. All the negatives against all the positives. I have to balance them."

He couldn't be going where she feared he was going with this. She had to head him off at the pass, and she knew "intangibles" would not be the weapon of choice. "But Jeremy, the good will we generate is priceless, and a recent study about good will—"

"It's simpler and easier to just write a check—"

He really was saying it. At a gallop, too. So much for small talk about children and office décor.

"—even if it's a big check. Which it doesn't need to be. Yesterday's concert did very well, bravo, but it was the final benefit. I don't know if you're planning another one, but you can stop."

She'd been primed for praise. She'd thought he might stick in some little dig about her benefits being more successful than Lipsticks & Scarves, but she'd been prepared to forgive him. In her imagination, she'd been gracious.

She'd always known the charity-benefit program had to be evaluated as part of a bigger picture than just the amount of money raised. In fact, seen in a certain way, a very narrow way, what he was saying was sort of … well, sort of true. It just didn't look at the whole picture. Dean understood about the name recognition and good will. She'd have to explain it to Jeremy. Remedial Marketing. First, inhale.

"But it's not just about—"

"It's simple. You need to spend all your time on launches. Profitable launches. Grand slams. More focus on profit, less on non-profit. Time for order and discipline, not emotion. Have to be fish or fowl." Tongue-dart. "Can't be both."

There seemed to be no air in the room. This was much worse than a hot flash. It was a vacuum.

He turned to face his computer and circled around the keyboard with his index finger—'here comes the airplane, into the hangar'—before he hit the "send" button. "I've spelled it all out in an email." He turned back to her and looked at his watch ostentatiously.

"It explains the changes in charitable giving as well as some other ideas for reorganizing. I'm sure you'll agree when you see the numbers. They're very persuasive. They always are. That's why I like numbers so much. They line up and stay where they belong. Right where they belong." His lips did their impersonation of a smile.

"It's a done deal. You have to expect changes with new management. But I just wanted to give you a heads-up in person. You know, as a favor. Thanks for coming up." He stood up to shake her hand, then went to the wall to straighten the crooked blank frame.

She must have left Jeremy's office, taken the elevator, and walked across the floor on the way back to her office, but when she got there she couldn't remember any of it. All she could remember was thinking, I can't believe this, I can't believe this, I can't believe this.

At her desk, she tried to deepen and slow her breathing. She went to Jeremy's email, both dreading it and furious at what she knew she'd find. Sure enough, there it was. With one stroke of a keyboard, he eliminated her favorite part of her job, the part that reassured her she hadn't sold out. Not only was it the source of countless awards, for her and for the company, it was also her defense when the judge in the Cosmic Courtroom asked her to justify what she'd done with herself. Poof, gone. She couldn't believe it. After all she'd done.

She didn't bother to read the charts and graphs with Jeremy's well-behaved numbers. She didn't need to, she knew what they'd say. She liked numbers too. Some of her best friends were numbers. She knew that, looked at from one angle, they told exactly the story Jeremy was hearing. But there were other angles, too.

She stared at the Crayola blue sky, then down at the traffic patterns. She spotted a spider on the orchid plant in front of the window. Absentmindedly, she broke off one of the threads on the web he was building. The spider slipped off the broken thread and righted himself on the one below. I know how you feel, buddy, she thought. The benefits were a really important thread in my life. An anchor. I feel unbalanced too.

Enough metaphors. She got up and paced while she thought about Jeremy, smart but stupid. Someone who has to do things in a certain way, even if the way is wrong, just to show it's his way, Mr. Three Piece Suit and horn rim glasses with the insipid family pictures and control issues. Narrow. Unimaginative.

How to handle a guy like this?

As she paced, she entered and exited the stripes of light coming in the window. Funny how her blouse could be a bright blue when she was in the light and a deep blue when she was in the shade. She stopped pacing and shifted her weight back and forth, in and out of a shaft of light, trying to spot the moment of change. She wondered which of those colors, the bright blue or the deep blue, or maybe a third or even fourth she wasn't seeing, was the true, objective color of the blouse.

The horrible thought came to her as she tried to catch the precise moment of color transition: Maybe I *should* retire after all. Maybe David is right; maybe this is the handwriting on the wall. The very thought increased gravity, slowed her down.

But she soon changed her direction and her tune, picking up the pace and revving herself up again. No way, nuh-huh. Sorry, David, I'm not retiring, not like this. If I retire, it won't be because Jeremy took away my charity benefits, it will be on my terms.

Now she had to figure out exactly what her terms were.

5

Unwrapping the Big Idea

RUTH'S SECRETARY CAME IN WITH AS JAUNTY A BOUNCE as her platform sandals would allow. Colleen's exuberance for her job splashed over into an exuberance for Mimosa's products, and for trying as many of them as she could, often at the same time. This day, under her asymmetrical helmet of sun-yellow hair, she wore rakish slashes of chartreuse eye shadow.

Colleen had proven her competence and her loyalty many times, and Ruth tried to look at her personal style with a sense of humor, even with some envy for its youthful abandon. Ruth loved and trusted Colleen like a daughter.

"Ruth, are you okay?" Her quizzical look, head tilted to the side, showcased the bright pink lipstick that extended slightly past the physical boundary of her lips.

"I'm in good health, let's put it that way."

"Okay, but, like, what's going on?"

"I just found out Jeremy is changing the benefit-event program. Not changing, exactly. Eliminating."

"Eliminating? No way, he couldn't do that. Could he? Why's he doing it anyway?"

"He says we spend more money raising the money than we should, and it would be cheaper to write a check."

"But wait a second." Colleen flopped into one of the chairs at Ruth's desk, then adjusted her cropped top and miniskirt. Ruth was glad to see her belly pierce-hole was closing up nicely, after she'd insisted on a stud-less belly or no visible belly at all.

"Doesn't he realize about the good vibes? And the, you know, publicity and all that? It's not just about the money, right?"

"Too intangible for him, I guess."

"What do you mean?"

"Just don't say anything to anyone."

"What are you gonna do?"

"I'm working on it. Remember, mum's the word."

"Okeydokey."

Colleen dropped off a package that had just arrived, then went back to her desk with a little less bounce.

Ruth opened the package and looked briefly at the sample pump-bottles without much interest. Most of her attention was looking here and there for inspiration. She couldn't do an end-run around Jeremy, even if she'd wanted to, because he was the top of the line. Should she pretend to be his version of a team player, waiting for her opportunity to trip him up? She probably could, but didn't think she wanted to live her corporate life that way. Could she stomach just going along with it all?

Her hyperactive train of thought eventually jumped the track and, unbidden, turned to the big idea she'd been playing with for some time. The idea turned one of the commandments of the cosmetics industry on its head, so she'd wanted to give it time in her mind's greenhouse until she was good and sure it could take the exposure.

The way she saw it, a youthful appearance was the holy grail of the cosmetics industry, the consummation devoutly to be wished, the be-all and end-all. But there were women in her age group who didn't go along with the "looking good means looking young" equation. Some of her best friends were these very women.

Ruth's idea was a product line for mature women who wanted

to look like attractive middle-aged women, not like women who were trying to look younger. This makeup wouldn't cover, wouldn't hide, it would enhance. It would celebrate. It would help women have the confidence to be themselves.

The irony of a cosmetics company helping women feel authentic was delicious. But she also smelled the profits.

Maybe it was time for the unveiling. With Jeremy's latest move, her identity would now have a hole where the "doing something socially worthwhile" part had been. Maybe a product line that helped women feel better about themselves would fill it. Can selling something count as doing good?

Yes it can, she answered herself. If the product helped women feel good about themselves. In an authentic kind of way. Empowered. It definitely can count.

She started one of her "plusses and minuses" charts on a piece of the heavy stock white-on-white paper used at Mimosa.

The plusses:

First was that it was a good thing to do, "Good" as in "Moral," something she could really be proud of. She'd be helping women feel better about themselves.

Also, it would bring a lot of new women to Mimosa, those who didn't usually buy cosmetics. It would make a ton of money.

Third was that it was an "aha" sort of idea, really different. She liked that.

Fourth, a big splashy success would be the best defense against disparagement of the Lipstick & Scarves results.

The minuses:

It was very risky.

Also, things weren't exactly copacetic between her and Jeremy. He was interested in numbers, not imagination. Doing good for middle-aged women would not be of any interest to him. And, she had to admit, that wasn't completely unfair. He was an orthodox corporate guy and wanted the corporation to make money. He wasn't the corporate odd-ball here, she was. Perhaps he sensed that faster than she gave him credit for.

Playing around with her two columns, she knew, was a stall. Mulling was easy, taking action not-so.

Action. What kind? With Dean she'd have talked about the value of innovation, of cultivating brand awareness with a certain demographic group. With Jeremy it could only be about profits. She needed numbers, lots of numbers, all lined up and behaving themselves.

A job for her friend Terry, a self-described "data nerd" over in Research.

She dialed Terry's extension and, after chatting with Terry's secretary about her baby's ear infection, she got through.

"Sorry about my numbers for the scarf deal, Ruthie. At the meeting. Great event, though. As usual."

"No problem. Numbers are numbers. And thanks."

"Are you recovered?"

"Yeah, I'm fine. I haven't seen you for ages, though, not counting yesterday's meeting. How about lunch? Soon?"

"Love to. I miss you too, but you sound like you have something up your sleeve and on your mind. Hmmm?"

"Moi? What's good for you? Next Thursday? I'd love to try that new bistro down the block. I hear the chef's the brother-in-law of some famous chef in Paris."

"Okay, Miss Mysterious. It'll be fun to catch up and ... and whatever else we're going to do."

Ruth pushed away from the desk and thought that, while the die wasn't exactly cast yet, she had a die-casting date. Time to talk to David about all this, too.

Of course, if she really got to create the line, it could be a big, splashy failure. Then she'd really have to go. With her tail so far between her legs, they'd all think she was doing somersaults. Oh well, who cares?

I care, she answered herself. Not about leaving. About putting herself out on a limb and falling.

No, no, it would succeed. She knew it would. Lots of profits, lots of good vibes, as Colleen put it. She envisioned what a star she'd be around the company, how Jeremy would have to be careful about his disrespect and power-plays. Most important, how the new product line would quell her feeling of not fitting in here, not feeling true to herself. Be a miracle drug for anxiety and uncertainty. Hers and everyone else's.

Whoa, girl. Slow down, get yourself under control.

But she'd held this idea in for what felt like a long time and now that she was thinking about letting it out, it felt like finding a bathroom after a long car trip: when relief is in sight, self-control is excruciating if not impossible.

What in the world am I about to do?

PART II

6

Fear of the Cosmic Courtroom

BETWEEN DAVID'S BOMBSHELL ANNOUNCEMENT, her encounter with Vivian, Jeremy's shake-up, and her tentative ideas about a new product line, she'd been chasing sleep for two nights, finally catching it last night around three-thirty. She lingered in bed, feeling she deserved it, and knowing today was the day to sort out her feelings and talk to David, who had, unfortunately, not forgotten about retiring.

Outside the bedroom window, the sun seemed less ephemeral, more intentional than usual because she'd slept late. Except for the gentle movement of the branches and the shifting sunlight through them, she might have been looking at a painting.

Surrendering to the day, she got up. David's shorts-and-sweat-socks drawer was open. He must already have gone jogging. Hoping he'd made the coffee before he left, she wrapped herself in her thick white terry robe, belting it tightly, and shuffled downstairs to the kitchen, enjoying the feel of the carpeting under her feet even as she knew her cold feet would punish her for not wearing slippers.

In the kitchen, the Mexican wall tiles were sun-bathing. Seeing the pot of coffee at the far end, she silently thanked David and repaid him by overlooking the open silverware drawer directly below it. Grabbing a heavy white mug, she prepared her morning jumpstart, then settled herself at the small round table in front of the window, contemplating the unexpected cheerfulness of the vase of forsythia. David's cup was still there, next to the newspaper, which was opened to the sports section. "Yankees Look Strong in Spring Training," cheered the headline. Well, she thought, David will be in a good mood today. It doesn't take much.

She idly flipped the pages and looked out at the neighborhood activity. Her neighbor was getting an early start on planting a lilac bush. Shirley jumped up on the shovel with both feet to force it into the earth. It took two or three jumps. By then it was in so far, she couldn't lift it out with all its dirt, so she had to lift a little dirt at a time. Struggle to get the shovel in, struggle to get it out, but never do it half-way. Spunk to spare.

She realized her feet were cold. Damn, she knew this would happen. And why did her feet have to keep acting like cold appendages stuck crudely to her mid-calves? She was tired of being cold. Old and cold.

Then her body treated her to her first hot flash of the weekend. The speed with which it took over caught her by surprise, as always. The power of her hormones—or, rather, their lack—felt as much a force of nature as gravity.

Rather than stand in front of the refrigerator, she tried a friend's suggestion: visualizing herself on a beach, where the heat would be pleasant and accompanied by the nurturing sound of waves. No dice. The heat on a beach came from outside her body, whereas this heat was definitely within.

Enough. She closed the paper and went upstairs to get showered and dressed.

"Hi hon," David said, returning from jogging, as she emerged from her shower. "I had a great run. It is really gorgeous out there. You know how you can *smell* spring before it's actually… And the flowers are starting to… It's just a great day."

She caught herself smiling a robotic half-smile.

"How about if I go into town?" David seemed determined to bull through her mood, even though that approach had never worked in the past. "I'll take the grocery list and get some stuff for lunch, too. I want to check out the new deli. I'll stop by the dry cleaner and the post office. While I'm at it, I guess I'll go over to Millwood and drop off those papers at the accountant's office. Anything else?"

"Not that I can think of."

He dropped his sweaty running clothes on the floor and headed toward the bathroom in his underwear. "Remember," Ruth said. "We decided to cut down on fat in our diet after Max's little… episode. So go easy at the deli."

"Got it." He closed the bathroom door behind him, then re-emerged. "While I'm gone, why don't you try to find some time to relax? You could use a little … " He tried to maintain eye contact and took a step towards her.

"A little what? Relaxation? Is that a joke?" She sidestepped, walking toward one side of the bed. He followed her lead and walked to the other side. They removed the pillows, then simultaneously pulled the covers up toward the headboard and straightened them out, just as they did every morning, not even noticing what they were doing. She waited for him to smooth a wrinkle in the blanket on his side.

"No, I've got way too much to do. I've got to pay bills, do laundry, return at least a dozen phone calls. Including one to Josh, to see if he's called that guy."

"What guy?"

"Don't you remember? That school superintendent Diane told him about, a friend of hers? I could ask him tomorrow at lunch, but I'm afraid it'll piss him off and I don't want that to spoil our time together. So I have to think of a reason to call today."

They fluffed the pillows and replaced them on the bed covers. "And then I have to push and pull some numbers into line for Jeremy."

What she really wanted to do in the worst way was escape into a crossword puzzle. A really hard one, the kind where she'd make inroads bit by bit. "If this letter goes here in the Across word, then that must mean the word going down is… " And after awhile, the world having taken a back seat to the challenge, every box would have the letter that belonged in it.

"But I'll put relaxing on my list and maybe that way I'll get to it—in my next life."

He headed back to the bathroom and she heard him turn on the shower, then call out, "Okay, you do your stuff, I'll do mine, but let's do lunch."

She forced out a curt "It's a date." Neither of them mentioned the elephant in the room waiting to be discussed.

While David was gone, Ruth loaded the stereo with Brahms' Violin Concerto, Joan Baez's Diamonds and Rust, and the Carole King record Josh had called Weally Wosie. She turned up the volume and occasionally hummed or sang along as she neatly slid check-writing and phone-calling between washer and dryer cycles, enjoying the solitude and the steady progress. While she tackled tasks, she also churned around her major dilemmas, David and Jeremy. Yin and Yang. Scylla and Charybdis. Rock and hard place.

She hated the idea of retiring. It was about being old. She wasn't in denial, she knew her body was aging, especially since the so-called "Change of Life." She hated that euphemism for menopause. Menopause needed some marketing. If it were her product, she'd call it "Freedom from Mess." Or maybe "Babies Be Gone."

And her spirit was older, too. She sensed it at work, especially around the snippy young MBA types who thought they knew everything.

Lurking somewhere in there, she knew, was the facts of her parents' deaths, two years apart. She was surprised how much she missed them, considering she hadn't gotten along with them all that well. The other day, she'd caught a glimpse of herself in the mirror at the gym and, fleetingly, saw her mother's face. The sagging cheeks and tired eyes, the graying eyebrows. Did she really look like her mother, she'd wondered with horror? Or was she just missing her?

And raising Josh was over and done with, too. David was right—she should let him run his own life, make his own mistakes. But, oh, she liked it better when he was five or six and she was more … more what? … more important.

Running into Vivian last night didn't help, either, especially since Vivian had remained so "pure."

So, no, she wasn't denying she was aging, she just didn't want to honor it.

David returned from his errands before she'd begun to focus on Jeremy. They unbagged the groceries, working side by side, mostly silently. Each item removed from its bag was like a brick removed from the wall between them.

David unwrapped each lunch element from the new store in town as dramatically as if it were a Christmas present.

"Don't these white beans with olive oil and oregano look terrific? We don't have beans that often and they seem so, I don't know … so … like sitting in a café? Like that time in France with… ?"

Ruth grabbed the stepladder, then silently went to the cupboard over the stove at the far end of the kitchen. She stood on her toes on the top step and grabbed the blue celadon dish they'd bought and shipped home from a pottery factory in Thailand.

"Now here's something you don't see every day. Marinated … Jerusalem … Artichokes," David said, trying to roll the "r's" and waving his hands in the way of a magician with brightly colored scarves.

"What are *they*?" Ruth asked.

"I'm glad you asked. It turns out Steve of 'Steve's Deli' was in Paris during the war. He said food was really scarce because the Germans ate all the good stuff. Except they didn't like Jerusalem Artichokes and left them for the French. Now they're back in vogue."

She walked back to the pantry, flattening herself out as much as possible as she passed David along the way, to retrieve Aunt Alice's practically-unused wedding gift platter with sparkles.

David, still playing Santa Claus, presented the curried lamb balls and dilled new potatoes. When he was finished, he said, "Not too much fat, right?"

"Mm-hmm, you did good, sweetie." Another dropped stitch in the marital fabric reknitted.

They set the food on the round table by the window, rearranging the vase of forsythia, and the salt, pepper, oil and vinegar so everything would fit. Ruth looked at the choice of platters as a montage of their life, foreplay for their discussion. Later.

Next door, Shirley wasn't digging any more. It looked like the hole was done, but the lilac bush wasn't yet in it, and Shirley was gone. The shovel was lying next to the hole, though.

David tasted a little bit of everything in sequence, sometimes combining two items in one bite. Ruth went through one item at a time. "Did you see anyone in town?" she asked.

As they ate, he filled her in on the goings-on. Who was running for mayor, who was resigning from the Town Board, who had had a face lift.

Out on the street, it turned out Shirley wasn't the only one teasing the season. The new family across the way was getting their yard ready, picking up twigs and pruning. It was their first spring in the house, and they were obviously raring to go, energized by the newness.

David had put down his silverware, had his elbows on the table, and was twirling his wedding ring. Ruth wondered why he was nervous. She was the one with the dilemma.

Ruth ate her beans, savoring and stalling.

They sat in silence for awhile. Without looking up from her plate, she said, "I have been thinking about what you said, honey, like I said I would. It was a shock, you know, and I—"

"I guess it was crummy timing to drop it in your lap on the way to the concert. I did try talking about it before, but… " He bit his lip. "When you asked me what the meeting was about, I just didn't want to…"

She cut the two dilled new-potatoes that remained on her plate into pieces, then into smaller pieces, then arranged them as a face. She dragged her eyes off the potatoes and looked up at David, wrinkled her forehead and frowned slightly, tilted her head, then looked out the window, into the middle distance, her eyes not focusing on anything in particular.

"I guess I can see how you might be ready to retire. You've done exactly what you've always known you wanted to do, and you've done a great job and you've been fulfilled by it and so I guess you're ready to let it go. And, besides, you love golf. You're lucky that way."

He nodded slowly.

"Retired people become marginalized, hanging out around the edges of things, looking in to where it's all happening. Like my folks. To the point where an exterminator visit became enough to plan a day around."

"It doesn't have to be—"

"And retirement is about endings," she continued. "I hate endings, even the good ones. I'll just torture myself about my choices. And besides, I just feel like I'm not finished yet."

"Do you suppose there might just be something in between Mimosa and retirement?"

"Then there's that whole thing about accounting for myself and realizing that all I ever did was sell makeup. I didn't cure cancer, I didn't wipe out poverty, I didn't teach children to be better human beings. Except for Josh, of course. I sold makeup, period, the end."

David, with a gentle voice and a gentler touch, pointed out the obvious, that staying at Mimosa wouldn't help her cure cancer or come up with some other dramatic answer for the

Grand Inquisitor. All it would do was put off the moment of questioning her choices. Which she shouldn't do anyway.

He shifted from compassionate to upbeat. "I'm just talking about the next chapter, a fun chapter."

"It may be 'just a chapter,' but it's the *last* chapter, isn't it?"

David's concession—not the one she'd been hoping for—was that he'd retire before her and stop pressuring her to join him.

The clock ticked, a few cars crawled by, and a neighborhood dog barked.

"You're saying you're going to do it whether I do or not? As if it didn't affect me?"

David let go of her hand, moved his chair away from the table and crossed his legs. He thought for a minute, then said, "Time to be honest. Okay?"

She nodded.

"I've never understood why you stayed at Mimosa this long. At the beginning, you kept saying you were only doing the whole corporate gig so we could afford to send Josh to any school he wanted."

"But I got into it."

"Don't get me wrong, I don't care that you stayed even after Josh's tuition was saved up, I…"

"I guess it was Dean, he was such a great boss. The freedom, the creativity. It was kind of heady."

"And now…?"

She pouted, mashing her remaining potato pieces into oblivion, then moving the mush around her plate. Her eyebrows reached for each other, then raised in surprise. Her mouth moved to one side of her face, then returned to center. She bent her nose with the back of her hand.

David asked, "Who just won that argument? And who was arguing with whom? About what, exactly?"

"Can we really afford to retire?"

They discussed their finances, thrust-and-parry. Ruth said they were inching toward the magic figure established by their financial planner. David insisted that was just a tool and they could overrule it. They could live on less and sell their wildly-appreciated home. He started to clear the table and said he was just plain tired of working and thought she wasn't enjoying it much either.

"Not true. I only tell you about the crummy parts because I need to vent. But that's not all there is to it." She was glad she hadn't told him about Jeremy and the charity benefits.

"Isn't it okay to just have some freedom and some fun?"

"Fun? What would I do? I've always worked."

"You don't need to have it all planned out before you make this decision. We can just...."

Outside, an insistent car horn startled her. They both looked out the window but saw nothing. The horn stopped.

"I *do* want to talk about this, Ruthie. But I want to talk about what it's really about. You know it's not about money ... or playing golf with the ladies. What is it?"

"I guess you're sort of right. I don't want to play golf and I do worry about money...."

"And?"

"And I hate change."

"And?"

"Well, there's something else, too. Something happened at work yesterday."

"A good something or a bad something?"

"Not so good. But maybe something good will come out of it. I don't know."

"I knew there was something bothering you last night. What's going on?"

"You have to promise not to use it as a reason I should retire."

"Okay. I won't. Really."

Ruth told David about Jeremy canceling the benefit program. He, more than anyone, knew the extent of the blow and was appropriately horrified. After just the right amount of proxied self-righteous anger, David said, "I'm trapped. I can't say what I want to say because I promised I wouldn't."

"Wait, I haven't told you the part about 'Maybe good will come out of it.'"

"Ah, right." He put his elbows on the table, leaned his chin into his palms, and raised his eyebrows.

She described her recent thoughts about a new product line for older women. It wasn't just about looking back and accounting for herself, she said. It was also a good offense-is-the-best-defense regarding Jeremy. If it were successful.

While it was true that she was never entirely comfortable in her corporate skin, she admitted he'd been right about how she liked being good at what she did. And with this, she could be very good at what she did. She talked about values and the demographics of middle-aged women, their increasing dominance in the population and affluence curve.

The best thing about it, though, was that it was about the idea of authenticity. She spoke louder and faster, losing her sense of David as audience, gesturing grandly to the appliances and cabinets. David followed her with his eyes.

"Authenticity has become very important to me, like there's no more time left for bullshit. You know what I mean by authenticity?" Standing up, she put her hands on the back of the chair, feeling the power of her own enthusiasm make her feel tall.

"Well, I think it's—"

"It's having an 'outside' that matches your 'inside.' It's being real. Everyone's dying to be real, and I am too. And this will help me feel more authentic and—I don't want to be grandiose about this—it just might help other women to feel a little more authentic too, like they don't have to pretend to be something they're not. Like they can just walk down the street and be who they are." She stopped pacing, looked up at David, and added, "And I've got a working name for it." She scrunched up her mouth, as if part of her wanted to keep from saying the name and going public.

"Yes?"

"I'm thinking of calling it 'Violins & Wine.' Because those are things that get better with age."

She lowered her head as she sat down. After a moment, she looked up and said, "What do you think?"

David said it was obvious that she had a different kind of passion for this idea. More than the scarf set or the color bubble-bath or any other product he could remember. He also agreed that it was a good idea and a good name. Between the idea itself and her passion for it, he was willing to concede that she should pursue it. While he pursued retirement.

She started to object, but he cut her off.

"Surely you're not suggesting that I work three extra years so you can pursue your ambition at Mimosa. Right?"

"I guess not. No, certainly not. Not that I'd mind, though. But you're right."

"Ruthie, you've always said you wanted to be more of a risk-taker. So here's your chance. You do the new idea. Be creative and innovative. Be risky. Meanwhile, I'll take the retirement deal. We'll start out that way and see what happens. I'll have dinner on the table when you get home. But ... no ironing."

She asked if he'd consider waiting until the last minute to tell the school officially, just to help her get used to the idea. He agreed to think about it.

"Now," he said, "since I worked my fingers to the bone preparing lunch, you think about your stuff and I'll think about mine while you clean up." Registering Ruth's open-eyed look of surprise, he ran out of the kitchen, scooping up the newspaper on his way.

7

The Brain Trust Weighs In

ARRIVING EARLY AT RUTH'S HOUSE FOR THE HASTILY-CALLED meeting of The Brain Trust, Blanche accepted a glass of wine without any of the usual polite hesitation. She seated herself on the green leather couch directly in front of the cheese platter, arranged her amber-bead necklace so it hung symmetrically on her plush velvet top, then took a generous sip and sighed loudly.

"I'm so glad you broke the rule. I don't care what anyone says, girl, nuts and chips may be easy for the hostess but they're not food. Cheese is food." She moved the throw pillow at her right elbow, putting it behind her head, then flopped back onto it.

"This is the nicest part of my day so far. No customers looking for just the right pencil with just the right eraser in just the right color. No vendors insisting that chartreuse notebook paper is going to be really really big next year and I should stock up. No employees who need to change their schedule because their second cousin's girlfriend's daughter is graduating. Just wine and cheese and friends. Heaven."

"Seems only fair. You come over on short notice, I thank you. Or maybe you should consider it a bribe in case there's a next time," Ruth said.

In the three years since this group of menopausal women had started their monthly meetings to share information and feelings, this was only the second special session. The first, ten months ago, had helped a member sort through the overload of information about treatment options after her diagnosis of breast cancer, providing emotional support along the way.

While Ruth thought her reason for assembling the group seemed trivial compared to cancer, she'd asked anyway. Talking to David had convinced her she needed to put up or shut up. Now she had a goal and a ticking clock, as motivating a combination as a wind-up key in her back. The Brain Trust would be a unique source of information, so she'd asked them to help her with "an important work problem." Four of the five could come.

Blanche finished her cracker, brushed the crumbs off her leather pants and eyed the platter. "You certainly were mysterious about it on the phone. And now I see video cameras? As my mamma would say, the plot she do thicken."

"As soon as everyone's here, I—"

"Don't mind me, I'm fine and oh-so-happy to sit quietly and make a pig of myself." She took a cracker and over-loaded it with cheese, looked at her cheese-mountain, then at Ruth.

"Too much cheese, right?" Before she received an answer, she put another cracker on top of the cheese. "There, that's better." She put her hand on her belly and said, "Ruth, I promise to name my pot belly after you."

As curious as Blanche was, Ruth was eager to hear her input, since she was an uncommon intersection of two-feet-on-the-ground common sense, new age spirituality, and a bit of vanity. Plus she was the only African-American in the group.

Ruth walked around the room, fluffing cushions, lighting lights, and closing curtains. She made sure the two video-cameras covered the couch, the loveseat, the overstuffed armchair, and the wooden rocking chair she'd brought from the den.

Charlie and Sarah arrived within a minute of each other. Blanche got up to join in the hugging. They complained about the busyness of their days keeping them from seeing one another more often, caught up with each other's lives, commented approvingly on haircuts, weight-loss and jewelry, and headed greedily for the table with the cheese.

Ruth-the-marketing-executive saw the group of four, including herself, as an iconic collection of various middle-aged shapes and sizes. Their unifying force was menopause. Some were "only" peri-menopausal, the run-up to the main event, feeling all the symptoms but not yet eligible for chemical relief, others were in the throes itself.

The great divide was between those who believed menopause was a natural wisdom-enhancing part of life, and shouldn't be medicated as if it were a disease, and those who held that wisdom was fine but suffering was not, especially if medicine could help. Whatever their beliefs about menopause, though, they helped each other in the way that women do well.

When Ruth returned from depositing coats, the chatting was in full swing. Blanche was finishing the story of her mamma's not realizing that "Blanche" meant "white" in French, or she'd surely have picked another name. Sarah was telling how she called her first private therapy patient by the wrong name and he was too timid to correct her and the subject of his timidity carried them through the next few sessions. When she sighed and put her hand on her chest, she realized she was still wearing her ID badge from today's pro bono work at the Rehab Center—"Hello, I'm Sarah and I want to help you"—and removed it.

Charlie said, "Jane's going to be a little late and she said not to wait for her. Something about 'No Child Left Behind.' Or maybe it was 'Whack No Child's Behind.' Or 'The Behind of the Child on the Left—"

"Let's start." Sarah's fog-horn voice often said what everyone was thinking. "But first, Ruth, maybe you want to tell us about those video cameras? Are we live on TV?" She pinched her cheeks, tilted her head, batted her eyelashes, and assumed a false smile. "Or are we just being taped for broadcast later on?"

Ruth plopped herself into one of the armchairs and explained that the cameras were just to provide a record—a better record than a tape recorder—of what everyone said, so she didn't have to take notes. "They're just a mechanical aid for someone who can't retain anything ...."

"Except water," came the boisterous chorus. Amid laughter at their oft-repeated joke, they said the cameras would be fine.

Ruth announced the subject of the meeting was makeup. Skincare, too.

"No surprises there," Blanche said.

She wanted to know who used which products, why they used them, and what they wanted the products to do for them. "And after we talk about that, I'll tell you why I'm asking. It's something I'm cooking up at work. And I'll want to hear what you think about that, too."

While Ruth went outside the brightly-lit seating area to turn on the video cameras, the three who remained looked at each other. Sarah said, "Who wants to start?"

Charlie leaned forward as if she were serving up the ball in a hotly-contested tennis match. As a weaver whose work commanded high prices, she dressed as the high-class artist she was. "I'll start." As she spoke, she nodded, and her dangling silver earrings shimmered and caught the light, an effect that looked particularly good with the snowy whiteness of her hair.

"I wash and tone my face and then use moisturizer. I use any old product, usually the drugstore kind. I do it in the morning. I know you're supposed to do it at night, too. Before you go to sleep. But I'm usually too tired."

She looked around from one woman to the next as she spoke. At first, she glanced at the camera occasionally, but by the time she finished what she had to say, she'd forgotten about it completely.

"Makeup's another story. I draw the line at makeup. Cleanliness is good. It's healthful, right? But it seems like makeup is a way of saying you don't like how you look so you want to try to look different. Want to hide yourself. Know what I mean? It's a kind of self-hate. It's very anti-feminist. I just don't know if I could do it." She raised her eyebrows and brought both palms up. "Hey, I went to Berkeley in the sixties and I can't help myself. It's marked me for life. But if I thought it would really work…."

Even though Charlie's gaze eventually settled on her, Ruth avoided it. She'd learned long ago, when driving Josh and his friends in her van, that keeping quiet allowed others to forget about her and talk as if she weren't there. She was sure if she stayed invisible for awhile tonight, she'd get good material to use in the meeting she'd set up with Jeremy for the following Tuesday. Maybe even a few of his beloved numbers.

"I don't agree," Blanche said. "It's not about self-hate. Any more than choosing flattering clothing is about self-hate. Actually, choosing clothes that make you look fat is more like self-hate. In my opinion. Makeup is just like that. It's about looking your best."

Meanwhile, Jane had arrived, amid chants of "Run, Jane run. Sit, Jane, sit. Have cheese, Jane, have cheese." She settled herself on the rocking chair and took some cracker and cheese snacks while they filled her in on the topic.

Blanche continued, though she first made sure the clasp of her necklace was in the center of the back of her neck.

"I for one like to present myself in a good light. And it's not just because I want other people to think I look good, but also because it helps me *feel* good. So, to answer your question, Ruth, I use cleanser and toner and moisturizer, too. But I also use foundation and blush and mascara. Oh, and lipstick, too, of course."

"'Of course'? What do you mean, 'lipstick *of course*,'" Sarah boomed. "I don't wear lipstick, or any make-up. Because that's just buying into a false image of female beauty. And the main effect is to make most of us feel terrible about ourselves. Because, really, very few of us measure up to the media image."

The founder of the group, Sarah was also the oldest and least ambivalent about her opinions. "I've worked with a few anorexic girls and let me tell you what the ideal of female beauty has done for them. They just want to present themselves in a positive light, too, you know."

"It's not always—" Jane was pointing her index finger at Sarah, looking every inch the schoolteacher.

"Let me finish. I was also going to say that it's also too much trouble to do all that stuff. Especially since it doesn't do any good anyway."

"What if it did?" Blanche looked over her red glasses with an impish half-smile.

"What do you mean?"

"Suppose, just for the moment, that all the goo did what it says it does—sorry Ruth, I don't mean to imply it doesn't, it's just a way to frame the question for Ms. Sarah the supremely sincere and authentic. Suppose it did make you beautiful and young-looking. Then would you go to all the trouble?"

"Troublemaker." Sarah put her two hands out, palms up, like a balance scale and alternated lowering one, then the other. "Politics. Vanity. Politics. Vanity. I have to think about that one." Her serious face transformed itself, with a girlish grin surrounded by wrinkles and listless gray-brown hair.

"A whole new side of Sarah," Blanche said. "Interesting, very interesting."

"You know," Jane said as she rocked back and forth, "I think it's very hard to draw the line between self-acceptance and self-help. You know?" If Sarah was the conscience and the sage, the stern mother-figure of the group, Jane was the understanding one, the loving aunt you'd go to when you had to talk to someone about the kids in school who were picking on you. Her round face, short curly hair, and front-tooth-gap gave her an androgynous air, which contributed to the role. So did her voice, soft except when provoked. She was the teacher they all wished they'd had.

"Like when you look at yourself in the morning when you're getting ready for work. Come on, now, is there anyone here who wants to pretend that they look in the mirror and they don't see something they'd like to change?"

Silence.

"Right. See? That's what I mean."

"I'm pretty happy with the way I look," Blanche said. "Except for the belly, I guess."

Sarah said, "You're belly's just fine, Blanche."

Jane shot back, "I thought we were talking about how we *feel*."

"You're right. Sorry," Sarah said.

"Maybe my belly's okay and maybe it's not, but I feel like I wish I could just slice that belly away."

"It's like what Sarah said, sort of," Blanche continued, pantomiming a balance scale as Sarah had done. "Vanity. Denial. Vanity. Denial. On the one hand, I feel like it's unrealistic to want to look twenty-five when I'm fifty-five, and I should just accept myself and not do that whole rejection thing. I tell myself I should be more spiritual than that."

Baritone Sarah jumped at her opening. "That's just what I'm talking—"

"Don't validate my spiritual side until you hear about the other hand, which is that I feel like I should be going to the gym and working out."

"And while we're on the subject of the other hand, and the sound it makes when it's clapping," Charlie looked pleased with her littleturn of phrase, "I hate the way my face and especially my neck, are turning into corduroy. I wish I could iron them."

"You think wrinkles are bad?" Jane asked. "I'll tell you what's really bad. Folds. When you get folds like I'm starting to get—" she stretched out the skin on either side of her mouth—"then you'll wish you had wrinkles again."

"Except maybe for those little ones around your mouth," Charlie said, "that make your pucker look like an asshole."

After a quick high-five from Jane, she added, "The way I see it, there are saggers and there are prunes. Jane may be a sagger, but I'm more of a prune. But I have sagger tendencies, too. Like how my face kind of seems to melt off my skull when I lie on my side or, god forbid, face down. Right? Am I right? Know what I mean?" She nodded and widened her eyes, looking for universal agreement, which she got.

"It's gotten to the point where I never want to be on top because I don't want Gary to see how bizarre it looks when the skin on my face stretches down. In the olden days, I *wanted* to be on top so my boobs would look bigger, right? I guess there must have been a middle period when everything was just the right size and stayed where it belonged. But I don't remember it. Because, as you know, I can't retain anything."

"Except water," came the chorus.

Everyone took some food and a few refilled their glasses. Jane continued, "Everyone has some vanity. Even the little kids in my class. You should see the pictures they draw of themselves."

"It's just a question of drawing the line," Charlie said. "Some people draw it at flattering clothes. Some people draw it at makeup. Others think the line comes just beyond plastic surgery but before cryogenics."

"But it's all connected to our limitless ability to feel bad about ourselves," Sarah said.

"Wait a second," Blanche said. "Isn't the topic something about products?"

"Good girl," Charlie said. "*Someone* can remember the topic. Are you sure you're old enough to be in this group?"

All eyes turned to Ruth. Sarah spoke for the group. "So what's up? Why'd you want to know all this?"

"Remember, at the session when we talked about our work, I said I've always been ambivalent about working at Mimosa?" Ruth noticed her hands were wet and her breath was reluctant. She was going public for the first time—David didn't count—about an idea she'd been nurturing like garden peas in April. And these women were her target market, too. What would they say? And what would they think of her? Sure, they offered relatively unconditional acceptance, but still she wondered what they'd think.

"Yeah, I remember," Jane said. "Ambivalent about a good job with good money. Talk about crazy."

Ruth nodded. "That's me. But one of the reasons is exactly what Sarah said before, because my life's career is in an industry that can make women feel bad about themselves. And I'm part of it. So I was thinking about us, you know, us middle-aged women who are so beautiful on the inside and also, really, beautiful on the outside, too, just not like Isabella Rosselini."

As she explained her idea for the new product line, she warmed to the subject and had no idea if she'd been speaking for five minutes or an hour. She poured herself a glass of wine and forced herself not to look at her watch. "So, I hope I haven't gone on too long, but I'd really like to know what you think. If there were such a product line for mature women, would you be interested? And do you think your friends would? Tell me true. Don't spare my—"

"I like it," Blanche said. "I know I'm never gonna look like Naomi Campbell or Angela Bassett, so I like the idea of being appreciated. 'Cause that's what it is, it's being appreciated instead of discarded. Right? Like years and years ago when they started having ads that actually showed … horrors!…black people in them. Isn't that what we've been talking about? Being included. Being visible. Being accepted. It's kind of revolutionary, so who knows what the corporate movers and shakers might think. But me, an unmover and unshaker, I like it."

"What I'm wondering, though," Sarah said, only slightly louder than the general hubbub, but loud enough for everyone to stop talking, "is about the products you're talking about. What are they? Are they really different from the rest of the stuff out there? Or is this just a scheme for some new advertising campaign to try to lure us holdouts? 'Cause, to me, it sounds like a way to fool the few of us who don't use makeup into finally buying some. And I wouldn't have anything to do with it. It's still about what you look like, not who you are, it's still about covering something up instead of letting something show. Isn't it?"

"Funny," Blanche said, "I think you could look at what you just said in exactly the opposite way. It's only about changing your skin, not about trying to change who you really are. So maybe you don't need to be so … so defensive or … or so judgmental about it."

"Nice try," Sarah said. "I don't buy it. And I wouldn't buy this stuff."

"Well anyway, I figure there are product lines for Asian women and African-American women, so why not older women. Besides, we're here to try to help Ruth, aren't we?" Blanche looked around.

"Ladies, ladies, Ruth knows I love her," Sarah said. She looked at Ruth, who nodded. "But she wants to know what we think. And now she knows what I think."

"And I'm with Blanche," Charlie said. "I think it's a great idea. Just don't forget something for the neck, okay?"

"Me too, I like it a lot. I think it's safely on my side of the line between self-hate and a legitimate desire to present your best face. And there's your answer, Ruth." Jane's summing-up voice and discrete look at her watch announced that, for her at least, it was time to go home. "One of us isn't sold, three are waiting for free samples."

Everyone helped carry dishes and glasses into the kitchen and the meeting ended the way it had begun, like a film played in reverse. They hugged, they chatted, they sent regards to husbands and children.

Three to one, thought Ruth. Not statistically significant, to be sure, but as a testing-of-the-waters, it's not bad at all. Even Jeremy would like those numbers. I think.

8
Some Things Never Change

THE TRIP FROM RUTH AND DAVID'S HOUSE in Northern New Jersey to Vivian and Carlos's apartment in Brooklyn crossed two rivers, three decades, and a state of mind. Ruth asked David to take the Parkway, slightly longer than the Interstate but more beautiful. Usually, his approach to life was the scenic route while hers was the Interstate, but this trip was different. She needed whatever balance the scenic route could provide. Also, it would take longer.

The brilliant yellow forsythia that crowded the northern end of the road's central island provided some good cheer right off the bat. As they traveled south, the bushy forsythia gave way to the stalwart daffodils, then the virtuoso fruit tree and dogwood displays, and finally some early lilacs. Seeing the mauve blooms on the way south meant she'd soon see them in her yard, an annual miracle.

She adored the lilacs, perhaps because of their short season and the fleeting allure of their scent. She always wanted more of the aroma than she could hold onto. Her other favorite was the daffodil, paradoxically, for the opposite reason: they were so easy, coming up every year with no effort, more of them than the year before. They were valiant, they were loyal. People fussed too much over their roses, over-valuing every little bloom, while daffodils didn't get their fair share of esteem because of their dependability. When she felt neglected, she liked to think of herself as a daffodil. Unlike her sister Marge, the prodigal, whose every rare smile was cherished.

Vivian, too, was more like a rose—unpredictable, hard to please, more independent, therefore prized. Before she knew it, she was reliving the fight at the Chinese restaurant, this time with the brilliant comebacks she'd composed afterwards.

"Oh, perfect. This is exactly what you do. You fall in love with someone, they're your best friend, then you drop them when you fall for someone else. You're still trying to reject your parents before they have a chance to reject you. Grow up."

Or, "I guess you just can't stand someone who's different from you. It's too threatening to your neurotic need to be right all the time. Get used to it, you're not right all the time."

It was easy now to look back and see the retorts, not so brilliant after all, for what they were, attempts to return pain. But it was still shocking that Vivian had been so willing to discard her.

Besides all the complexities of the friendship with Vivian, there was Carlos to be nervous about. He used to be so holier-than-thou. Was it youthful idealism? Could he have calmed down by now? Or was it in his DNA?

And she was embarrassed about having become such a straight arrow, "one of *them*," as they used to say in the wisdom of their 1960's hippie-dom. At least her blue denim pants and white cotton sweater didn't look too suburban. Or did they? Anyway, here she was, Ms. Suburban Corporate Executive, while Vivian and Carlos were still making the world a better place.

"Are you okay?" David asked after awhile.

"Mmmm, I guess so."

He looked over at her. "Meaning… ?"

"Just wondering again about what will happen today. Wondering about what Vivian's like. And Carlos too." She kept her gaze straight ahead.

"It'll be fine."

She explained, with only a hint of a whine, that she kept seeing herself through their eyes and felt self-conscious. They'd stayed so pure, with their ideals on the outside where everyone could see them, whereas hers, while they were still there, were covered up. "I'm afraid I'm going to feel like I need to prove myself."

"You're assuming we've changed and they haven't. And it also assumes they'll look down on us suburbanites."

She turned to face him. "Right. But I'm assuming it because it's true. We *have* changed. And you should have seen Vivian in the women's room that night. She was—"

"You're putting them in a category, you're prejudging them. Just what you're afraid they'll be doing to us."

"But—"

"Let's not assume anything, just see what we see." He rolled down his window, sniffed, and said, "Doesn't that air smell great?"

She returned her body to its forward position and her gaze to the speeding lilacs by the side of the road.

"I have to chew on that one. But you're not supposed to be able to reason with your emotions, you know. That's why they're called emotions."

"Like you said, I'm just amazing." He beamed.

Ruth realized David thought she'd complimented him, but the truth was that she suspected David's emotions weren't as "real" as hers. How could they be, if they could be corralled so easily? Before she knew it, she was imagining a vigorous "My Emotions are Bigger Than Yours" debate. Maybe a TV game show. She giggled.

"What?" David asked.

"Oh, nothing," she said. "Just thinking about someone at work."

They crossed the first bridge, the mighty George Washington. Whoever dreamed up suspension bridges sure didn't have Jeremy for a boss, she thought. What an idea, hanging the roadbed from cables running between two towers instead of stretching it from one side to the other. It reminded her of a giant mother with open arms supporting everyone's troubles.

As they continued down the East Side of Manhattan, Ruth

watched the woman in the car to their right. She was about Ruth's age, with long hoop earrings that bobbed as she shook her head, which she did constantly. Ruth realized the head-bobbing was accompanying the kind of lusty singing an empty car invites. And then she saw the woman was singing along to the same music she and David were listening to on the radio, a station that played rock and roll from the sixties and seventies. Ruth enjoyed how she remembered every word of every song, even those she hadn't heard for years. She started singing, too, hoping the woman would look over. When she did, they had a good laugh as they sang together, neither one able to hear the other. The virtual duet lifted Ruth's spirits and kept them elevated the rest of the way, over the Brooklyn Bridge, to Brooklyn Heights, and into a lucky parking spot practically in front of Vivian's apartment.

Carlos opened the door. There was a breathless moment while the three old friends squared their memories of the other faces with the reality.

He was much older. His hair was still long, but not so thick, not so dark, and he now wore it in a ponytail. His long, thin face was lined and tired, though his dark eyes were still steel-bright under stern brows, and his gaze was firm. Tall and trim as ever in what looked to be the jeans he wore in the Peace Corps—like him, a little older, a little more worn—he hunched over just a little, as if something hurt.

Ruth imagined a video of Carlos's younger face gradually aging until it got to its present state, like police projections of kidnapped children's faces. It didn't feel like her life passing in front of her eyes, exactly, the way people said happened at times of great urgency, but it *was* coming up against the passage of time.

Ruth let out her breath first. "Carlos, I'd know you anywhere, you look exactly the same. You haven't changed even the tiniest little bit."

Carlos looked down. "I don't know about that," he said in the husky voice she'd last heard in Africa, now with the addition of a slight Spanish accent.

David said, "Oh Carlos, allow me to let you in on Ruth's code. Now you're supposed to say, 'Neither have you, Ruth. You look exactly the same as you did when you were twenty-five. Actually, you look even younger. And thinner.' Not that she's lying about your looking good, though. You do."

Carlos looked back up to meet David's eyes and smiled gently, as if to say he got the joke, but wasn't playing the game. "It's good to see you two. It sure has been a long time. I remember once, maybe it was the last time the four of us were together, when we were at the Café de Paris. In Dakar."

"Probably playing Scrabble," David said.

"Even though half the pieces were missing," Carlos said.

"And we were probably arguing about something," Ruth said.

"Like whether 'beatnik' is allowed in the game," David said.

"Which it was, just like I said. I looked it up later on."

"I can't believe you did that. Okay, okay, you win."

"We were probably also wrangling about who'd pay for the beers," Carlos suggested. "I'm pretty sure it was your turn."

"Or about how long it would take us to save the world," Ruth said. She instinctively stepped forward to hug Carlos. He was so stiff she felt like she was hugging a coat rack.

Carlos and David shook hands energetically. "Come on in. It's *muy bien* that you're here. Vivian's so excited, she's been telling everyone we know. Talking even faster than usual."

As they entered the apartment, Vivian emerged from the rear. "Ohmygod David. Oh. My. God. I can't believe it. It's so incredible to see you again. Incredible. You look terrific, you haven't changed at all. I'd know you anywhere. Oh, I can't believe it, here you two are, in my house. I'm sosoSO happy to see you." She hugged David warmly, standing on her toes, patting his back, breaking away from her hug to take a step back and look at him, then hugging him again.

She approached Ruth. "It sure is lucky we were in the same place at the same time and both had to pee."

Vivian showed them around the apartment. A floor-through on the bottom of the brownstone, a half-level below the street, it was dark, even at mid-day. As she led them into the living room, she turned on the lights.

Crammed among a couch covered with threadbare Indian-print fabric, two painted rattan armchairs, and pine desk was a hyperactivity of objects. Photos filled the walls, the bookshelves, the desk. Ruth and David walked around and watched Vivian and Carlos's daughter, Ida, grow up in pictures. The proud parents silently observed their rapt attention. Ruth gave an occasional "Aaahhh."

There were also photos of Vivian and Carlos at work, she with her clients at the Brooklyn Shelter for Women, where she was a counselor, he at his desk as the Assistant Executive Director of the Prisoners' Rights Foundation. Some photos showed them at political rallies and retreats where the causes and the clothing changed, but the energy remained constant.

When she saw the photo in the African print picture frame on the windowsill, Ruth brought her right hand to her chest as something between a sigh and a gasp escaped her mouth. There she was, twenty-five-year-old Ruth, in the hut she and Vivian had shared in Djembering, surrounded by crintin, Ada the refrigerator, the orange crate bookshelves, and a bunch of smiling children who would now be about thrty-five years old. She turned to look at Vivian, who was already looking at her. Vivian's silence was more expressive than her words ever were.

Besides the photos, there was a traffic jam of African art on every wall and horizontal surface, as well as on the floor. There were wood sculptures and masks, some with metal trim, some with straw, some with cowrie shells. There was an assortment of fabric hangings, the black and white mud-painted Korhogo cloth from the Ivory Coast, the brightly-colored Abomey toiles with fabric appliqués of animals and traditional symbols, and the striped blue Malian weavings. All the art was African, even after all these years. Houseplants added to the frenzy, big ones on the floor, smaller ones competing with the photos for room on the desk and bookshelves, and hanging baskets. The small space was filled to bursting.

The clutter didn't bother Ruth as she would have expected. Nor did the water stains on the walls or the creaking and uneven planks in the ancient wooden floor. She knew this place was very different from her own orderly home and recognized the irony of her envying a life that had yielded fewer material possessions than her own. Carlos and Vivian had taken a different path than she had, and she wondered what it would have been like if she'd chosen that path too. No fancy house in the suburbs, no debt-free tuition for Josh, no corporate perks, but maybe idealism. Maybe passion.

"It's beautiful," Ruth said.

"Well, we like it here, we really do. It's kind of funky, sort of like us. But we can afford it and it's a decent commute to our jobs, so that's good too. I know you probably live someplace that's much more—"

"And the neighborhood's great," Carlos added. "The block association holds pot luck dinners every month. And a great public library a few blocks away. Too bad Ida's grown up, because the public school's terrific, a nice mix of middle-class and working-class kids. Very progressive program."

They continued through the living room and out the other end, careful not to knock over any of the items they slalomed around on the way. The apartment was laid out in a long line from the living room on the street side of the brownstone to the kitchen at the back. As they entered the next room, Vivian turned on its lights while Carlos doubled back to turn off the ones in the living room.

The bedroom had only a bed in the middle, a dresser on the wall to the left, and a floor-to-ceiling bookcase, stuffed full and running over, on the right. The bedroom's comparative emptiness brought its shabbiness into relief. The paint was peeling badly, and the bed was supported by three legs and a pile of books. They continued into the kitchen, where the chaos that was missing from the bedroom had taken refuge. A long narrow battered oak table was in front of them, set with four unmatched places. The cooking area was to the left, and a counter filled with jars, collectible chotchkies and telephone paraphernalia, was in between. Beyond the kitchen was a neglected garden in an interior courtyard that provided a little natural light.

"Well, now you've seen it." Vivian spoke louder than she needed to and shrugged. "Believe it or not, it's a big step up from our place in Washington Heights, but that place went co-op a couple of years ago, so we had to leave. We were lucky to find this, boy we had to look and look, and you wouldn't believe the places we saw and turned down. So here we are, all snug and at home."

David said, "Hey, this place is fabulous. I think if we'd seen a place like this when we were looking around for—"

"So, *mi amigos*, have a seat everyone." Carlos turned out the lights in the bedroom and led everyone to the table. He took his place at the narrow end near the door, while Vivian directed Ruth and David to his right.

"Carlos, my friend," David said, "you seem to have gotten more Spanish than you used to be. I know your father's Puerto Rican, but is this some kind of time-release ethnicity? Or have you changed parents?"

"A lot of people at work have Spanish accents. I guess it's catching," Carlos said to the table top.

"Anyway, I hope you still like Bloody Marys, 'cause I still make the best ones you ever had," Vivian said. "Really and truly, the best. You'll see, the very best." She reached into the refrigerator and took out four glasses and a pitcher, all thick glass with bubbles trapped inside, a blue stripe along the top. She stuck a celery stalk in each filled glass before passing them around. Ruth held her glass out and said, "In the immortal words of those wise volunteers who preceded us… "

"Don't let the bastards get you down," came the enthusiastic chorus, followed by clinks and gulps.

Everyone sipped until Vivian insisted they bring each other up to date on their lives. "You can go first, then us. We have all day. Moderate bragging about kids is allowed, okay?"

Ruth pointed her celery stalk at David. "You do it, okay?"

"Where should I start?"

Vivian jumped right in. "Start with how you went from being friends, you know, the platonic kind of friends, which you always insisted you were even though I knew better, even back then, and wound up being married and proving that I was right all along, even though I had to wait for you guys to catch up to my superior wisdom."

"Right," Ruth said. "Superior wisdom. Honey, start with the trip to Woodstock and how we got turned back by the State Police and arrived at my parents' house, covered with mud."

He took a big sip, then launched into the oft-told story of their muddied arrival at her parents' house where, because of a houseful of guests, they'd had to share a bedroom. Since they were platonic friends, no one thought much of it, but the sleeping proximity resulted in a seismic shift in their relationship. The new relationship took root quickly and grew.

He took the scenic route for the story of their lives and Ruth herded him back to the chronological thrust whenever she felt a side-trip was only marginally relevant. When he started telling about their visit to John and Janet, mutual Peace Corps friends who'd become sheep farmers in rural Vermont, Ruth burst in. She pointed out that, though it had been more than thirty minutes, he was only up to 1983. So David left John and Janet in the lurch and switched to Josh, indulging in the allowable bragging, showing the three pictures they'd brought for this purpose. He summed up their work lives by describing his work at the high school and his new plan to retire soon, then Ruth's work as the means through which she'd been able to express her creativity, plus put Josh through college.

"I made it in under an hour," he announced. "Your turn." He pointed his glass first at Carlos, then at Vivian, then drank.

"First, let's fill those poor empty glasses," Carlos volunteered.

"And how about some food to absorb all that alcohol? Who's hungry?" Vivian and Ruth brought platters of bagels, cream cheese, and lox from the refrigerator to the table and passed around the chipped plates and mismatched silverware.

"Anyone want coffee yet?"

"Right after I finish this Bloody Mary," Carlos said, taking a big gulp.

Vivian told how she and Carlos had continued seeing each other after Peace Corps, as they worked for the same anti-war groups. They got married and continued to work for "the movement" for about five more years, he as an organizer (and part-time bartender to pay the rent), she in a printing shop that produced leaflets and brochures. Carlos contributed a description of their economically marginal and sometime nomadic existence, while Vivian giggled and looked nostalgic.

Then she turned to Ida's birth and neo-natal emergency surgery to repair a hole in her heart and a malformed esophagus. Ruth occasionally stole a glance at Carlos. He fingered a silver and turquoise bracelet on his right wrist, rubbing it one stone at a time. Once, he looked up at her and they remained locked in eye contact for a long three seconds. For most of that visual game of chicken, Ruth had the feeling he wasn't looking at her so much as through her, to the past, but then he snapped out of it and saw her. He shrugged.

Ida's problem was completely corrected with her surgery. "The doctors told us she'd have one permanent side effect," Carlos said solemnly. "She'll never be able to eat upside down. So she can never be an astronaut." Passing pictures of Ida around, Vivian added, "I can live with that."

Sometime after Ida's birth, around the time she started school, Vivian and Carlos got their more sedentary jobs. "And here we are," he concluded, "regular middle-class Amuricanos. Sort of."

Vivian reached for the full coffeepot at the far end of the table. She poured four mugs-full and passed them around. Her fingernails were bitten down to the quick, and two of them had bloody cuticles. Were her fingers that way when she started the story of their lives? Ruth wondered. Or did this story cost her a few fingernails?

Carlos crossed his legs in a lotus-position on the bench as he said, tight-lipped, "There's just one li'l bit I don't understand, Ruth. You work at a make-up company?"

Her stomach tightened. Oh no, here it comes. "Yup, I do. Yes." She kept an even tone, concentrating on not feeling apologetic or defensive.

"You're a manager?"

"Mm-hmm, I am. Yes indeed, a manager."

Vivian put her hand on Carlos's arm. "Carlos," she said more slowly than Ruth had ever heard her speak. "Have some coffee. Don't do this." She raised his mug to his mouth.

"I wanna ask one more thing, okay, just one, pretty please?"

"Go ahead Carlos," Ruth said, forcing herself not to look away from his gaze and not to furrow her brow into a headache.

"I was just thinking that it's bad enough you're management on the backs of labor, but in an industry that, well, let's just say it's … not food, not clothing, not shelter. Just something that goes along with the Barbie Doll image women seem to be persuaded to buy into." He looked at her and raised his scraggly eyebrows.

Vivian rushed in with "Oh Ruthie, don't mind him, really, it's okay, you know Carlos has strong feelings about everything, I'm sure you're not surprised, right? That's the way he was and that's still the way—"

"Hey guys," David said. "You know we're just here to get reacquainted and have a nice time, have fun, not to solve the problems of the world."

"That's just the point. Solving the problems of the world is fun for us. Always has been. And," Carlos added, "it used to be fun for you too. So what happened to you guys?"

Ruth took as big a sip of the hot coffee as she could and forced herself to speak slowly, thinking she'd sound confident that way. "So I see, when all is said and done, you're still not the most tactful guy in the world, Carlos."

"Si, I've been told that. But tact isn't important to me. Truth is."

She thought back to her anxieties in the car and was at least glad that they'd been justified. "Is this Marxist shorthand? The workers should own the means of production, capitalism is evil and all that?"

"Bingo."

"Ruthie, why don't we—" David put his arm around her.

She shook it off. "No, David, why don't we *not*? Don't do that. That's you, not me."

Then she turned to Carlos and forced herself to make eye contact. "Just for the moment, let's ignore your smug superiority, and just talk about what you said." Her mouth seemed to have a mind of its own, but at least it covered the sound of her heart knocking at her chest to get out. "You're pretty glib about the evils of capitalism, but communism hasn't exactly worked out so great."

"*Si, si*, that's true in some parts of Eastern Europe. But you need to take a look at Cuba. It's different there. You know, we went down there for the Venceremos Brigade." The twinkle in Carlos's eyes had returned, giving Ruth the clear impression that he was enjoying making her mad. And that just made her madder.

"Cuba? You're talking about Cuba?"

"There's Sweden, too, if you prefer. Socialist more than communist."

She knew that if he weren't so arrogant, she might tell him

she agreed with a lot of what he said. Well, some of it anyway. And, besides, he wasn't an innocent bystander when it came to capitalism. He bought those paper towels over there, and the coffee, the peanut butter, the newspaper, and everything else in the house, including the film for family photos, all from companies with bosses and workers. And that bit about being on the backs of labor was ridiculous. She was a great boss.

"Did you ever stop to think about—"

"Calm down, love. Maybe that's enough for now?" David asked.

David didn't have to join in the argument if he didn't want to, but at least he could stop being Mr. Reasonable, Mr. "We Can Discuss This Like Mature Adults." He could at least be angry at Carlos, couldn't he?

"Ruthie seems to be holding her own, David," Vivian said.

"It's just that—"

"David, you don't have to argue if you don't want to, but I *can* if I want to."

"So when did you get so smart, *senora* Ruthie?"

"And Carlos, when did you get so condescending? Oh wait, I forgot, you were always condescending."

If they only knew. She was like an M&M: hard shell on the outside, all gooey and melted on the inside. David knew. Was fooling people this way good? Or was it self-defeating, she wondered.

Vivian asked if the caffeine was starting to kick in. Silence was her answer. She looked from Ruth to Carlos. "You two picked up right where you left off, didn't you?"

Again, silence was the answer.

"I'll clean up," David said.

Ruth thought she'd kill him for that. Did he think he was being a good guy? Or did he want to get away from Carlos as much as she did? Or did he want to try to force the two of them to make up? In the living room, where he didn't have to hear it? It didn't matter, she was still going to kill him.

"And I'll help David," Vivian said. "And see if I can't draw him into the fight just a tiny little bit."

"Lots of luck," Ruth said.

Vivian raised her mono-brow as she looked over at Ruth, but then went to the sink, handing David a dishtowel.

In the living room, Ruth made a bee-line for the photos along the far living room wall. At least she could avoid eye contact that way. Carlos came up beside her and they stood shoulder-to-shoulder.

"We really have had some good times, Viv and I," he offered.

"Mmm-hmm, I can imagine."

He shrugged.

Did he think he'd just apologized? She needed for him to know that he hadn't. They moved a few paces to the left.

"Where was that one taken?" Ruth asked, staying in neutral conversational territory.

"We used to go up to our friend's farm upstate for weekends. That one was a weekend when a whole bunch of us went up to help him paint the barn. It was a party for a whole weekend, I remember. Sleeping bags, beer, paint, rock 'n' roll. The good old days."

She moved to the left again, in front of a series of Ida's school portraits.

The phone rang and Carlos answered while she stared at Ida's pictures and imagined how it might have been if she'd known her while she was growing up.

"Ida is the love of my life," Carlos said, and silently returned to her side. He fingered the bracelet again. "*Mi amor.*"

"Clever of you guys to mount all the school pictures in a row like that." She straightened a crooked photo. "This one looks like … third grade?"

"Something like that. I guess."

"You know, Carlos, it's not just *what* you say. It's *how* you say it. Like it always was."

"I believe what I believe. Passionately. It's my religion. Peace. Justice. Equality. Fairness. That kind of stuff. And they're more important to me than making nice with people who don't believe them. Or who aren't doing a good enough job."

"I believe in them too, you know."

He turned to stare at her full on. "Then why are you peddling makeup, *chiquita*?" He put his hands on her shoulders. "You were one of the good guys and—"

"I still am." She left his hands where they were, though they communicated weight more than warmth.

"Last time I saw you, you were a Peace Corps Volunteer. Now you're a manager in a big corporation. Maybe you've accepted the change gradually, but I only just found out."

"You don't need to accept anything. It's *my* life. And it's more complex than you're making it sound." She stepped back, out of his arms' length.

"Okay, *bueno*. But I don't see how you can believe in those values, really believe in them, and not be part of the movement."

"The movement? Like in the sixties?"

"People are still working for justice. Lots of people. Really good people."

"I do my part, in small ways. I'm not trying to change the whole world, it's true, but I do some things that make incremental changes. I guess I don't think it's realistic to think I can change the world."

"And I feel like I *have* to try to change the world."

"And I respect that. But I don't think it's the only way to be. And I don't like having to defend myself like this."

"I just call it like I see it."

He bumped her to the left, to the series of Peace Corps photos.

"Don't you think there's more than one way to be a good person in the world?" Why couldn't she let this drop?

"No, I don't."

Vivian and David came in. "At least they're not hitting each other," Vivian said. "Is it safe?"

"Yeah, sure," Carlos said quickly. Ruth looked up at him, seeing again how he'd aged.

"Did I hear the phone? Who called?" Vivian asked.

"Casey. Asking about his loco plan for a sit-in. He said he wanted my opinion. But he didn't like it when I gave it."

"Really? How can that be?" She kissed him on the cheek. "Why don't you show David the bookshelf project in Ida's old room, and maybe get his advice? But don't yell at him if you don't like his ideas, okay?"

Carlos and David couldn't get out of the room fast enough.

Ruth and Vivian leaned back on the arms of the couch so they faced each other. Each pulled her feet up under her, as if they were pony-tailed fifteen-year-olds listening to their favorite Frankie Avalon records and talking about the boys in school.

"Finally," Ruth said. She slowly looked around, this time letting her eyes go out of focus to get a total effect. There was so much stuff, with so little space between the individual elements, that it looked like a jigsaw puzzle whose pieces had been pulled apart from each other just a little bit. Her eyes were drawn to a photograph of the three of them when Ida was about eight years old. They must have been at a street fair, because Ida's face was painted red, blue, and green, and it radiated a childlike unguarded happiness. What was striking was that Vivian's face and Carlos's face, though unpainted, radiated similarly. She mourned the lost years of their friendship.

"I really like your place. It's so *you*." Ruth was warmed by the old intimacy. Not that she would mind a little regret from Vivian for throwing their friendship in the garbage in the Chinese restaurant. She wondered if Vivian even remembered the argument. She probably thought they'd just drifted apart, as friends sometimes do. Oh, well. Some parts of Vivian were easier to take than others. Just like everyone else. A package. Take it or leave it.

"So, you two seem pretty happy," Vivian said, somewhere between a question and a statement.

"Yeah, we are. Life is good for us. We mesh. We keep each other balanced. And you?"

"We're good too, but not in that way. Obviously, neither one of us is exactly a pussycat, so we've had our fair share of times when we went at it like cats and dogs, oil and water, Nixon and Mao." She looked thoughtful. "To tell you the truth, I guess I wouldn't have it any other way. It's part of the passion. The good things are better than I ever thought they'd be, and the bad things are worse."

"I think all marriages are that way, don't you?"

Vivian cracked the knuckles on her left hand one at a time. "Maybe. Carlos can still be an attack-dog sometimes, but believe it or not, he's gotten a lot better. What can I say? He thinks what he thinks, and most of the things he thinks are enlightened. Or at least tending in that direction. And at least he's not a hypocrite. Like the time when he thought monogamy was a crock, but at least he thought it was a crock for both of us. And anyway—"

"You mean—?"

"Never mind. We straightened that one out eventually. It was one of our bigger fights and it took a few ultimatums. It was not a happy time, but it's over. As far as you're concerned, he doesn't mean to be obnoxious. Well, maybe he does. But like I said, we're not pussycats."

"Well, you always knew where you stood with Carlos, and I see that part hasn't changed. There's a certain comfort in that. No complexity, no ambiguity. I wouldn't admit this to him, but… "

"What?"

"The truth is, I'm not always so thrilled about what I do either."

"What do you mean?"

"Well, it's sort of like what Carlos said, but don't you dare tell him I said that. I used to be a Peace Corps volunteer, making the world a better place, and here I am, five minutes later, or so it seems, management in a cosmetics company."

"So change."

"It's not so simple."

"But it is. If you don't like it, find something else. It doesn't have to be complicated. You always thought things to death and I see you still do. You're your own worst enemy."

"Like I said, it's not so simple, especially not now. I've got this new boss. What a pain. I might have considered leaving before he came, but not now. It would give him too much pleasure. And for another—"

"The way I see it is that if you don't like what you do, you should do something else. Or retire and volunteer. Like, for me. Or Carlos. Only kidding. But seriously, you could—"

"Don't mention my retiring in front of David. His school district is offering early retirement and he's probably going to take it. And he wants me to retire too."

"Really? What would he do?"

"I don't know. If it were me, I'd make lists of alternatives with the advantages and disadvantages of each, then formulate my plan. But not David. He'll figure it out as he goes along."

"I don't know if I'd go so far as to make up a list and a plan, no I definitely wouldn't do that, but I'd have lots of ideas, too many of course. Like there's traveling and there's studying and there's volunteering and, you know, I've always wanted to sing, can you believe it? Do you think he'll—"

The men came into the living room, reminiscing about their days in Kaolack, laughing about Carlos's meltdown when his new roommate ate the canned apple pie filling he'd been hoarding since his mother had sent it.

There it was again, David's aggressive niceness. Sometimes she envied it but sometimes, like today, it was aggravating. Even if she and Carlos made their peace, it's not as if nothing had happened. Wasn't it better to be mad and make up eventually, to let someone know he did something you didn't like, than to never notice that something was wrong?

David had papers to grade; Ruth had a community meeting. As they left, the four made another date to continue catching up with each others' lives. Ruth had two weeks to figure out how to either get along with Carlos or not care about it.

9

What's Wrong With This Picture?

JEREMY LEFT HIS JACKET ON THE BACK OF HIS DESK CHAIR, patting it as he emerged from behind the protective wooden mass with measured steps. He pointed to the less formal seating area of his office. He didn't say "Sit," "Stay," or "Heel," but Ruth half expected it. He offered coffee from the urns he kept on the table by the couch and, while asking about cream and sugar, made small talk about the weather and the stock market, masquerading as a casual person. He even complimented her on her shoes.

Meanwhile, she studied his appearance. Decent-looking enough, kind of an EveryMan, with fairish skin, light-brown hair, small ears, unobtrusive nose. None of his features gave offense, but none stood out either. They just did their part individually, like good soldiers.

Handing her one of the mugs, he folded himself into the chair facing her. He tugged his freshly-creased pant leg with his right hand, then flung that leg over the other, like a marionette. He asked innocently, as if he hadn't cut her heart out ten days before, "So, Ruth, you wanted to speak to me about something?"

Here goes. No turning back.

Ruth had brought a mountain of data with her: financial, demographic, psycho-social. Terry had helped her with a lot of it, even after Ruth had worried aloud that any anti-Ruth animosity from Jeremy might now spill over onto her.

"Not to worry. All this stuff existed in our databases. I just rearranged it. Like pulling out the right pieces in Pick-up

Sticks. Besides, I think his current target is Martha, over in Communications."

She'd also approached Roger from Research & Development. Big and gruff, he'd been at Mimosa as long as she had, and was even older than she, with a shock of white hair exploding from his head to prove it. He'd come up with something that might be an approach to an approach, a previously-abandoned foundation that sank gently into a woman's wrinkles and changed shading, rather than staying on top of them and trying to cover them up. It was a start.

Plus she'd brought testimony in the form of quotes and photos she'd extracted, with permission, from her videos of The Brain Trust meeting.

"Jeremy, I've got a big idea. Big profits. Even better, it would carve out a new niche. Shift the makeup paradigm."

"Shift the make-up paradigm?"

"Like when luggage with wheels changed everything? Or remote control for TV? It's like that, something to change the market, get people to rethink their whole view of make-up."

"A new make-up paradigm? Like maybe a paper … a paper covering … sort of like a thin mask? I gather from your office décor you like masks."

She assumed this was a joke and smiled quickly but so did he and, in terms of smile-speed, he was the champ. "But really, Ruth, I don't know about a new, a new paradigm. We just need good products."

"I wouldn't disagree. Let me show you some of the women who would be our target customers." Ruth displayed the poster-boards.

First, Jane, age fifty-four, teacher. "I like to take care of my skin and I like to present the best me possible, but I resent being told that the only way to look good is to look young."

Then Sarah, fifty-six, therapist, looking old and tired, her listless hair pulled back in a clip behind her neck. Not like Mimosa customers. "I don't wear any of that stuff because I don't buy into the corporate idea of female beauty. It's totally unrealistic and it pisses me off."

Then Blanche, fifty, entrepreneur. "Cleanser, toner, moisturizer, yes. Lipstick, yes. Everything else, no. Why? Because I don't need to look like someone else, I need to look like me. A me with lipstick is just fine."

Charlie, fifty-three, weaver. She was wearing one of her creations in the form of a scarf and one of her earrings was in mid-twinkle, echoing the mischief around her eyes. "If I thought makeup could help me feel good about myself instead of feeling bad that I don't wind up looking like those models in the ads, I'd buy it in a second."

Thank you, Charlie, thought Ruth. I couldn't have said it any better myself.

"Let's face it, Jeremy. The underlying assumption of all our products is that young is good, old is bad."

"It's not rocket science, Ruth. Young *is* good. Old *is* bad."

"Not exactly. Deep inside, women are dying to be real and, for middle-aged women, young is not real. That's why the working name is 'Violins & Wine: for the woman who gets better with age.'"

"Better with age? Come on, Ruth. We're in the make-up business, not the therapy business."

She started presenting Terry's data, leading up to the dramatic finish, two pie-charts. One showed the effect of luring non-cosmetics-buying women into the market. The second assumed fifty percent of these new buyers—even though Ruth thought it would actually be closer to 100%—would buy Mimosa's products. Sales increased by eight percent, from $300 million to $324 million.

Ruth said that since it would be the first major launch under his leadership, and the profit potential was so big, she wanted him to be involved immediately. She wound up her flattery-as-pitch with how important it would be for Mimosa to make a big splash right after becoming a B&D company. She was pretty sure she looked sincere.

Without a word, he got up and walked around his office. Every once in a while, he'd ask a question, usually about numbers. He finally settled in front of the windows and opened the drapes to expose the view of Central Park. One hand tugged at an earlobe, then at his lower lip, as he stared out. No darting tongue. Ruth knew she had to sit quietly, even through a hot flash, and let him think.

She'd taken her best shot, had her say in her calculated and respectful way, let herself be vulnerable. But this moment was lasting forever. Was he going to give her a lecture about scatter-brained ideas? Or suggest she find a company whose do-gooder values were more aligned with her own? Was he trying to figure out how to get rid of her and steal her idea? Or wondering whether she'd dare threaten to take it to the competition? Or maybe he was hoping she'd do exactly that so he'd be rid of her?

She resolved to count five more complete breaths before breaking the excruciating silence, but in the middle of her fourth inhale, just as she was noticing the previously-empty frame now had a striking black-and-white photograph of the Statue of Liberty that looked out of place in the middle of all the blandness, he turned to face her.

"This is interesting, Ruth." He put on his jacket and stayed at his desk. Was she supposed to go over and sit opposite him? She stayed where she was.

"Calling it a paradigm may be a stretch. And twenty-four million dollars in increased sales is completely unrealistic. Out of the question." Smile. Tongue dart. "But the old gals do have gobs of money. If we could separate them from some of it by telling them it's okay to look old—assuming they'd actually fall for it—that would be interesting.

He walked over to her side of his office. "What would you see as next steps?"

This man was direct, she had to give him that. Even when he was right for the wrong reasons. She rattled off some suggestions about research and focus groups, about timetables and milestones.

When she touched on possible project partners within the company, she impishly proposed Martha in Communications.

Jeremy said, "No, let's think of someone else."

Ruth used raised eyebrows to put a discrete question mark on her face, but Jeremy only said, "I just don't think she's the right one for now."

"Okay, how about—"

"When you get back to your office, just write it all up, everything we just said and any other thoughts, as well as projected timetables. As precise as possible at this preliminary stage."

This was much more than she'd expected. "You bet," she said on the way out.

When she got back to her office, her sanctuary, everything felt different from the way it usually did. Lighter, sort of. Not exactly lighter, more like there was more space between things. No, that wasn't it, either. Less substantial? More contrast?

She knew she didn't need to, but did an inventory anyway. The masks, photos and carvings were where they belonged. Her desk, neat but productive, with her calendar and to-do lists right where they belonged.

Colleen's desk was still directly in front of her office. To the right was Tom, with his phone balanced between his ear and shoulders, taking notes with one hand on one of the many scattered papers on his desk, keeping his hair out of his eyes with the other hand. Pat was at her desk, too, also on the phone, absent-mindedly dusting her silver-framed pictures of horseback-riding and ballroom dancing competitions while she nodded her head and looked around. Judy wasn't at her desk, but her potted plants stood guard with their leaves shiny and their blossoms perfect. Tom got off the phone and turned to his computer. Pat hung up and stood. Life went on.

It had only been an hour or so since she was last here. She knew nothing was *really* different. It just seemed that things had shifted because her idea was now out in the world, no longer just a rose-colored fantasy. It felt like the time a little sheet of wrinkled blue paper informed her in stilted language that she was pregnant. All of a sudden, abracadabra, presto chango, the world was not what it had been.

Mimosa was now going to be the place where she put herself directly in the line of fire, making herself 3-D visible. Now "they"—the great massive "they" out there—could find out how inadequate she really was.

She knew it was David's prep period and he'd be in the teacher's lounge, available to take a call. "Hey, honey. Guess what?" she said.

"Are you calling from the Unemployment Office?"

"He sort of said okay. Didn't jump up and down with joy, but said we can do some preliminary exploration. I can't believe it."

"I can. Because it's a great idea. Congratulations, Ruthie. I'm really happy for you."

"Thanks."

"Aren't you?"

"Of course." Tom started to make another phone call. Pat walked to the elevator. Judy returned to her desk, brushed off the chair and sat. Colleen waved to someone. "I'm just a little breathless. And a little distracted. Oh, also, he said I have to change the name."

"Really? Just so you couldn't get your way completely?"

"He was kind of snotty about it, too. I think his exact words were, 'You're just going to have to do an about face on that name.' About face, that's what he said. Can you believe it?"

"About face?"

"About face. Wait a second. Wait, wait, I just had a thought."

"Me too. Same thought? About a name?" David asked.

"Could be. But, then again, I don't know… "

"How about I'll make us a nice dinner after my parent-teacher stuff, and we can compare and contrast our thoughts. Can you wait?"

"Can you get some nice wine, too?"

"I love you," he whispered.

She heard some teachers in the background yell, "We love you too, Ruthie."

She smiled. "Me too."

She let out her breath and swiveled to face the window and watch the traffic patterns. Continuous and hypnotic, the urban equivalent of waves at the beach, they aroused a powerful longing to be at the shore, sitting on the sand and watching the ocean.

She was glad her facts-and-figures approach had been successful. But now the prospect of actually starting to work on the project—research, battles with R&D, packaging, and, eventually, advertising—seemed enormous. Such a lot of work. And it would take years. Did she really want to be in all this for years? Was David right after all?

Maybe her usual self-medication for anxiety would do the trick. She took a stack of her beautiful paper and markers to start a fresh To-Do list, complete with columns and color-coding. But it sat blank on her desk while she gazed outside. She couldn't bring herself to construct it. Odd, very odd.

She would have expected to feel very excited after this kind of success. Fast heartbeats, uncontrollable smile, inability to sit still. But there was none of that. Things felt different, yes, but not exciting. She felt empty. Tired? No, not tired, empty.

What's going on here? she thought. I wanted this so much. It's the right project at the right time. Women are ready for it. I'm ready for it. The company is ready for it. Twenty-four hours ago I was thrilled at the idea. Wasn't I? I think I was. Is this fear? Am I afraid of having to prove myself, afraid of failing?

No, she knew what fear felt like and would recognize it in an instant. It wasn't the presence of something negative like fear or doubt. No, it was more like the absence of something positive.

Right, that was it. She expected joy. Where was joy? Why was she so unaroused, so un-joyful? She was unmoved. Numb.

She tiptoed out to the void, confronting the possibility that her emotional disconnection meant she didn't really want to do this revolutionary product line after all. Maybe the fantasizing and planning were the fun part, but the prospect of actually devoting a few years to it was something else. If what she'd thought was her professional heart's desire wasn't, then what was?

She'd never had such difficulty looking inside herself and sorting out what she was feeling. This was not a recognizable sensation. She had no name for it. That was especially frightening.

Should she take this unexpected lack of enthusiasm as a sign to retire? David's thirty days were ticking away. Was she feeling pressured by that? No, don't be silly, that's not it. It's just that the project is so huge, her system was just protecting her. The excitement would surely come. Soon enough. It had to. As soon as she got started on the To-Do list. Maybe tomorrow.

PART III

10
Knowing When It's Right

SHE FOUND HERSELF ALONE WITH COLLEEN in the elevator at the end of the day. Like Pavlov's dogs, they responded to the "ding" by exiting in lock-step. But then Colleen held back.

"Something wrong?" Ruth asked.

"I know you're probably, like, in a rush to get home, so maybe you don't have time? And this is not about business, it's personal? But could I maybe ask you for some advice, 'cause you kind of know what to do about stuff?"

"I don't really know so much, I'm just older and more experienced than you. But you can ask me anything. I'll try to help."

They started walking. "Well, I've been seeing this guy."

"Hmmmmm … interesting. And?"

"I really like him. A lot. And he likes me too."

"So far, so good." And no question marks at the ends of *these* sentences.

"But I don't know if he's, you know, 'the one.' How do you know? Do you think there's, like, one true love out there, a soul-mate kind of thing, and so if you don't know if he's 'the one,' then it means he's not? Like, did you know as soon as you met David … if it's okay for me to be asking you personal stuff like that?"

"It's fine to ask me. But it's a big question. Want to grab a cup of coffee?"

"Cool. But do you have time? I mean, you're always in such a rush."

"Today I have time. In fact, it would be nice to sit down, have some coffee, talk about anything besides work. And David's one of my favorite subjects."

When they were settled in a booth at the coffee shop, Ruth asked, "You want the long version or the short version?"

"Long. If it's okay."

"I love it. But, I warn you, I'll start at the beginning and wind around. Have faith, eventually I'll answer your question."

"My ears are open wide."

Ruth got lost in the telling of her own story.

AFTER FOUR MONTHS IN DJEMBERING, she'd changed. Her skin had darkened and hardened, the former from sun and dirt, the latter from Vivian. She no longer had a problem going to the bathroom outdoors. Even the flies had become a mere fact of life. Her life was no longer either a thrilling adventure or a desperate flight from her parents' expectations. It was just who and where she was, like a brand-new dress brought home from the store carefully wrapped in tissue paper that eventually becomes, simply, something you wear when you go outside.

When it was time for her first All-Country Volunteer meeting in the capital, she was eager to see the volunteers she'd trained with in Kentucky and compare stories about what they'd been doing. Plus she'd get to see the other Senegal volunteers who'd already been in-country when she arrived. And the idea of having more than one person to speak English to was downright thrilling.

After a predictably long and dusty ride to the capital, Ruth and Vivian found the Hotel du Port easily. Ruth saw the place through two sets of eyes simultaneously.

Her former eyes, the ones she'd used before she came to Senegal, saw a rundown building in a seedy section of town. Even the sign was missing the "r." The floor was mopped but shabby, with occasional cigarette butts tic-tac-toe-ing the black and white tiles. The beggars were at their stations in the corner of the lobby. The owner of these eyes wondered what in the world she was doing at the Hotel du Po_t.

Her new eyes, only four months old, elbowed out the old. First they saw lamps and a radio, which advertised the presence of electricity! Then these eyes took in the real walls, made from concrete, with pictures hanging from them. And glass windows. With retractable shades.

Using a pencil that had been sharpened and re-sharpened so many times there was barely anything to hold onto, she signed in, first brushing away the flies that seemed to consider the hotel registry their home. When the desk clerk asked if they preferred a room with a shower or a tub, she thought she was the luckiest person alive.

After bathing, they put on shoes that covered their sandal-line suntan and cotton floral-print dresses that wrapped the clean skin that was still puckered from water they'd made as hot as they could stand. They set out, giggling, for a walk through town. They went up-hill from the port, on the cracked sidewalk leading towards the ring of tall palm trees framing the Place d'Indépendence.

"Do you believe all these cars? And look, traffic lights too." Ruth knew she sounded like all the hayseeds she'd made fun of in New York. "I can't believe what I'm saying."

"But look at the stores. My God, there are even supermarkets. Want to go into one and look around?"

"No, not yet. I don't think I'm ready for that yet. I need to walk around some more."

"Yeah, I know what you mean," Vivian said. "Imagine, milk in packages being too much of a thrill. Can you believe it?"

As they walked up the narrow side street, they distributed small coins to the children who followed them. News of their generosity spread. Eventually, they told the gathered throng—using the local language and faces that were steeled not to show the pity they felt—to go away. They finally emerged from the shade of the narrow side street into the unrelenting sun of the Place, the center of the downtown, surrounded by big apartment and office buildings. Except for a few sedentary beggars and vendors, most people were headed someplace, whether in business clothes or traditional dress, carrying a briefcase or a basket.

The sun and heat were blinding. "Where should we go?" Ruth asked.

"Dunno. The meeting's in an hour. Wanna sit at a café? Wouldn't that be wild? Drinking coffee at a café?"

"Or beer?"

In the crosswalk to Avenue William Ponty, they passed a man on a bicycle with seven egg trays improbably balanced on his head and another walking with a bed on his head.

"You know what's so weird?" Vivian said. "Seeing all these people carrying stuff on their head looks amazing. But we see it every day. I guess it's being in the city instead of the village."

"Context is king."

They continued to walk, mostly in silence. The smell of burning leaves was ever-present, though fainter than in the countryside. Shops and vendors sold the exotic and the mundane. Mass-produced crafts for tourists were displayed close to authentic sculpture from villages where they'd been used for ceremonies. Batteries and key-chains were sold by kids, cigarettes and chewing gum by women. An old toothless woman sold peanuts, carefully weighed on an ancient balance scale and put into a newspaper cone. Modern shops sold imported French tennis and soccer clothing, electronic equipment, worsted fabric and lace, while outside them a vendor cooked pieces of an unidentifiable meat on skewers. The breezes blew the smoke right into his face, but he sat unmoving.

They were so tired from their walk in the exhilarating city, in the sun, with sensory overload, they decided to skip the detour to the café and just get to the meeting early.

When she walked in, Ruth was taken aback by all the white faces. She'd forgotten. Even the black volunteers looked, somehow, white. Her misperception confused her, but she later heard from her black friends that they frequently encountered this kind of color blindness, especially from Africans. To the Africans, Americans were white, even black Americans.

"Hey, Ruth." It was Carol, a woman she'd trained with. They hugged as fervently as if they'd grown up together. "Wow," Carol said, "has it really only been four months since Kentucky? How have you been? Where have you been? Is it good?"

Their stories poured out. Even though one was a white twenty-two-year-old, stationed in the south of the country to run a medical dispensary, and the other was an "older" volunteer at twenty-nine, black, stationed in the north, teaching English, they found their experiences remarkably parallel. They said "Wow," over and over.

Ruth spotted Tom, another fellow trainee. He introduced her to his roommate. "David got here a year ago, so he's an old hand. He showed me the ropes. Literally, 'cause we've been digging wells. Talk about getting to know someone, try being down in a well with them all day. Marriage will be easy after this." Ruth and David shook hands as Tom was called over by another volunteer. They exchanged the "where" and "when" and "what" of their volunteer service, as well as their American geography, then each went to talk to someone else.

Vivian accosted Ruth. "So, who was that guy? Kinda cute, don't you think? He's not my type, so you don't need to worry, but he might be—"

"Tom? He's in some village outside of Kaolack. It turns out he and I grew up a couple of miles from each other, but since we went to different high schools, we never got to—"

"I don't mean Tom. I know Tom. I mean the other one."

"That's his roommate, David. Yeah, he seemed nice."

"And cute."

"Yeah, cute I guess, too."

"So?"

"So what? Get off my back. I'm not as hungry as you."

"That's what you think."

The next night, after a long day of discussion sessions and problem-solving sessions, then a meal of fish and rice at the Peace Corps offices, all fifty-eight volunteers tumbled into the Bar Americain for beer and rock 'n' roll.

The Volunteers stationed in remote villages, where there was nothing to buy with their monthly Peace Corps living allowance, had money to burn and a lot of partying to catch up on. They were happy to buy round after round of beer and feed the jukebox.

Ruth and David spent two beers' worth of time talking to each other, though each spoke to, and danced with, many others. Jacquie, the bar owner, finally kicked them all out at two AM.

As soon as they left the bar and started walking back to their hotel, Vivian said, "You were talking to that cute David for a long time. You want me to find another room for tomorrow night? I could force myself, you know. There's a really cute guy from Tambacounda I could maybe manage to get an invitation from."

"Feel free if *you* want to, but don't do it on my account. It's not like that with David. He's really nice, but it's not like that."

"Come on, don't give me that. It's always like that."

"No, really, it isn't. I liked talking to him a lot, but it was like talking to a girlfriend. Like you just feel comfortable and easy. You don't have to worry too much about what you say. Natural."

"But he's so cute."

"I guess he is. But he has a girlfriend back home. And anyway, that wasn't the main attraction."

"We'll see."

"I hate when you act like you know it all."

"Especially when I'm right."

"We'll see."

It turned out Vivian was right, but not exactly in the way she thought. Ruth and David became very good friends. After the weekend of that first All-Country Meeting, they saw each other at a few other volunteer meetings. They also each visited the other's village once, she with a bunch of volunteer buddies, he with his visiting parents. Every time they met, Ruth felt the same way, like she was coming home to something welcoming, something that fit. But it wasn't romantic.

David returned to the U.S. six months before she did, and they continued their friendship through correspondence. When she finally returned and they saw each other in New York, after he'd broken up with his girlfriend, the feeling of homecoming she'd always experienced with him was even more intense and the increased intensity eventually became, as Vivian had always predicted, sexual.

And the rest was, if not history, the more traditional part of the boy-meets-girl story.

"FINALLY, THE ANSWER to your question: No, it wasn't what they call love at first sight. I was a girl far from home—funny, we didn't realize back then that we were women—feeling very comfortable with a friend who happened to be a boy. But I think being good friends first allowed the passion to bloom later on. And to 'stick,' if you know what I mean."

Ruth dug money from her purse for the coffee they'd finished long before and said, "That might have been more of a story than you wanted, and I don't know if it helps, but it sure was fun to relive."

"Thank you *so*-so much. It's *so* not what I expected and *so* something I want to think about. Because you hear all these stories like 'I knew the second I met him that I'd be with him for the rest of my life' and you wonder if it's bull or if there's just maybe another way it could go. Oops there's my bus. Do you mind if I run?"

"Run, run, run. It's fine."

Funny how things turn out, Ruth thought. The white-hot friendship with Vivian couldn't be transplanted from one place to another. But the friendship with David had blossomed.

When they'd first become lovers, she'd thought they'd wasted a lot of time in Africa. But later on, after several couple-friends' mad infatuation subsided, only to reveal they didn't much like each other, she thought maybe it was better their way. The friendship part is harder. Better to get that under their belts, so to speak, before passion muddies the waters. Because when they did become passionate, friendship definitely took a back seat.

Was it the same with her work? Did she need to *like* Mimosa more before she could love *Violins & Wine*? Was it that her revolutionary idea was only good in the context of Mimosa because the cold hard truth was that it was just less phony than its surroundings?

Or maybe that wasn't it. Maybe middle age is just the time when it's not reasonable to expect that kind of passion from work. Is it time to give up and grow up?

11
Old is New

RUTH AWOKE SUDDENLY, WITH POUNDING HEART and sweaty body. Since the start of her hormonal seesaw, she'd sometimes awakened like this three or four times a night. Falling asleep afterwards was always an ordeal; thank goodness it was morning.

She sat up in bed, listening. The hum of the furnace reminded her of the sound of rushing water in her dream. She pieced it together.

The dam had burst at its base, with a hole like a seven-year old's missing tooth. The hoarded water crashed through the gap to the other side, where the red clay gladly soaked it up. No longer two of the four elements, dry earth plus water, they became a new element, a different kind of earth. It was moist, redolent, contented.

Miraculously, the walkway above the dam remained intact. Ruth walked across from south to north, chatting with her mother Helen about all the things they'd never really discussed while Helen was alive. They strolled arm-in-arm, speaking fluidly. Her mother, a child of the depression, told how she'd learned to grit her teeth and do what needed to be done. Ruth, a child of the sixties, had tried to feel comfortable with herself. They could barely hear each other over the roar of crashing water on their right, but the spray on their faces, the sunlight, the joy of emotional connection more than made up for whatever fragments they missed. Helen brought out a scrapbook of Ruth's childhood artwork that neither had seen for many years. They oohed and aahed; they were struck by its freedom and artistry.

The dream images evoked nameless feelings that flitted around her head and shoulders like a persistent mosquito while she tried in vain to catch them. They were there as she showered, dressed, inhaled coffee, kissed David good-bye, and headed to the bus station in her workhorse of a commuter's car.

The most unsettling dream element was the conversation. It kept drawing her attention against her will, like a car accident along the road. In real life, their conversations had always been transactional, centering on recipes or travel schedules or Josh's grades. Through them all, Ruth would try, usually unsuccessfully, to stifle her bratty annoyance.

"Ruth, darling, is Josh happy about getting into Cornell?"

"Of course, mom. Why else would he have applied."

"Harry's niece went there too, you know."

"I know. Because you've told me 100 times."

She wondered if the dream related to her mysterious emotional distance from her product line idea. She stowed the dream images on her growing list of things to think about later, and began her daily trek via the bus to the Port Authority Terminal, the cross-town subway to the East Side, and the five-block walk uptown.

SHE'D RESERVED THE EIGHTEENTH FLOOR conference room, alerted her team to devote the entire day to a meeting about a new project, arranged for lunch to be brought in, asked Terry to join them at two o'clock and Roger at three o'clock. Her objective—at least the one for public consumption—was to make substantive progress; what she *really* wanted was to pump herself up or, at least, prime the pump.

Gathering the things she needed from her office, she saw a group of people had closed off half the width of forty-seventh street between Lexington and Third. They erected tables, tents, signs and assorted booths on the now-pedestrian-only street. They must be setting up for a street fair. A mini-street fair, she thought. Lucky them; unusual for mid-town; unusual for mid-week. Inexplicably, she thought of the dam.

In the conference room, everything was ready. Colleen would hold everyone's calls. It almost felt like summer-camp. This was exciting. Finally, she thought.

Ruth announced they'd be starting the meeting with a game. They needed to approach today's subject with a fresh point of view and the game was a kind of warm-up.

Each person had to say three things about herself or himself that no one else in the room knew. Two of the details should be true, one a lie. The others had to guess the lie.

"But Tom has quite a significant advantage over us." Pat's voice was close to a whine. "His tenure here has been rather short, so we don't know much about him."

"Hey, Pat, it's only a game. Besides," Tom added, "I may have an advantage in terms of *my* lie, but I'm at a disadvantage for yours."

"We'll do this quickly," Ruth said. "I'll go first." She rattled off her details. In fourth grade, she'd purposely hung out with stupid kids so she'd feel smart. In high school, she was the third runner-up in the Miss Bronx Teenager contest. She'd once slept in the same bed Tom Cruise had slept in.

"Who's next?"

"I'll go," Judy said, who was more dressed up than usual in a black suit. She hooked the metal clip of her pen on the cardboard back of her pad, then balanced it on her lap as she slipped one hand under each thigh. Leaning forward, she listed her details, a bit more slowly than Ruth had.

"One, the woman I call my mother is really my aunt." She brought her hands out of their hiding places and used them to hook her dark brown hair behind her ears, then folded them on her pad.

"Two, yesterday on the subway home I saw Woody Allen. Three,

I broke the same bone in my body two times, about a year apart." She swayed from side to side in her seat with pleasure. "I'm done."

Tom brushed back the hair that had fallen in his eyes and avoided eye contact, focusing on the center of the circle. He used to stutter. He was dating his older brother's ex-girlfriend. He was the anchor on his university's four-man one-mile relay. "Next?"

Pat pulled her expensive brown silk sleeves down to her wrists and said, in a monotone, with no introduction, "Once on a vacation in Indonesia, I came close to marrying someone to help him in his quest for an American green card. Yesterday I was in Saks and I paid with a twenty-dollar bill but received change for a hundred. When I was a youngster, I had a pet boa constrictor."

They wrote their guesses, then secrets were revealed—Ruth never entered the Miss Bronx Teenager contest, Tom never stuttered, Judy didn't spot Woody Allen, and Pat never almost-married anyone. Points were scored for correct guessing and also for fooling the others.

"Nice going, Tom. Lunch on me, anywhere you want within ten blocks. We're all warmed up now, able to look at familiar things with fresh eyes, so let's get started. Today we're going to brainstorm the word "old." What it means, what it evokes, what it implies, anything at all." She turned to a page on the flip chart with the single word "old."

Ruth had allotted forty minutes for brainstorming. Wanting to get at the thoughts that were deeply buried, she reminded the team not to comment on or criticize any of the ideas until the end, and to wait out the silences.

Sure enough, the words, as well as the ideas they reflected, had gone from the predictable—"granny," "wrinkled," "prune," "dry," "boring," "weak," "sick," "death"—to realms that surprised even those from whose mouths the words came. Like "pearl," "pinnacle," "accepting," "diamond," "sparkling," "Aunt Sylvia," "valuable," "loving," "perspective," and even "beautiful."

At the end, breathless with mental exertion and discovery, Tom said he was amazed to find the ideas, or maybe values, he'd always carried without his knowing they were there. Judy agreed.

"Now let's take it a little further," Ruth said.

For the next two hours, the group delved into some of the ideas they'd generated. They wrote stories about imaginary older women, some beautiful, some not. They clipped pictures from magazines, sorted them into categories and compared results with each other. They tried to match the others' verbal descriptions with their clipped pictures.

Then they broke for lunch. Colleen brought in the caterers who'd been waiting outside, and Ruth took down the flip chart sheets containing the brainstorming results, the pictures and the descriptions. She rolled them together, rubber-banded them, and stashed them in the corner.

While putting together their salads and sandwiches, they returned to the game they'd played, diving into the details of the "truths" and "lies" as Ruth had hoped they would. She revealed that David's cousin was a movie director and, when they'd once stayed in his guesthouse in Hollywood, they'd found out afterwards who had preceded them. Tom was somewhat reticent about his juiciest tidbit, the older brother's ex-girlfriend, saying only that she was someone he'd known a long time and that his brother wasn't upset by the new constellation.

Judy spoke of her aunt-mother and uncle-father matter-of-factly. "It's no big deal, really. My mom died in childbirth and my father couldn't handle it, so he 'gave' me to my mother's sister and her husband, who had been unable to have their own children. My father died about a year afterwards, in a car accident. But Diane and Arthur have always been "mom" and "dad" to me, even though they always told me the truth. She asked Pat about Saks.

Pat fussed with her salad fixings, adjusted her ham three times so it was lined up perfectly on the rye bread, and determined that three was the perfect number of ice cubes required by her ginger ale before she finally admitted that she hadn't returned the excess change to the cashier at Saks. "Don't be silly. It's Saks we're talking about, not a shoe-shine guy. Saks doesn't need the eighty bucks."

"But neither do you," Tom said.

"Don't pretend you'd have done it any differently," Pat said, as she changed the subject to the boa constrictor. She was just confessing that it had lasted only one day in the house before her parents made her return it to the pet store, her consolation prize being a horse, when Colleen poked her head in the door.

"I know you said to hold your calls, but Roger said it was really important and you would really, like, *want* me to disturb you. But then it's not disturbing, is it? Or is it?"

Ruth heard the gloom in Roger's gravelly voice immediately. "Look, I hate to break in on your planning session, but we got a problem that won't wait."

"What?"

"You know those new high-density plastic bottles we ordered for the 'Mauve Magic' Buy-and-Get-a-Bonus samples for the holiday promotion? The ones with the mini-pump?"

"Mm-hmm. New vendor, sexy color, fast delivery, good price."

"Right. Well, it looks like there ain't no free lunch after all. We just got a MayDay call from Packaging. The formula is breaking the seal on the pumps. More times than Quality Control allows. They say they could change the pump, but that would mean a different bottle, which means ordering from a whole other vendor, and that means time tick-tockin' away. Or we could change the formula, and that might do the trick, but the testing would mean great big monster delays. And the posse has to figure out what to do right away, like yesterday. I know if there are delays, yours is one of the asses that will be bit, so I just thought…."

"When are we meeting?"

"Twenty minutes. Twenty-sixth floor conference room."

She'd been crazy to think she'd get through the day without an interruption. But it was a good first go-around, she reassured herself, and would provide material for creative thinking about marketing.

She asked Colleen to coordinate everyone's schedules and reserve a conference room to continue today's work. As everyone left, she overheard Pat stage-whisper to no one in particular, "Sheesh, I sure hope we don't have to start with more fun and games."

12
Running Into Herself

WHAT A DAY IT HAD BEEN. THE DREAM, THE MEETING, the pow-wow with Roger. And then, as if that weren't enough, just before she left for the day, Colleen told her about a disturbing conversation with Jeremy. He'd been slumming on the eighteenth floor while Ruth had been up with Roger. He'd said one of the ways new management would be cutting costs was through secretary-sharing.

"He said he was sure I must have, like, heard about it through the secretary grapevine. He made like it was no big deal."

Then he gave her a list of five people she could choose to work for, in addition to Ruth. Because of Ruth's seniority, he was giving her first choice. And he'd try to limit her to two people instead of the usual three, but he couldn't guarantee it.

She needed to tell him her preferences within two weeks, though the changes wouldn't go into effect immediately.

"The thing of it is, I've asked some of the other girls, you know, my friends, and no one's heard anything like this from Jeremy. Or anyone else, neither. So it's not really a company-wide policy, right? Is he punishing me? Or, did you … you know … like, complain about me? It's not about my messy desk, right?"

Ruth was so tired, her anger could only energize the major bones in her body, though she breathed a little faster and shallower at the audacious power-play. A school-yard bully ploy. He didn't even try to disguise it by doing the same with some of the other secretaries. She explained that it wasn't about Colleen at all, it was about her. He was trying to squeeze her. First he eliminated the charity events, now he was trying to eliminate half of Colleen.

"But what should I do? Maybe I should change companies because these Big Daddies are so really annoying and part of me *so* wouldn't mind. I'd miss you like crazy, but still. But would that hurt your, you know, prestige-stuff more? If I left?"

Ruth said she'd think about what would be the best move and get back to her. She knew that right now, though, thinking about anything having to do with work was what she was trying *not* to do.

When she finally left, she forced herself not to march or stride, tried to stroll. Half-way down forty-seventh street a mime from the street fair appeared beside her. She hated mimes and the way they imitated you with annoyingly relentless cheer; they were like a piece of toilet paper you couldn't unstick from your shoe.

This one didn't have a white-painted face or a suspendered black jumpsuit and she didn't do rubbery-body mime routines. She was dressed like a French café-singer with black beret, dark red lipstick, and dangling cigarette. She played Edith Piaf's "Je Ne Regrette Rien" on her accordion as she shadowed Ruth.

The mime removed her hands from her accordion and dramatically adjusted her beret, tucking in a wisp of dark black hair and ensuring the angle was just right. But the accordion's bellows kept opening and closing, the keys depressed themselves, the music continued.

Even Ruth was impressed. I've heard of player-pianos, she thought, but never a player-accordion. As others gathered to watch, Ruth saw the mime's face mirror the surprise on her own. Finding herself publicly mimicked, she shifted her face into neutral, or so she thought. The mime's face changed, too, with prominently contracted eyebrows creating a washboard in her forehead and a tight stern mouth holding her cigarette. A child commented to his mother on how "the lady was making the same face as the other lady."

Is that me, she thought? Fierce? Angry?

Her surprise appeared on her face, then on the mime's, so she tried even harder for facial neutrality, and saw another angry-lady imitation. They became like a pair of face-to-face mirrors generating an endless series of reflections. Ruth finally escaped by dumping a few coins in the mime's basket.

As if to spite someone—herself or the mime?—she marched over to the fair, determined to be carefree. Tonight was the meeting at which David was submitting his official request for early retirement. The thirty days weren't even up, but he thought it wasn't fair to the administration to make them wait since he knew he'd be taking the deal. She was in no hurry to get home and talk about it. Unless he'd changed his mind.

She meandered over to a "Do It Yourself Mask" table sponsored by the mid-town homeless shelter and did it herself, painting and decorating a mask that covered the top half of her face. She chose a hot dog and ear of corn from a vendor and congratulated herself on making a spontaneous choice. No pros and cons.

It came to her that she would choose a new bottle and pump from her ace-in-the-hole vendor—reliable, speedy, expensive—for the leaky seals. Time was, as Roger put it, "tick-tocking away" and she'd take budget flak instead of schedule flak. Mauve Magic would be only a little late and more than a little expensive but totally safe. She'd make up some of the budget bulge with her other Buy-and-Get-a-Bonus program, the "Color Me Beautiful" line.

The Colleen situation would take a little longer to figure out.

She moved on to the booths selling handicrafts. A dark, round-faced woman explained her "worry dolls" in halting English. If you took the six tiny dolls out of their yellow oval box and put them under your pillow at night, they'd absorb all your worries for you.

Ruth was drawn to the woman as much as the business: make the dolls, get a booth, sell them. No Buy and Get a Bonus, no office politics, no dress for success. She bought one set for herself and one for Josh.

She couldn't put it off any longer. On the trip home, she'd focus on setting up the Violins & Wine focus groups and, maybe, the meaning of her dream. And Colleen.

"HELLO?" SHE EXHALED into the phone as she ran into the house, fearing it was David worrying about her.

"Hi, Ruth, it's me."

"Vivian, how are you?" Ruth took off her coat and deposited it on the floor. "I really had fun on Sunday, and I've been meaning to get back to you, but it's been—"

"No problem, you don't have to worry about the polite thank-yous, I know you had fun, I did too. It was so great to see you guys together after all these years. And Carlos ... well Carlos may not have seemed to you to have a good time, but you have to understand he never does anything that isn't political. That was a lot of progress, and he enjoyed it. Believe me, he did."

"Okay, if you say so." She took off her sneakers and dropped them on her coat.

"I'm calling to ask a favor. It's funny that you're really the perfect one to help me out with this, and if I hadn't bumped into you last week, I don't know what I'd do. Because, really, I need help and there's no one else I could ask."

Ruth took the bait. "What could I possibly do that nobody else could?" Her suit jacket landed on top of the sneakers, then, with some one-handed acrobatics, the pantyhose.

Vivian explained that she and Carlos were going to another of Ida's concerts in a couple of weeks. She just found out that Ida's boyfriend would be there and he was bringing his parents.

"Who's the boyfriend? Do we like him?" She threw her legs over the arm of the chair.

Vivian painted a verbal picture of Ida's boyfriend, his good values—meaning the same values as hers—and the fact that he made Ida happy. She wasn't so thrilled about his being a lawyer for a big corporate firm, but was dedicated to getting him to switch to litigation so he could do pro bono work. The problem was his parents.

They were investment bankers and, according to Vivian, the kind of people who think the poor are responsible for their own hard luck, who think anyone who wanted two BMWs could just roll up their sleeves and work hard for them.

"These people have no patience for people with a hair out of place. Like me."

Ruth remembered meeting David's parents for the first time, when they came to visit him in Africa. They were conspicuously white, even compared to white people. Colorless. His mother carried a leather purse that smelled brand new, and she carried it with the strap at her elbow so her arm was folded in front of her, as if she were at a cotillion. And David's father kept leading her around with his hand on the small of her back, calling her "Mother."

"Oops," Ruth said. "So how do you four manage to be civil in front of the kids?"

It turned out Vivian and Carlos hadn't met them yet. But she knew exactly what they'd be like.

"So, the favor?" Ruth asked.

Ida had asked them, just this once, if they'd wear clothes like everyone else wore. "Not your hippy clothes," she'd said.

She knew it was a lot to ask. But she thought that, the first time they were meeting the Danforths, it would be easier on everyone if they could tone it down, just a little, maybe help things go a little more smoothly.

Carlos, of course, refused immediately. Vivian mimicked his Spanish accent as she told of the interchange:

"You didn't think we were so terrible when you were arrested for demonstrating outside the student union and we were the only parents who were on your side. Then it was all right to be alternative, right? But now that you're hooking up with Mr. Country Club, we embarrass you? You want us to change who we are? Not on your life. If he loves you, he just has to live with who we are. And so do his parents, chiquita."

Vivian agreed it shouldn't matter what they looked like, they were who they were. But she also wanted to help Ida out. She succumbed to Ida's argument that it wasn't the same as pretending to be someone else. They'd just be trying not to ignite knee-jerk prejudices with their clothing. They had plenty of time to ignite the prejudices later. Her attempt to placate Carlos was a refusal to change her hair.

"Of course, I wouldn't know how to calm down my hair, anyway."

"Sounds reasonable," Ruth said. "Some parents have to work two jobs for their kids, sweating and slaving and not getting any sleep. Others have to dress up. We all make sacrifices."

"Very funny."

"The favor?"

Vivian told Ruth that she sewed her own clothes. She had trouble finding things she liked that fit her and, besides, she enjoyed the freedom to visualize herself the way she wanted and turn the vision into reality. She'd been doing it for so long, though, she didn't know where or how to shop for clothing anymore. And she certainly didn't know how to shop for "regular" clothing.

"And I think you probably do, right?"

"You're asking me to go shopping with you?"

As if she were confessing her crimes to a judge, she said, "Yes, I'm asking you to help me shop for something to wear to Ida's concert so I can look like one of the regular people."

Ruth laughed.

"You can just say 'no,' you know, you don't need to make fun of me. God, I can't believe I actually built up my courage to ask you and—"

"No, Viv, that's not why I'm laughing."

Meanwhile, David had gotten home. He held the tea kettle up with a raised-eyebrow question on his face. Ruth nodded as she continued. "It's because I always feel like *I'm* the one who doesn't know what to wear to these things."

"I'm sure you know better than me."

David held up three kinds of herb tea. She pointed to Apple Cinnamon.

"Why don't you sew something?"

"It's a lot of work to sew something I'm only going to wear once, at least I hope it's only going to be once."

"I'm happy to help you. Want to go on Saturday?"

"This Saturday?"

"Day after tomorrow. Before you change your mind. And before Carlos talks you out of it."

"It's a date."

"Write it down."

She joined David at the kitchen table. They blew into their cups and sipped, silently at first. After a day at work and then a phone conversation with Vivian, Ruth drank in the silence as much as the tea.

David spoke first. He had indeed notified the district of his retirement plans. She didn't like it, but was mostly reconciled to it. Even so, when he told her he'd done it, she sucked in her breath and blinked back tears.

"Hey, come on, honey. We talked about this, you knew I was going to do it. Right?"

"You're right, no problem. It's just so final. The end of something."

David opened his mouth to speak but Ruth jumped in.

"I know, I know, it's the beginning of something, too, the glass is also half full. Let me just wallow for a second. I'll be fine."

"That's not what I was going to say. If you're going to finish my sentences for me, finish them correctly."

"Sorry."

"I was going to say that I know what you mean about it being the end of … "

"What do you mean?"

"When I left the meeting, I started looking at people and seeing the ones I'd miss and the ones I'd be glad to be rid of. I sort of jumped into the future and saw it all in the past tense even though I'm still in the present. Kind of spooky."

"Yeah, spooky," Ruth said. Thank goodness, she thought. It wasn't that she wanted David to be unhappy, but she was glad he was experiencing some upset, that the thought of ending the career he'd loved for years wasn't like rolling out of bed. Made her feel a little less crazy.

"Why don't you tell me about your day?" he said. "Wallowing of a different sort, just for distraction."

She ran through her day as they finished their tea, went upstairs, and went to bed. She let him put two of the worry-dolls under his pillow. She kept four.

13
In Shopping Veritas

IT WAS UNUSUALLY WARM, AND RUTH finally chose light gray slacks with a short-sleeved green knit top. No scarf, no jewelry. Not too suburban, but also not too hippy-dippy as if she were imitating Vivian. She gulped her coffee while returning two phone calls, then took out some frozen chops to defrost for dinner. She checked to see if the lettuce was still good or if she needed to get more on her way home. Thank goodness it was all right; one less chore to remember to do. She rushed out the door.

Forty-five minutes later, Vivian emerged from the depths of the subway exit at 17th Street, red-faced, short of breath, hair and eyes wild. She stood out from the crowd because of her loud voice and louder Hawaiian shirt, whose reds, yellows and purples argued with each other over who got to be the boss.

Ruth wished she'd worn something less goody-two-shoes. She looked at her watch; eighteen minutes late, even though the meeting place was a ten-minute subway ride from Vivian's place, while she herself had managed to get there on time from Jersey.

Vivian said, "It was hard getting out of the house. Fifteen minutes doesn't count as late, though, does it? Carlos needed to run his latest crusade past me for feedback and when I made a few suggestions, which was what he'd asked me for in the first place, no sugar-coating or anything, exactly the way he gives it to other people, he got all defensive and upset, so that became a whole big thing. Then—"

"No problem, I just got here."

"So where are we going? And can I afford it? I told you about my budget, right? Carlos is upset enough, without my spending a lot, and even if he weren't upset—"

"Down girl. Relax. I heard everything you said, you can trust me."

Vivian shook her head and exhaled loudly. "I'll try." She kissed Ruth's cheek then grabbed her arm and whistled "We Shall Overcome" as they walked north in lock-step, arm-in-arm, just as they had done hundreds of times before, long ago, in a village far from New York.

Three old women with beseeching eyes and empty tin cans sat on a bench. Vivian took a few coins out of her pocket and gave it to one of them. The recipient smiled, enlarging the view of her few discolored teeth.

"Only one?"

"She was the ugliest."

"Still give preference to the ugly?" Ruth said.

"They still need it, don't they? Everyone's still drawn to pretty people, aren't they? It was true in the village and it's still true. And it still stinks."

"I thought we'd go to Loehmann's first because—"

"I'll tell you what; when I see an ugly person's support group, I'll know my little affirmative action isn't necessary. But there never will be, and you know why? Because no one wants to be a member. It's lookism, plain and simple. Hey, you work for a cosmetics company, you know what I'm talking about. Why don't you do something like makeup that makes everyone ugly so the people who are naturally ugly won't feel bad?"

"All I said was—"

"I can't remember the last time I was at Loehmann's, probably it was when my mother took me to buy a dress for my junior high school graduation. I remember it perfectly. Pale pink dotted swiss, capped sleeves. I must have looked like a tuna sandwich. Thank God there are no pictures. Also I remember that dressing room."

They walked past the easy chairs where men—mostly older, mostly reading the newspaper—waited until called upon for their wisdom.

"Yes, Doris, it's pretty."

"No, it doesn't make you look fat."

"I like the red one better."

They passed the casual wear department, with oceans of minimally-varied jeans and T-shirts, continued on past the jewelry, purses, and hats, to the back of the store, to the racks of "evening wear."

Vivian put her head down and squared her shoulders as if she were gathering her courage for hard labor. She strode to the size sixteen section and went through the offerings at a manic pace. The hangers clicked as if they were angry. Ruth stood off to the side and watched silently as Vivian quickly rejected the first fifteen choices at warp speed, then looked up and saw Ruth watching her.

"'Evening wear' is a category I have no experience with. 'Late afternoon' is the dressiest I ever get. Or maybe 'Afternoon milk and cookies.'"

Ruth was about to suggest a second look at the rejected gray pants suit four hangers back when Vivian said, "Look, Ruthie, you go look at stuff yourself and I'll look at stuff myself, and then we'll do show and tell."

"But it's really better to decide about each piece together." This was going to be tougher than she thought. Vivian was really wired. Wired and weird. "That way—"

"Nope, too methodical. Can't do it that way. You go down that aisle, I'll go down this one and then we can meet in the middle. Believe me," she said as she rolled her eyes, "I can live with the life-shattering possibility that there just might be one perfect outfit here somewhere and we might miss it if we're not together, God forbid."

She remembered that this was exactly how Vivian used to make her feel—half of her wanting to slink home, the other half wanting to smack her. She reminded herself that Vivian was a compassionate oxymoron, caring deeply about humanity but less so about individual bits of humanity. "I just thought the whole point was that you wanted my help."

"Sorry, try not to be offended, Ruthie, I do appreciate your help; this shopping must be making me a little loony."

Ruth looked up and waited for the rest of the explanation she thought she was entitled to.

"First of all, this whole idea of dressing up for Ida is wacky to begin with and is becoming an issue between Carlos and me and he's getting nutty about how I'm choosing her over him." She closed her eyes and shook her head like a wet dog.

"I've never gone shopping with a girlfriend, I hardly go shopping at all, shopping is not something I do, I have no experience with this, so consider my behavior the behavior of a beginner, okay? I just don't know how to do something that I don't really know how to do. If you know what I mean. I'm kind of a mess; bear with me."

"No problem."

They split up and spent the next fifteen minutes wending their way towards each other from opposite sides of the "evening wear" racks. Ruth rated each garment according to her checklist of criteria. Budget. Not too self-consciously dress-up. Vivian's size, and what would flatter or at least downplay it.

Vivian, more intuitive and more negative, covered ground faster than Ruth. When they met, like two tunnel-diggers who wind up face-to-face, Ruth had ten hangers over her arm to Vivian's two. At their summit meeting, they saw they'd both chosen the same black pants suit, so eliminated one. Vivian then rejected five of Ruth's choices. "Too Republican. We're down from twelve to six. Let's go face the music."

The try-on room's monitor must have been selected by the same central casting agency that used to hire the matrons in the movie theaters, the ones who made the kids take their feet off the seat in front of them. With her slightly humped back and her sensible shoes, she enforced the "five garments per person" rule as if she were dispensing divine justice.

The huge room had mirrored walls and a community of overhead fans. Each woman had the illusion of having her own territory by virtue of two hooks about eighteen inches apart, while, in truth, everyone undressed, dressed, and preened in front of their neighbors. It was a lesson in the infinite varieties of female anatomy and the uselessness of modesty.

They chose two adjacent spaces far from the entrance. Vivian was on Ruth's right, and had the temporary luxury of an empty space on her other side, so she could spread out a bit. They hung their garments on their respective hooks to maintain the charade that they had each selected three.

Vivian started with the electric blue dress that was a second cousin of the flowing robe she'd worn to the concert where they'd encountered each other in the bathroom. Ruth wondered if Vivian had selected it because she actually liked it or as a strategic move, to stake out an extreme taste-baseline from which she'd only budge so much. It was hideous, really. Its shapelessness would usually be camouflage for a large woman, but the color overruled any softening effect. It looked like a huge neon sign.

"I don't know nuthin' 'bout evenin' wear," Vivian said, "but I sure think it looks like a tablecloth. I know Miss Scarlett looked great in a curtain, but somehow I don't think this works for me."

Ruth tried to hide her relief. "I agree."

Vivian slipped the dress off, let it fall to the floor, and side-stepped out of it, like a snake shedding its skin as it continued its thrust forward. She looked through her hangers to choose what would be next. Ruth picked up the blue tent and put it back on its hanger.

"Excuse me?" A woman in bra and thong undies had walked

over from the other side of the room, seeming unconcerned about the amounts of her body that couldn't fit into those two small pieces of cloth. Ruth didn't know whether to avert her eyes from her overflowing body or her skewed teeth.

She asked if they'd be taking the blue dress and, if not, could she try it? As Ruth gave it to her quickly before she changed her mind, the woman handed over one of her own rejects. "Here, take this in exchange? Then our numbers will be the same as when we walked in and we won't get in trouble with the Wicked Witch of the West? When we leave?"

Vivian tried the black pants suit with her own riotous Hawaiian shirt. She stepped back from the mirror, arranged her hair, put her hands at her sides, widened her eyes, and thinned her lips together, pushing them out for the "moue" look that full-length mirrors seem to demand. She tugged on the bottom of the jacket to make it longer.

"Vivian, stop fussing, stand still."

"Yes, mommy."

"What do you think?"

"I have a little trouble with it being black, which is what ninety percent of the women at the costume party—excuse me, I mean concert—will be wearing. And I wish the jacket were longer."

"The shorter jacket is actually what makes it nice. Otherwise it would just be a pair of black pants and a black jacket. You could wear it to work."

"Maybe *you* could wear it to work."

"What I mean is, this cute little jacket gives it enough style to be dressy. You look great in black. And you'll be able to get a lot of use out of it. Certainly the pants."

"Let me tell you about these pants." She pulled at the pants' legs and pushed the waistband lower. "This is why I started sewing my own clothes. Pants aren't made for women like me. They're made for anorexics. These pants feel like they're trying to get in my pants. I know you're thinner than me, but you're not one of those stick-figure girls. Don't the seams ride up into your crotch and drive you crazy? How do you sit for more than fifteen minutes?"

"It's true. And it's not just what you said about the crotch. It's also the growing waist and—"

"—and getting the waistband to fit means that when you sit down, it slides up to your armpits."

The little old lady to the left of Ruth's space took a step towards them, with her carefully coiffed white hair, a spot of red on each cheek, and stockings with seams. She said, in a conspiratorial tone of voice, "The suit looks very nice on you, dear, but I know what you mean about the pants being uncomfortable. It's the price of being a woman, I guess."

Vivian smiled sweetly. "Screw that. But thanks." The little old lady went back to her stall, cheeks a little redder than before.

"If this suit turns out to be the best of the lot, I'd open up the crotch seam and put in a little insert, what tailors call a gusset and I call a crotch-patch. It's a little roomier, and there's no central seam to be so insistent. It takes the pressure off the waistband, too, when you sit down."

She took her own pants off the hook and showed Ruth the crotch. "See, that's how I make all my pants. I don't understand why everyone doesn't."

"But it would be hard to find matching fabric, wouldn't it?"

"Exactly how many people would be in a position to see the contrast between the crotch-patch and the rest?"

"Good point."

Vivian stepped out of the pants, leaving them on the floor, then set the jacket on top of them. Ruth reached down and scooped them up. She looked for their hangers among the tangle on the hooks and, like a hot flash, resentment overtook her. Why did Vivian expect her to pick up after her?

"Vivian," she imagined calling over to the chubby woman who used to be her best friend, "I'm not here to be your maid."

"Who said you were?" Vivian would probably say.

"So hang up your own discards."

It would feel so good to say it that way, giving herself over to it, like eating whipped cream from a spoon. Like Carlos?

"I didn't leave them for you," continued the imaginary-Vivian. "I'd have picked them up in my own sweet time. You just couldn't wait."

"Sooner or later you'd have gotten mixed up about which ones were which. You should pick them up as you take them off, not leave them on the floor."

"Maybe, maybe not. But if I *should* have picked them up, that's *my* should, not yours. You, on the other hand, *should* stop cleaning up other people's messes. Especially when they don't want them cleaned up. It just distracts you from your own messes. Or maybe that's why you do it?"

Pretty bad when she couldn't win her imaginary arguments. Of course, Vivian had help: Ruth, not the imaginary one, the real one, gave her the sharpest truest blade.

"Hey, Ruth, you don't have to do that, really," said the real Vivian. "Thanks just the same, but you're not my mother. Thank God." Vivian's naked hips swayed as she walked over and took the black slacks from Ruth.

"You're right." She knew Vivian thought she was talking to her, but she was really talking to the imaginary Vivian, too.

Vivian held up a black and gold dress in front of her in the mirror.

"I thought I had trouble with black, but now that I see black and gold, I'm thinking black isn't so bad." She put the dress on the "reject" hook.

Ruth wanted to object, but decided to stifle it and tried hard for a neutral face, not the one that she'd thought was neutral but now knew was angry.

Vivian turned to a white-skirted suit with gold buttons and trim. A definite no.

Next was a mid-length black dress with subtle black and mauve embroidery on the bodice. With a seam under the bodice, it was gently fitted, not too tight. But not a tent. Vivian unzipped it and slipped it over her head, stood back from the mirror and assumed the moue.

"Are you thinking what I'm thinking?" Ruth asked.

"Only if you're thinking that this actually looks better on me than it did on the hanger, and that it's only slightly too hotsy-totsy for the likes of me, and that even Carlos might not hate it too much."

"That's pretty much it. And also that you could borrow my great big mauve scarf to wear like a shawl and then it would look even less like a black dress that all the ladies are wearing."

"Oooh, scarf. Oooh, mauve. Good. Let's get it."

"Wait," Ruth said. "There's still the red suit. Gorgeous color—not black, you notice—and feel the fabric. Soft and rich and lush. And not expensive."

"Color's good, but, no, the jacket looks military. Military is a definite no-no."

"But don't you want to try everything before you decide?"

Vivian put her hands on Ruth's shoulders. "I think if I like something, I can just like it without evaluating every single option I could possibly compare it to. I can just like it because I like it. Things aren't so complicated for me. Right now, I like the black pants suit and I like the purple and black dress. The pants suit involves alteration work, the dress doesn't. Plus the dress costs less. I'm getting the dress. I'd like to borrow the scarf. I'm happy. Isn't that enough?"

14
Unmasking the Truth

SHE LOOKED AGAIN AT THE SUMMARY of the concept-testing focus group results. With faith in the "aha" quality of her idea, she'd let the P.R. firm run the groups with Pat's supervision, planning to jump in afterwards. But this report was a blow.

Of course she'd expected some of the women to hate being middle-aged. And she'd been right about that. But she'd also expected there to be some who saw it as a time to profit from a lifetime of experience. And to be beautiful, too, but in a different way. And she expected the holdouts to moderate their views during the course of the group, especially after looking at possible spokeswomen like Sharon Stone and Sophia Loren. But the view-changing went the other way around. Most had eventually chosen the youthful faces of Uma Thurman and Natalie Portman when asked for examples of beautiful women.

The transcribed verbatim statements were the worst.

One woman said: "Some of us need all the help we can get. I've even been known to wear a girdle in my time. I know they frown on that, now. Think it's better to exercise all day long or even have liposuction. Frankly, I think a girdle's easier. And so is makeup, if you want my opinion. If makeup can take ten years off my face, I'm all for it. Hell, I'll settle for two years off. They say all these wrinkles are about wisdom, but I think I can be just as wise with a smooth face, thank you very much."

And another said: "It's not just about the media images. Young means healthy, with a big fat future ahead of you, and lots of energy and passion. Young means having enthusiasm and lots and lots of choices. And even if you aren't young, it makes sense to want everyone else to think you are."

David called to tell her his meeting was cancelled and he'd be home for dinner after all. He must have heard the tone of her voice and asked what was wrong.

"Maybe this is a New York kind of thing. Maybe it will be better outside the glamour capital of the world," he suggested.

"I hope so, but I don't know. This is definitely not what I expected. Who *are* these people?"

"They're your customers. They've always been your customers. *They* haven't changed. *You* have."

"Great. Now I've got a product line I might have to call The Kiss of Death."

"So I guess this isn't the time to segué into the idea that maybe it's a good time to re-consider retiring?"

"DA-vid … "

"Plan B: Want to spend some time brainstorming a little, maybe after some wine, and see if we can come up with anything? Like we did that time with the … what was that thing?"

"Some holiday promotion. Dinner and brainstorming, it's a date. Gotta go."

She read and re-read the two-page summary, trying to come up with a way to explain things to these women so they'd understand. She got up to pace, trying to distract and comfort herself. She stared at her African masks, touched them, traced their features.

The Dogon mask had its subtly carved, perfectly-arched brows that rose from either side of the small nose, over eyes that were little more than slits. Small and dark, tarkly beautiful. Ruth couldn't imagine anyone not responding to this little mask.

The Bakota mask was flat and trimmed with silver-colored metal. Its sculpted hair was reminiscent of an elaborate Japanese style. She'd always liked Bakota-lady but never knew why.

Her long-time favorite, though, was the Chi-Wara, the stylized antelope profile that was all about agricultural fertility. Ruth's specimen was quieter than the better-known variety, simpler, not calling quite as much attention to itself, yet reminding the viewer of what all the fuss was about.

The smell of the wood-fire smoke that lingered in the Chi-Wara hijacked her attention from the focus groups to the marché where she'd bought it.

A MYSTERIOUS KIDNEY AILMENT with no symptoms other than blood in the urine had required observation in the capital. The volunteers she'd stayed with were busy all day teaching English, while all she had to do was present her kidney for observation once a day, so she did all the household errands and shopping. After having lived in Djembering, where the closest thing to a marché was a guy selling sugar, tomato paste, tea, and, occasionally, batteries, she loved going to the Kermel Marché.

The kids would start to approach her about two blocks before she reached the market. Since this was the smaller and more picturesque market in Dakar, it attracted more white people. Toubabs. And these kids were ready. They were buoyantly persistent, with gangly limbs punctuated by knobby knees and elbows. They had a singsong routine for Toubabs. "Hello Madame Toubab, tu veux des oranges? Pretty oranges, good price Madame Toubab." "Madame, I have pretty dresses, bon prix pour toi, best price. Viens voir." Continuing to throw in a little English, just in case, they trailed her all the way, good-natured in their failure to sell her anything. At first, they made her uncomfortable, but after a while she didn't mind them.

The closer she got to the marché, the more beggars there were. They sat on mats displaying their deformities prominently, even cheerfully, as if the worse the deformity, the prouder they were. And they were right, because the syllogism was obvious: "I have so much, they have so little, it's the least I can do." As she walked, she distributed the small change she'd brought along for this purpose, a ten-CFA piece to the legless boy, another to the man whose arm was twisted like a paper clip, and two to the blind mother of twins.

Her favorite marché denizens were the cut-flower ladies. They were tall, dark and impossibly graceful with babies tied on their backs and bouquets balanced on their heads. They strode through the streets in and around the marché, gliding smoothly, their heads swaying side-to-side independently of the rest of their bodies, which moved forward as through water. They dressed in bright colors and smiled profusely so their gold teeth accented the bright bunches of blooms perched on their headdresses like a second face. Without saying a word, they fairly screamed "Photo Opportunity," an opportunity for which there was, of course, a charge.

The tomato vendor she gravitated towards would see her coming and start to weigh tomatoes in her ancient balance scale. Her wrinkled skin was practically falling off her face, but her sparkling eyes and flirtatiousness belied her skin's age. Her head-cloth was usually wrapped with one corner of the print, today's being orange and blue, sticking out of the top like a ponytail.

Ruth would start the usual routine by saying, in French, "Good morning Madame. How much for the tomatoes?"

"A thousand francs the kilo."

Knowing tomatoes are six hundred francs a kilo, she'd respond "No, no Madame. You must think I'm one of those rich Toubabs, but I'm just a Toubab ordinaire. I can't pay so much."

The tomato vendor betrayed her amusement with the slightest upturn of the upper left corner of her mouth. "How much will you pay?"

"Five hundred francs."

She waved her arms excitedly, then settled them on her hips. She frowned. "Madame, I have three children! And five grandchildren, all living with me. But you can have them for nine hundred francs the kilo." She smiled sweetly.

"No thank you Madame." She tried to look serious, even though she loved this gentle duel. "But I'll buy a half-kilo for three hundred and twenty-five francs. It's my last price."

"Last price?"

"Fo-fu-lie-em, last price."

Her face melted every time Ruth used this bit of the local language, as if it were the first time. She was delighted, too, with the extra twenty-five francs, worth about ten cents. Ruth thought that excess amount was enough to avoid guilt at getting the very best price nor so high as to be foolish.

"Okay, good." She wrapped them in age-softened brown paper. Ruth tried hard not to think about where that paper had been, knowing that, regardless of the paper, she would wash the tomatoes in iodine-water when she got home, a standard Toubab health precaution.

She had a variation of the same conversation when she bought a woven lampshade from the ancient, one-toothed man sitting on his narrow prayer mat, surrounded by baskets of every shape and size imaginable. And when she got lemons from the giggly eight-year old girl whose mother put her in charge of her precious yellow pyramid. It was a kind of dance, each partner having precisely-choreographed steps, each step a combination of theatrical poses and words.

After shopping at Kermel for a while, though, she noticed something. The shirt she *had to have*, made from brightly colored woven strips sewn together—Kente Cloth, "the cloth that cannot be broken"—cost her double her "final price." Even though the vendor took great care to measure her, tying a series of knots in a single piece of string to indicate her shoulders, waist, arms, and even though it fit her perfectly, she always thought she should have been able to buy it for less.

But the Chi-Wara, the one that she thought might be different enough from her other two to be worth buying, was offered to her retreating back at a rock-bottom price. When she *really* wanted something, she didn't get as good a deal as when she wasn't so interested. Maybe her desire made her tense and inhibited her ability to bargain well. Or maybe she unknowingly communicated her desire to the vendor.

As a bargaining ploy, she tried to feign indifference. It didn't work. The vendors were too experienced at reading Toubab body language for pretense. Finally, she got it: the best way to bargain for something she wanted was to convince herself that she really didn't care about it. She needed to give it up before the fact so she might be able to have it.

Twenty years later she discovered the Buddhists knew this long before she stumbled onto it. Craving is the problem; letting go of the craving is the solution. At Kermel, she just knew it helped her shop.

Walking around her office, Ruth thought back to her first attempt at trying out her bargaining lesson.

"Madame, how much are the bracelets?"

The vendor looked up from her work of stringing beads on wires and slowly fanned her plump face with a fragment of dirty newspaper, taking Ruth's measure. Flies scattered. Her right earlobe had two sections, like a rounded letter "W," perhaps from a baby pulling too hard on her earring long ago. She was surrounded by a hundred tomato paste cans in varying stages of rust, all filled with beads. There were Venetian trading beads, gold-weight beads, and glass beads of every color. She had strung the finished pieces on horizontal wires along the sides of her stall. They caught the sun, looking like a neon Venetian blind.

"Three for fifteen hundred francs," she said casually, flicking a fly from her arm.

"Oh, no," Ruth said sadly, with much head-shaking. "I can't pay that much."

"How much will you pay?"

She thought. "I guess I could pay seven hundred and fifty francs for three."

"Seven hundred and fifty? No, not possible." She swept her arm around her stall, showing off her handiwork. "I made all these bracelets myself, they're one-of-a-kind. I support my family, I must have twelve hundred francs for three."

"Madame, it's true that you are skillful and the bracelets are beautiful, but I can't buy them for twelve hundred francs. If you want to sell them for eight hundred and fifty, I'll buy them. Fo-fu-lie-em."

"Eleven hundred and fifty francs Madame. It's a good price." She sat down.

"No thank you," she said, meaning it. She walked away.

"You can have them for nine hundred and fifty," the vendor said to Ruth's back. She kept walking. "Okay, nine hundred."

She returned, selected three bracelets, and paid, happy with the deal and with the lesson she'd learned. The vendor wrapped the three bracelets in newspaper and, from her eagerness to finish the transaction, Ruth was pretty sure she liked the deal, too, so her conscience was at peace. The vendor squeezed the packet into Ruth's basket among the pineapples, tomatoes, carrots, shrimps, and parsley.

And then, as if to underline the lesson, the vendor burst out in a laugh that seemed to push the heat and humidity away more forcefully than her newspaper. She selected a beautiful blue bead with flecks of gold deep inside and put it in Ruth's hand. "A present, Madame."

They shook hands and smiled. "Merci, au revoir, Madame."

SHE WAS STILL SMILING at the memory when she looked back at the masks on her wall. Were they telling her there were many ways to be beautiful, the Dogon way, the Bakota way, the Chi-Wara way? That American women can be beautiful in different ways, too?

Or was it the bargaining lesson that was the point, warning her of the danger of craving? Was she too desperate for women "out there" to see her light, looking for the validation that comes with unanimity, like religious converts who want everyone to believe?

She shook her arms and hands, willing herself to release the urge to corral everyone's thoughts, and looked again at the lethal sheaf of papers. Then she decided to watch the tape of the focus groups, a time-eater she rarely could afford. That's when she saw the problem. And she was pretty sure she knew what to do about it.

15
Money Talks

"WHEN YOU'RE YOUNG, YOU THINK MONEY doesn't matter," Jane said to the gathered Brain Trust, twirling a clump of her curly hair around her right forefinger. "You think changing the world is what it's all about."

She released her curl. "It's not like I think money is the most important thing in my life, now that I'm all grown up. Obviously, or I wouldn't be a teacher. But today, not five minutes after I was talking to the kids about the 'a' sound in 'made' and the 'a' sound in 'mad,' I found myself talking to the school secretary about my pension plan. Kinda surreal."

She looked at the hairs remaining on the finger that had done the twirling, removed them with a slight expression of disgust, and discarded them in a tissue that Blanche, sitting next to her on the couch, had ready for her.

"I picked this pension plan when I first started teaching, but I didn't care about it. Didn't think I'd ever care. Not that I thought I'd die young or anything, I just never ... just never saw myself being anything other than what I was, I guess. God, we were so arrogant. 'Never trust anyone over thirty' and all that. Now I care about my pension in a big way. I understand all that stuff about defined benefits and defined contributions and payouts and annuities. It's even worse. I actually think it's interesting. Want me to explain it?"

"No thanks," was the politest of the many replies.

"Well it *is* important. Money, that is." Charlie's long thin fingers played with her trademark woven belt as she spoke. She told about the time her father-in-law sat her down, gave her his 'I-lived-through-the-depression' speech, then walked her through the ABC's of pricing.

"I'll never forget what he said." She stood and pointed to her imaginary self in the chair she'd just vacated. "'CharLENE, my dear dear girl, it's practically criminal that you're not assigning a value to your time.' That's what he said. Criminal." She flung her scarf over her shoulder as she reseated herself.

"Valuing my time. What a concept. Made a big difference, too, 'cause weaving really takes time. So now I feel like I can care about money and also care about making beauty or changing the world. I can care about creativity and also afford double-thick toilet paper."

"Money is not the root of all evil, ladies," Sarah said. "The *love* of money is the root of all evil. We can like money, just not love it." She nodded as she brushed the peanut debris off her sweater and onto the floor.

While The Brain Trust had originally formed to help each other evaluate approaches to health and menopause, they'd soon become bored with dry discussions of pharmaceuticals. They started tiptoeing into discussions they couldn't have anywhere else, about shifting bodies and faces, about sex drives, about feelings of worthlessness, about death. About anything.

Tonight, they filled Maria in on the meeting she'd missed and she weighed in with enthusiasm. Then they talked about money: how they earned it, how they spent it, how it fit into their value system. At times they became practical, touching briefly on investing and even clarifying, for those who needed it, the difference between stocks and bonds. Jane was eager to explain the difference between defined benefit and defined contribution pension plans, but no one would let her.

The liveliest sub-topic was how they shared money—or didn't—with their partners. Some had elaborate schemes for who-pays-for-what and which-account-does-what, while Ruth and Charlie were the only ones for whom all money was joint money, no matter who earned it and who spent it. Everyone was interested in the others' systems, having previously thought their way was the only way to do it.

The first significant pause in the conversation didn't come for an hour. Sarah broke the silence by observing that neither Maria nor Blanche had said very much. "For heaven's sake, ladies, we talk about our orgasms here, is there a problem talking about our money?"

Maria, staring at the hanging plants on the wall opposite her as if the answer were encoded in the macramé holders, said, "It's just that ... I was hoping we weren't going to talk about *how much* we all have. And I can't believe I just introduced the topic." She smacked her head with a flat palm.

"Why?" The question came from three mouths at the same time.

She removed her shoes and folded one leg under her, then hugged herself and spoke to the wood-burning stove. "It's not that I'm embarrassed about being broke. I like my work in the flower shop and don't mind that it doesn't pay very much. I think there's even a part of me that thinks it's virtuous to be broke. And Jim lives close to the earth, very close, growing our food and all. So we live a good decent life and have enough to do what we want."

"But ... ?" Sarah said.

"But maybe I'm afraid seeing myself through your eyes, would make me mind being broke." Looking at the circle of women, she added, "Nutty, right?" She shook her head so hard her long red hair smacked Charlie, sitting next to her, in the face.

"Really, it's the same damned thing we obsess about all the time," Blanche said. "Even when we think we're talking about something else, we're talking about holding onto who we truly are no matter who we're with. Isn't that what we always talk about? In one way or another?"

"Is that why *you* haven't said anything tonight?" Sarah asked.

Blanche cleaned her red-framed glasses and put them back on. She stood up abruptly, frowning, and pulled her tight silk slacks down at the hips, then settled herself again on the couch. She confessed that she hadn't said anything for a similar reason, except she was on the other side of the coin, so to speak. Knowing she probably had more money than some of the others, she wouldn't want to feel as if she were showing off. And she also didn't want to feel, saying the numbers out loud, as if she'd sold out.

"Like how Maria said there's a certain virtue about being broke. And I'm not."

"What in the world are you talking about?"

"Sold out? By working your ass off?"

"Is this a black thing?"

"Or a sixties thing?"

"Or a nice-girl thing?"

The pause was long gone as they picked and prodded at the question of their inhibition about the "how much" question.

Sarah's voice cleared the air like a plow through soft earth. "The reason for everyone's discomfort is shame. Having too much, not having enough. Spending too much, being too frugal. Let's face it, we are one fucked-up bunch of ladies."

The summation was accepted unanimously. And they agreed not to talk about numbers.

"Except," she added, "we're all middle-aged and we all have whatever we have. So, can we talk about retirement?"

And they were off.

Sarah couldn't even think about the subject until she got her kids through college and could start to think about saving. "Which means never," she said. "But it doesn't matter because I love my work. Usually."

Blanche had the traditional fear of becoming a bag lady if she stopped making money, and wondered if the fear persisted as a result of feminism or in spite of feminism.

Ruth told of David's early-retirement deal. And of her extreme reluctance to join him. "I'm not exactly sure why. It's not the fear of being a bag lady."

"We know it's not because you love your job so much," Sarah said.

"I think it's more about what I'd do with myself. Here I am doing something I'm good at. I like that. David calls it my 'addiction to competence.' And I guess it is like an addiction, because feeding it just fuels it."

"Come on, Ruth, you'd find lots to do. You can't sit still," Maria said. "It's ironic that I have lots of ideas about what I'd do.... but I'll never be able to retire."

Charlie groaned. She said she didn't want to hear anything like those motivational lectures on PBS or NPR about some older woman whose first screenplay won an Oscar or who just started painting and, voila, has a solo show. "There's that irritating implication that we all could do those kinds of things if we just wanted to. Man, that pisses me off. We're not all gorgeous and healthy and we're not all talented. Well, you all are, of course." She rolled her eyes. "Hey, I'm a good weaver and I make some nice stuff—and I now value my time—but otherwise I'm actually pretty ordinary. I'm tired. I'm depressed. I'm bitchy."

"Particularly tonight?" suggested Maria.

"Well, maybe," Charlie said with a shrug and a toss of her white mane.

"There's always drugs," Jane said. "I've said it before and I'll say it again: Estrogen is the best drug ever invented. We used to think it was marijuana. We didn't know. It's not like being stoned. It's better. It's being normal."

Ruth said, "I'm thinking about throwing in the herbal towel, too. I haven't slept through the night in months and it's catching up with me. But maybe I should take a sleeping pill. But are sleeping pills better than hormones?"

"Maybe you should quit your job?" Sarah said, almost tenderly but not quite.

Okay, Sarah, I get it, thought Ruth. "This has nothing to do with work," she said.

"Don't be so sure. Emotions play a large role in the health of our bodies. I held my peace when you called us together to talk about makeup—"

"And skin care," added Ruth.

"That's what you call holding your peace?" Blanche cleaned her glasses again.

"Well, some of my peace, anyway. But the way I really see it is that you're an intelligent and sensitive woman who's devoting her energy to a male-dominated capitalist machine that's all about oppressing women." The almost-tender tone of voice was gone. "It's enough to screw up your emotions and your body."

Charlie said, "I don't agree. But I don't think you need to agree about economic philosophy to agree about hormones."

"Or chin hairs." Maria stroked her chin. I agree with you, Jane, I don't think corporations have anything to do with how much I hate—I mean I really really HATE—them. Just yesterday, I made Jim promise that if I get hit by a bus and I'm unconscious, he'll come to the hospital and secretly pluck. I even showed him which tweezers to use. If I knew hormones would put those hairs back where they belonged, I'd take them in a New York minute."

"Okay," Sarah said. "I'm a little more … let's say, ardent, than you all. It's just that we're all struggling to be okay with who we are." She looked at Ruth. "And I'm just saying I don't think you're okay with who you are at work. What I see is that *you* don't think you belong there, not me. Well, me too, I guess. But still…."

Ruth waited for someone else to challenge Sarah, but no one did.

"Okay, Sarah. I get it." Ruth said.

WHEN RUTH CRAWLED INTO BED AT HOME, DAVID WAS HALF asleep. "Good meeting?" he drawled.

"Thought-provoking. I have a lot to think about."

"About money?" He rolled over to face her, but without opening his eyes. "I thought this one would be kind of cut-and-dried."

"Wrong again."

He opened his eyes. "Now *that* sounds interesting. Can you tell me?"

"Maybe tomorrow. But, then again, maybe not."

"Okay, good night. I hope you get some sleep."

"Me too. One of these days, I'm sure I will. Good night."

16
Refocusing

THE EARLY-MORNING QUIET AT WORK was different from other kinds of quiet. It wasn't like the succulent quiet of the natural world, a peace hovering over the earth. Nor was it like waking up in the middle of the night and feeling that something is missing.

It was more like suspended animation, being in a place that had been removed from the normal world. What made the interlude so precious was knowing that all the dormant computers, copiers, phones and coffee machines would soon be called into service and the white-noise of office chatter would soon be inescapable. Or maybe it was being surrounded by work but not the people associated with the work. No matter how many people were at the office, early morning was always a sacred time of quiet and individual concentration.

This morning, Ruth's only distraction was the team of upscale flower arrangers with their intensely focused, painstaking work. They drew from several large boxes of blossoms as from a palette, selecting one stem at a time, placing it in its vase deliberately, stepping back to examine its placement, sometimes moving it a few times until satisfied. What seemed like a haphazard, even random, addition of blossoms became a harmonious creation.

She fantasized about being their apprentice. She'd be able to concentrate on grace, nature, and beauty, not on who said what to whom. She'd devote her attention to how the gentle arcs of the long stems related to the shape of the vase, to finding the perfect combination of blossoms.

She liked the idea that most people wouldn't actually see *her*; they'd only know she'd been there because of the beauty she'd created and left behind, like the shadow on a swimming pool floor cast by the all-but-invisible dragonfly on the water's surface.

She got up and closed her door, then reviewed the focus group results again, thinking about how she'd present them to Jeremy. He'd called the day before and asked her to stop by his office after lunch today to update him on Violins & Wine. It was a reasonable enough request, she guessed. He was, after all, the CEO, and she reported to him, so he had a right to ask. But still, only one day's notice to present her progress?

"It doesn't need to be a formal presentation, more like a conversation," he'd said. "Just bring some back-up data." But she didn't believe him. He wasn't a "conversation" kind of guy. It might look like a conversation, but she'd have to be careful.

She'd prepared data on budget, R&D, timelines. The trickiest—and probably most important—part was the concept testing with focus groups. She could just hear him. "Disappointing, very disappointing." He'd say he always knew makeup for old women was a dumb idea no matter how you spelled it.

She wanted to make sure her reaction to the tape she'd watched was grounded in what was actually on the tape and not on what she wanted to be on the tape. She'd told Judy, Pat, and Tom to drop everything for a one-hour high priority meeting this morning so she could test it out. If they arrived exactly at nine-thirty, she promised they'd be out by ten-thirty.

Waiting for them to arrive, she talked to Colleen: She should pick the one person she'd least hate working for. This secretary-sharing scheme might never happen. And even if it did, it would only be temporary. Of course, if she *wanted* to leave, then that's what she should do.

"But, like, how will you get everything done?"

The truth was, she didn't really need a full-time secretary, but didn't want to give half of Colleen up in a power-tug-of-war. If Jeremy had only asked her for suggestions about cost-cutting, things might be different. But Ruth was going to have Jeremy eating out of her hand with Violins & Wine, and getting Colleen back would be her first priority. She promised.

She looked out through the rain-streaked windows, trying to follow the traffic patterns, settling on the yellow cab that was weaving his way into the right-turn-only lane. She raised her eyes from the street to the sky. The persistent low clouds sucked the color from buildings, streets, and even trees, leaving only a nondescript gray.

But over in the northeastern edge of the sky, the monolithic moist cloud was separating from the earth a little, letting in something that resembled light—not the sun itself, but evidence of it. That hint of light at the edge of the sky, even while most of the sky was still blanketed, made the scene less gloomy. After days of unrelenting gray, just the promise of something different and better was thrilling.

Tom arrived first and chose the end of the three-seat couch. Then Judy and Pat walked in, chatting about a movie that Judy had seen but Pat hadn't. Judy sat right next to Tom, presumably to leave the third space for Pat. But Pat declined the couch and chose a chair, leaving Tom and Judy next to each other.

Their comfort with physical proximity was very different from her own experience on the subway that morning, when she'd been lost in thought, inventing lives for the usual subway denizens: The scruffy teenagers in their too-long pants and backwards baseball caps, lost on planet Walkman, came from homes where they were ignored by career-oriented parents, so they took comfort by numbing out to music. The androgynous businessmen and women couldn't get taxis, so were daring and took the subway, looking to their left, to their right, and at their watch with anxiety. The slow-moving senior citizens who talked to each other too loudly must be on their way to museums and lectures about ornithology. The young mothers, harried with strollers and baby-paraphernalia, were trying to expose their children to the cultural wealth the city had to offer.

At forty-second street, everyone on her side of the subway car left except her and the man next to her. Five minutes earlier, surrounded by other commuters, their touching thighs had meant nothing. Now she felt monumentally uncomfortable. She got off one stop early.

But Tom and Judy stayed. They didn't even look uncomfortable. Strange. Interesting.

"I promised to get you out by ten-thirty, so let's get started." She distributed the focus group results.

Ruth knew Pat would be defensive about anything resembling criticism, since she'd supervised these groups. In fact, though, she'd done a good job and what had happened was not her fault. Once she was reassured of that, she'd probably concentrate on feeling vindicated by the results.

Ruth asked for their reaction and out-waited everyone's reluctance to go first until Tom eventually started by stating the obvious. "These results are surprising."

That was enough for Pat. "I'll say," she said. "Surprising but interesting. Our customers are telling us they're not interested in this product. It's a good thing we tested first, so to speak. It will wind up saving the company a lot of money."

"Pat, sometimes it feels like…." Judy's blinking ended with closed eyes instead of open ones, so she wound up speaking with shut, trembling eyelids. It was disconcerting, like watching a movie whose sound and video are out of sync.

"… feels like … you've *wanted* this project to fail from the get-go."

Impossibly, Pat got stiffer and straighter. "No, Judith, I haven't wanted it to fail from the get-go, as you put it. I will admit I wasn't quite as enthusiastic as the rest of you. Maybe I'm enthusiasm-challenged, who knows. Instead of jolly-jolly-jolly."

Judy locked her eyelids in their full-open position. "Pat, are you—"

"I'm just saying, everything we need is right in here." She held up the sheaf of papers. "If you take someone's temperature and you don't like what it says, you don't doubt the thermometer, do you?"

Judy glared at Pat. Ruth didn't like Pat's smugness, either.

"Maybe yes, maybe no. I want to show you something that might help us decide whether to doubt the thermometer."

Ruth showed excerpts from a few of the focus group tapes. Judy saw it right away.

"That skinny one with long hair … it's like she's … I don't know … like she's some kind of … magnet."

It was subtle, and Ruth was surprised Judy saw it so fast. But as soon as she pointed it out, Tom saw it too.

During the background part of the session, all the women seemed to be perfect middle-aged target customers. But the next part was a "projective techniques" designed to elicit under-the-surface attitudes that people aren't always able to locate and articulate on their own. The moderator distributed pictures and asked respondents to invent stories for them. Things shifted and kept shifting for the rest of the session, including the part when the Violins & Wine concept was presented.

One woman—very attractive, very articulate, a former model—had profound problems with aging. She came across loud and clear and negative. She didn't seem to be *trying* to sway others' opinions, but they lined up behind her. Who'd not-mind looking their age when they could imagine looking like Ms. Model?

The moderator should have seen it or sensed it and changed course.

"It's not exactly 'group think,'" Ruth said. "But it's not independent thinking, either. And the same thing happened in one of the other groups."

She showed two more excerpts. Tom got as excited as the one who's first to find Waldo in the crowded picture. "Look, look. That blonde one. She's the lodestone. Right? Don't you think?"

"I do. She's not a model. She's a dancer. Just as bad."

"I'm not so sure I agree with you all," Pat said. "Maybe we have some group think going on right here? But I suppose this means you're going to want to run more groups. Can the budget tolerate that?"

"No to group think. Yes to more groups. Yes to budget."

Three hours later, getting to Jeremy's office was more of a trip than she'd expected. The local elevator that would have taken her from the eighteenth floor to the twenty-sixth was out of service, so she had to go down to the lobby in the elevator that stopped at all floors between one and twenty. Then the one that went directly from the first floor to the twenty-fifth before stopping at all floors between twenty-six and fifty. The zigzag was an aggravating delay.

THE TIME SHE WENT from Djembering to Ghana with Vivian was worse. First they'd taken a bush taxi from their village to Dakar, where they met up with Vivian's friend from home who'd come over for a visit. The friend was a hippie-turned journalist, with long jet-black hair and blazing eyes to match. She was doing research for a story, she'd said. Maybe the story was about the Peace Corps, maybe it was about Africa, she wasn't sure yet.

"A journalist?" Ruth had asked Vivian. Does that mean I have to be careful about what I say? After living with you, I don't know if I can."

"Nah, she's one of us, she just happens to have that job."

From Dakar, the three caught a flight—an extravagance for Vivian and Ruth, financed with Christmas presents from home—to Abidjan, the capital of the Ivory Coast, a city with the only ice-skating rink in sub-Saharan Africa, where Ruth and Vivian knew a volunteer they could stay with. The volunteer borrowed a car from her Ivorian boyfriend, a colleague in the school where she taught English, for the drive to Ghana, one country due East.

It was sixty kilometers to the border, along the coast. Two-thirds of the way there, they found the direct road was closed and they had to take a long detour: 200 kilometers north on bone-jarring red-dirt washboarded roads to the next border crossing, then east to cross over, then south for another 200 kilometers back to the coast, only thirty kilometers due east of the "Road Closed" sign.

They had a grand time in Ghana, with the journalist paying for everything, including gas, from her expense account. They loved the food, they loved speaking English. They stayed in the old slave-trading castles along the water where, for a dollar a night, they slept on straw bedding on the dirt floor, ate whatever nameless meat the guardian cooked, inhaled the wood-fire smoke, and heard harrowing stories of the castles' terrible history. They visited fellow volunteers, all of whom welcomed them warmly. Finally, they returned the way they'd come, driving the 200 kilometers north to the border crossing, where they encountered a different guard from the one when they'd entered. Tall and handsome in a military uniform and red beret, he said they couldn't cross because they didn't have the right papers for the car.

"But we just came in a week ago," they protested.

He put his hand on his gun. "The papers were so good for the coming in, miss, but for the going out not so," he said. His lips moved, but nothing else did. His eyes were locked straight ahead, somewhere over their heads.

Ruth thought the guard might be looking for a bribe and

suggested, "Perhaps there's a fee we need to pay. We'll be happy to pay any fee that's necessary, sir."

The guard didn't look at her as he said, "No, miss, no money, miss, I need the papers."

The four women looked at each other in bewilderment. These were the only papers they had.

Vivian burst into noisy tears, remonstrating loudly that her husband and baby awaited her in Abidjan and she needed to get back to them right away. As she walked, she gestured wildly and cried real tears. Her hair flew around her face, some of it sticking to her wet cheeks. She walked in circles and got more and more excited, talking about her husband and her baby, over and over. The other women watched in wonder.

"My husband is having an operation tomorrow. I need to be there. Tomorrow." And on and on.

The guard's face melted from stern military man to bewildered boy, someone who wanted to be rid of a crazy white woman. "Just go, misses, go now." The women got back in their car and, as soon as they were out of earshot, laughed for 100 of the 200 kilometers back to the coast.

THE ELEVATOR DOORS OPENED.

She knocked on Jeremy's door and he greeted her with a big imitation smile but his usual wimpy handshake. They agreed the sun had finally broken through and the weekend promised to be fair. He didn't offer coffee this time.

He sat on the couch and indicated Ruth should sit there too.

"Do you have the data for me?"

So much for it being a conversation. She handed him a thirty seven page report, but hung onto a smaller packet. "How about if I give you a tour of the highlights, big picture, that kind of thing."

"No thanks. I'll look it *all* over. All over. Big picture plus details."

He read and she followed his page-by-page progress. Was he taking longer than he really needed to?

"Let me just say that the most important material is on—"

He looked up and seemed to choose his words carefully. "I prefer to look through it myself and make my own judgments about what's the most important."

Some conversation, she thought.

He continued to read. Sometimes he ran his finger down the tables of numbers, and sometimes he returned to a page he'd already read.

When he was on page twenty-six, he said, "This is just what I'd feared."

She'd been expecting it on page twenty-five. "I know what you mean. But there are a few interesting verbatims on pages twenty-seven to thirty. My team and I are convinced that—"

"Ruth, Ruth, Ruth." He looked up at her. "Focus groups are like science. Create a situation, test it, see the results. Data. Individuals may say one thing, but the composite data reveal the truth. And the truth, as I said, is just what I feared. We may or may not like the idea of makeup that's about ... about ... loving your wrinkles. But our customers don't."

"Let me just read one verbatim to you. It's on the bottom of page twenty-nine."

He returned to the precise point where he'd previously stopped, held up his hand in a "Stop" sign, and continued his plodding. She held her tongue and her breath.

Finally, he said, "It doesn't look good." He looked above and behind her.

Here was the tricky part of the so-called conversation. She had to explain that she wanted to run more groups, this time paying more careful attention to the selection of the respondents, but without implying they hadn't done a good job the first time around. She had to prove there were different results out there, waiting to be uncovered, that it wasn't a question of throwing good money after bad.

"Right. They don't look good at first, but there's is a nugget of gold. These women have shown us something very important. It's in that verbatim."

"I see it. 'After all these years of showing me beautiful young women in your ads, you're telling me you've changed your minds? So I've been making a mistake to listen to you? And why should I listen to you now?'"

"That's the one."

That comment had gotten Ruth thinking that maybe they were asking too much of women to disbelieve the old advertising messages and believe the new. It was conversion fervor, like brand-new EST idealogues who try to convince everyone to jump onto their magic EST carpet, only to find people crossing the street to avoid them.

She still thought her ideas about authenticity were right, but knew it wasn't enough simply to state them. So it wasn't *just* about new groups, which she was confident would yield the expected results. It was also about the message.

She told Jeremy about her plan for additional groups, with different screening techniques, and her new concept. She'd never prepared anything so fast and knew it wasn't as polished as she'd have liked. But, with a couple of "Oh well's," she'd patched together photographs and possible message statements.

When she was done, he said, "You think you're going to change their minds this way?"

"I'm sure of it."

"Before I was CEO here at Mimosa Inc, before I was SVP at B&D, even, I ran a project for my company, even though the numbers told me maybe I shouldn't. Like you. I let my hopes and dreams cloud my judgment. Feelings, the bad "F" word." He smiled in what was, for him, slow motion.

He's making a joke?

"We lost a bundle. I vowed never to do that again. When I *do* make a mistake, I try to learn from it."

He flipped through the rest of the thirty-seven-page report, then reached over for the smaller packet with the new plan, which he looked at more carefully. As he thought, he licked his lips, slowly and thoroughly, as luxuriously as if someone had told him to clean the sugar from a powdered doughnut off his mouth.

"On the other hand. . . ." He paged back and forth through the document, a few times, then snapped it shut. After a long pause, he said, "Maybe, just maybe. But be sure you keep me informed. And have you made any progress on a new name?"

"We're working on it."

That's it? An abrupt and unexplained U-turn? And then 'Keep me informed'? No questions? No snide comments about the slapdash presentation of the new approach? No deadlines or ultimata? Does he have another meeting he's late for?

She was glad he said yes, and didn't even resent the hoops she'd had to jump through. But she wondered why good sometimes felt bad.

PART IV

17

Profit or Non?

THE RED BRICK BUILDING THAT HOUSED The Brooklyn Shelter for Women could have been an old-age home, a nursery school, an apartment building, an armory. Square and squat, with no nod to decoration or beauty, its heaviness was slightly intimidating, which seemed fitting, as if the building welcomed its broken and bruised inhabitants and promised to protect them.

"No one can know about the shelter in a casual sort of way, if you know what I mean," Vivian said, as she and Ruth approached. "The women have to sign a confidentiality agreement. The residents are here so they won't be found by husbands, boyfriends, girlfriends even, not by anyone. We found out a little while ago that some people in the neighborhood think it's still a barracks, which it hasn't been for a long time, so every once in a while we blast some military music to keep the illusion alive. I love that."

A week ago, Vivian and Ruth had been talking about their jobs. They ventured beyond questions of exactly what they did to the satisfactions and frustrations therein. With uncommon restraint, Vivian didn't actually lecture Ruth on finding another kind of work; she just asked if Ruth wanted to see the Shelter or, as she called it, the BSW.

Ruth accepted the invitation partially as a way to get to know the contemporary Vivian better, but also for her periodic re-evaluation of her long-ago choice of profits over non-profits. Was it really just about the money and Josh's college fund?

David thought the visit was all about female bonding and she didn't disabuse him. He still wanted her to retire, she still didn't, and they rarely discussed it any more. But secretly she thought maybe she'd consider leaving Mimosa for something else. If it were the right thing. Just the exactly right thing. Something that fit her perfectly.

Vivian had to work for a few hours on Saturday and Ruth tagged along. Carlos was going to meet them, then Ruth would drive all three of them to her place, where David, at this very moment, was getting lunch ready for the four of them.

She'd been gratified that Vivian looked less like a vagabond than she did at the concert or the shopping trip, but not so much as to disguise who she really was. Her blue slacks were loose-fitting and, therefore, flattering as well as comfortable. The fabric was a second cousin of denim, but with a fine and handsome finish. On top of it was a colorful knit, not so colorful as to be wild, merely uninhibited. Her bright-yellow shoes matched her top in only the loosest sense of the word, with clunky heels that used to be found on old-country grandmothers' feet. Her hair was formed into a loose-weave single braid and was moderately well-behaved.

As they drew near the entrance, Vivian stopped to face Ruth. "Listen, Ruthie, visitors are sometimes really uncomfortable in here, and they just don't know how they should talk to the women and kids. There's only one golden rule. No pity. No 'Oh, you poor thing.'" She started fumbling for her keys. "Other than that, just do what feels right, what feels like you."

"Yeah, it's true that some of them are pitiable. They're physically and emotionally bruised and you want to scoop them up and say 'Poor baby' over and over, and rock them to sleep. But believe me, 'poor babies' don't really help them get their lives in order. We're protecting them and nursing them back to health, but we're also trying to prepare them for the rest of their lives. We've got three months to do it. Remember, these women are the lucky ones because they're here. Save the pity for the ones who are still out there."

She found a small brass-colored key with a red string, separate from the densely-populated and noisy key-ring that advertised its whereabouts in Vivian's huge tie-dyed canvas purse. She unlocked the ten-foot-tall metal door, heavy and thick, unadorned, unwelcoming. Ruth expected it to creak, but it didn't. They walked through a cavernous empty room with high ceilings and barred windows. Ruth could imagine troops practicing here, or school kids playing "Duck Duck Goose" during recess. They crossed to the far side of the room, footsteps echoing like a film noir soundtrack, to a cheerless stairway which took them to Vivian's office.

Vivian looked at her desk, piled with mountains of paper. She sighed and said, "As you can see, there's stuff I gotta get done. It'll take maybe an hour or so. Want to walk around and see what you see? Then come back and I'll give you an official tour and introduce you around?"

"Okay."

"Here's an ID badge. If anyone wonders about you, tell them you're my friend. Or tell them you're a potential corporate sponsor who needs to see the work we do. Or both."

Vivian's mind seemed already to be focused on her work as she turned to the paperwork on her desk. Ruth set off down the hallway, trying to keep her mind empty of preconceptions about what she'd find and her heart free of guilt about the disproportionate share of luck in her life.

The walls were a quiet nondescript speckled green, not the dull military or institutional green she would have expected, more like the living color of an algae-covered pond. The orange trim was also unexpected and curiously cheerful. At odd intervals along the way were hand-painted murals, about three-feet square, the bottom of the square being the floor. Frame and picture and wall in one, thought Ruth. Neat. Some had clearly been painted by children, others by adults, some by artists of unguessable age. She particularly liked the aquarium and the playground. A few were disturbing in their depictions of violence. Each panel was labeled with the artist's name and the date.

Everything was clean and very, very orderly, like the stacks of magazines with labels as to categories, sub-categories, and sub-sub-categories. Perhaps it was a way of having control over one's environment, a way of reining in emotional chaos through physical order. That made a lot of sense.

She idly looked through the glass panel in the closed door on the right and saw a group of nine women seated in a circle, as if they were a therapy group. But it might be a class, too, because the leader or teacher, also seated in the circle, was pointing to a flip chart. Everyone was taking notes. The windows in the room had whimsical yellow and orange curtains and lush potted plants. A few women looked up at her, their impassive faces registering her presence but shielding their own reactions. One had a large bandage on her cheek and almost no hair on her head. Another's arm was in a sling. Ruth walked on.

She was drawn to a huge bulletin board—The Bee Ess Double-You—dominating the end of the corridor, listing all the goings-on. By this time, she was not surprised that it was well-organized, nor that it was attractive, with cheerful hand-made decorations. What struck her, though, was the bubbling activity going on inside this building, yeast-like. It had looked so immobile and lethargic from the outside, yet was so energetic within.

There were counseling and therapy sessions, for individuals and groups, for adults and children. But there were also courses on personal and interpersonal matters, on parenting and workplace issues. She saw that the course she'd just looked in on was "Workplace Communication and Writing a Resume." There was AA, NA, and AlAnon. There was an elaborate schedule of home-schooling classes, as well as lawyers' visiting days. There were schedules of communal chores, including cleaning, cooking and repairing. Announcements and congratulations were scattered throughout:

one woman got a job, another stayed sober for ten days, one passed the GED, a child won a local spelling bee. And there were lectures, concerts, and movies. The current population was thirty-five women and their twenty-eight children, along with fifteen staff and twelve volunteers, all listed on the left with photos. It struck Ruth that, like Djembering in Africa, BSW was a thriving community that was hidden under the radar to most people.

"Do you belong here?" asked a loud, stern, monotonal voice that lingered on the second syllable of 'belong.' Ruth hadn't heard the approach of the small woman in jeans and a dark blue tee shirt with BSW in large white letters.

"Oh hi, yes I do. I'm here with Vivian. She's my friend." She pointed to her ID badge. "And I'm also a potential corporate sponsor. I'm from Mimosa. The makeup company."

She was glad she remembered the sponsorship cover story, but also immediately envisioned, listed on the bulletin board, the classes Mimosa could sponsor: Makeup for the Workplace, Makeup as Concealer, Talking to Your Daughter About Makeup, Makeup and Self-Image, Makeovers. Then she remembered "No More Benefits." But this wasn't a benefit event, it was different. Would Jeremy think so? Probably not.

The woman shifted her weight to her left foot as she studied Ruth for a moment with large, unblinking and unforgiving hazel eyes. "Okay." Her voice was still stern.

"My name's Ruth," she said as she extended her hand.

They shook. "I'm Elaine. I work here. Actually, I used to be a client, but the BSW helped me straighten myself out."

A skinny girl of about eight emerged from a room with a hand-lettered "Infirmary" sign. She looked up and down the corridor, then came over to stand close to Elaine, far from Ruth. Her complexion indicated ethnicity of some kind, though whether African-American, Semitic or Hispanic, Ruth couldn't tell. It was a perfect complexion, the color all people would be if everyone reproduced with everyone else. The ultimate answer to racism. Her hair was curly, about chin length. Several colorful barrettes did their best to control it. Like a puppy's paws, her adult teeth were too large for the child's face that contained them, giving her the illusion of wisdom and innocence at the same time. Her mouth was magically expressive, now smiling, now frowning, now wide open in surprise.

This child reminded Ruth of pictures she'd seen of herself. And of the children used in fund-raising photos for international aid organizations. Of the daughter she'd regretted not having after Josh. Of EveryChild. She adored her instantly.

"What's the matter, Joy?" Elaine asked. "Are you sick?"

"No, I had to get a needle cause I stepped on a nail. A turtles shot? But mom said she'd wait for me out here. Did you see her?" Joy's eyes were on Elaine as she spoke, but they made frequent quick jumps over to Ruth and back.

"I haven't seen her. And, by the way, it's a tetanus shot. This is my friend Ruth. She's Vivian's friend too. She's visiting today because maybe the company she works for will give us some money."

Ruth kneeled and said "Hi, Joy. Does your arm hurt from the shot?"

"No, it's okay. But if your company gives us money, tell them we need a new computer. And I could use some new shoes, cause I'm getting so big so fast."

"I'll remember that. And how about some books? Do you need some books, too? Do you have a library here?"

"Yeah, we do. And the books are really rusty-dusty old, and I've read 'em all. I like to read a lot. So yeah tell the company people we could use new ones."

Ruth unconsciously reached out to remove a strand of hair that was like a corkscrew in front of Joy's eye, but the child backed out of her reach.

Softly, Ruth asked, "What's your most favorite book in the whole wide world?" She wanted to keep this girl engaged as long as possible, so she could stare at her some more.

Joy folded her arms and rolled her round brown eyes up to the ceiling. "Let's see, I really loved it when mommy used to read 'The Runaway Bunny' to me. And 'Good-night Moon.' But those are baby books. Those are from when we lived at home. Long ago." She looked at Ruth solemnly. "Now I like books about magic places, like Wizard of Oz and stuff."

"Do you want me to help you find which classroom your mom's in, sweetie?" Elaine asked.

"Yeah," she said as she held onto Elaine's leg."

"It was nice meeting you, Joy," Ruth said. "I'll remember what you said."

"Goody." Her eyes danced, her mouth grinned. "Red ones would be good. Shoes, red shoes. With a little strap, like my friend Amy has."

"Bye." She waved, using all her restraint to keep from leaning over to try to kiss Joy good-bye.

Elaine and Joy walked off hand-in-hand, the child skipping and the small adult walking quickly to keep pace with her.

Ruth continued to wander the halls and went upstairs to see the dormitory-style sleeping rooms, the cafeteria, the gym. No one else asked her for identification. She returned to Vivian's office about an hour and fifteen minutes after she'd left and entered without knocking.

"Perfect timing," Vivian said. "Ready for the official tour?"

BY THE TIME RUTH AND VIVIAN got in the car, she knew in her heart the non-profit life was not for her. She'd always felt that way, though she thought she "should" feel otherwise, wished she did, and hoped that maybe she'd have changed by now. She certainly loved the work done by the BSW, thought the environment was stimulating and passionate, and knew there were many other non-profits about whose missions she felt equally enthusiastic. She was glad they were there and would do anything to help them. In fact, she already had plans for a computer and books for the library, although Vivian would not permit her to buy Joy a pair of shoes.

"That would be begging. Kids here are taught not to beg. You want to buy shoes for *all* the kids, fine. But not shoes for Joy alone. Great impulse, but rules are rules."

Ruth, in turn, understood the rule, even thought it was reasonable. If she were in Vivian's place, she might make the same rule. That's why she didn't want to be in Vivian's place. She wanted to buy Joy a pair of red shoes. Guess she was going to have to spring for twenty-eight pairs.

"So, how was the visit?" Carlos climbed into the back seat of Ruth's car.

"Great. I loved it."

"Vivvy does a great job. In a great place. Turn left here, the light on the next block takes too long."

She put on her turn signal and advanced into the intersection.

"You can go, just scoot in after this car; the truck's going slow so you can make it before him."

She waited and turned after the truck.

"The place was great, the kids were great. Did you ever meet the little girl named Joy? She's just irresistible. I—"

"Did Viv show you the list of 'graduates' and what they're doing now? Pretty impressive, don't you think? What a difference that place makes. And her, too. Watch out for the cop who watches that stop sign like it's a pot of gold."

"Very impressive."

"And did she … wait a second, you missed a turn back there. Quick, quick, make a left up there. But watch out for the yellow car coming this way."

"Enough! I know how to drive and I know how to get to my own house."

"Whatever you say."

"Children, children, play nice," Vivian said. "In fact, it *would* be a little better if you'd turn here, Ruthie. It's a little faster this way. But either way is basically fine."

She turned. "Now I know why you married Carlos," Ruth said. "You come off like sugar and spice next to him."

Ruth looked into the back seat, where Carlos was staring out the window. "Only kidding, Carlos."

"No problemo." He fingered his bracelet.

"WELCOME TO CHEZ TALBOT," David said as he opened the door even before they knocked. He was wearing his "Toughest Job I Ever Loved" Peace Corps T-shirt. His blue-jean shorts were nearly covered by a JFK Middle School apron from a long-ago PTA fundraiser. It displayed reminders of all the dishes he'd prepared while wearing it. He took coats and offered drinks.

"Man, I would loooove a beer. But wait, don't we get a tour?" Vivian asked.

David was the tour-director, so Ruth excused herself to make a few phone calls, but when she got back to the living room, Carlos was there. Oh no. Didn't he take the tour?

"I never was big on house tours," he said. "Don't take it personally."

He accepted a club soda and they listened to music, talking about their favorite artists, for awhile.

"You know, Ruthie, I'm this way with everyone. Not just you."

"What way?" She wanted him to say it out loud, to own up to being a pain.

"I think it's being direct, but other people call it different things. You called it 'tactless' I think."

"I used to think it was okay because you were so, you know, so … so passionate about everything."

He turned to face her. "I'm trying to say this in a way that won't piss you off. Which I don't usually bother to do. You're not the only one who gets pissed off at me, you know."

"Really?"

"Maybe I should say it in Spanish. People tell me I'm nicer in Spanish."

"Just say it."

His eye contact was laser-like. "I want to make an exception for you—to my world view."

"An exception to your world view? Excuse me?"

"The things we said last time. Helping to make the world better. Being political, not corporate. But I'm not good with compromise. I—"

Vivian's voice preceded her into the room. "Not good with compromise is putting it mildly. This is a man who uses organic peanut butter in the mousetraps. If he can't bring himself to poison the mice with chemicals, what hope is there for things of slightly more import?"

"You think that's not important, babe?"

"I didn't mean it that way."

They settled down in the living room, Vivian and David sprawled, shoeless, on the green leather couch, each with a long-necked beer bottle. Ruth sat on the bentwood rocker she'd inherited from her mother, salt-rimmed margarita glass in hand. Carlos was cross-legged on a fringed green-and-blue pillow he'd appropriated from the couch and placed in the middle of the floor. Joan Baez was singing "Diamonds and Rust."

Vivian told Ruth how much she liked the house. Especially the wall of photos, her favorite part. "And I'm dying to meet Josh. He looks yummy, like a combination of you guys. I always knew he would, back in Djembering when I could see the future and you couldn't."

David asked about the tour of the Shelter.

"You can't believe all the stuff that goes on there," Ruth said. "Classes and meetings and job counseling and lots of really interesting and valuable stuff. Vivian's done such a great job. And everyone loves her. It's inspiring, really."

"That's great," David said. "I hope you're proud of yourself, Viv. You should be."

"Yeah, well, proud. Okay, I guess I do feel good about what I do."

"Sounds like there's a 'but' coming?" David raised his eyebrows to accentuate his question.

"No, not a 'but,' well not exactly. It's just that I know that what I do is important, really I do, I see it every day, and I like doing it, sometimes I even love doing it, it's just that I sometimes have times when all the things that are frustrating get bigger and hide my view of the value so it becomes just a job and today was one of those days. You're a teacher, so you must go through that, too, don't you?"

"Babe, how can you say that? You do something that's so noble and valuable, something that helps people every single day, how can you—"

"Face it, Carlos, I'm not a saint like you and sometimes I can't manage to keep my attention fixed only on the good stuff and ignore the bullshit and the politics and the pettiness which gets me down. Call me imperfect, Ishmael. Or call me human. Trust me, this is not the day to lecture me about my contribution to humanity."

"Whatever you say."

Linda Ronstadt was just starting to remind them that "Love is a Rose." Ruth changed the CD player from "random" to one-at-a-time so she wouldn't have to yank her loyalties back and forth.

David said the worst for him was talking to people who get that woo-woo look on their face when they hear he's a teacher and talk about what a noble profession teaching is. As if appreciation makes up for pitiful salaries, huge classes, crumbling buildings.

"Do you get mad?" Vivian asked.

"Not really. I don't *have* to be a teacher, after all. I chose it."

"We are so very different, David."

"What made you mad today?" David asked.

Though she said she'd have preferred to forget about work and let the beer do its job, she also couldn't resist venting. Today's target was funding problems. Getting money from people to do the things that need to be done. Being in competition with other agencies that also need it, so you feel bad for yourself if you don't get the money but bad for the others if you do. Today's issue was a set of ethical-political-financial niceties surrounding a grant proposal.

"It just feels so grown up, so 'life is complicated.' I hate when life is complicated. Simple is better. Let's drink."

Carlos's voice softened a bit, though the Spanish accent got more prominent, as he talked about how great it would be if he were the one giving the money away for a change. Sitting somewhere with a pot of money. People coming to him to describe the things they do. Then his voice returned to its usual earthly self as he entered the next stage of his fantasy. He'd be the one deciding how much everyone deserved. Or he'd tell them how to do it better so they'd get more.

"A power trip?" mused Ruth.

"No. Not the power."

"Are you sure?"

"Don't get him started," Vivian said. "He's weird about power imbalances, even between teacher and student, shrink and patient. I even had to talk him into buying a dog."

"Really? A dog?" David asked.

"As if one living being could actually own another," Carlos said. "We adopted him, we didn't buy him. But no, it's not about power, just about giving money to good causes. A nice fantasy."

Linda's CD finished, and Ben Webster started playing a smoky saxophone number whose combination of pain and longing seemed perfect for the subject.

Carlos asked Ruth if she had a fantasy job. Realistic, not realistic, it didn't matter. "Come on, I dare you. Think big. Or small."

Ruth set her rocking chair going on a gentle trajectory.

"Yeah, Ruthie, what would it be?" seconded David.

"Let me think." Since she'd been asking herself this question every day for the last few months, she didn't really need to think of her answer, just how much of her musings she wanted to share.

"I'm not sure about the job itself, just some ideas about what kind of thing it might be. First of all, I'd like it to be something that's socially valuable. Like you guys."

Carlos made a noise that had equal parts snort and snicker.

"A snort? You're snorting?" Vivian asked.

"It's just that if it were important to her, she'd be doing it already. So maybe she just thinks she—"

"You're asking me to fantasize and then you're jumping on my fantasy? Excuse me?"

"You're right. I should wait before I jump on you." Carlos grinned. "Kidding!"

Ruth said she had an energy she could only describe as entrepreneurial, even though she knew it was a dirty word to them. She didn't mean making a ton of money, though, she meant it in terms of creative energy, personal power, having an idea, acting on it, using all your wits and energy, and then seeing in concrete terms if it's successful. A marketplace.

"There are other measures of success. How many clients you rehabilitate. How many kids you help graduate. How many contributions you solicit to your foundation. Stuff like that," suggested David.

"Good point. I was just going to say the same thing," Carlos said.

"I know, but those just don't seem to do it for me like the thrill of the marketplace. And, damn it, I'm good at it, too. So that's the outline of my fantasy. Doing good and also being entrepreneurial. You want to jump on that Carlos?"

"No. It's not too-too bad. Even with the bad-e word. What about you, man?"

David confessed that, while he considered himself a world-class fantasizer, most of his fantasies about professions had to do with the past, as in people he'd love to have been, people like Jim Henson, Mickey Mantle, the guy who invented Velcro or Post-it Notes. But as for his present life and what he'd like to do next, retiring and playing golf seemed like a fantasy to him, and yet that was just what he was going to do.

"But right now, lasagna that isn't dried out and lettuce that isn't soggy would be a nice bite-sized fantasy." David faced the group and started walking backwards toward the table, saying "Come on, follow me" with his hands.

Ruth followed Vivian to the table. Her eyes were grabbed by the generous waistband of Vivian's pants. They had to be elasticized, she figured, or they wouldn't fit so well and they'd move up and down as Vivian walked. But they didn't have that obviously-elasticized look that advertised middle-aged waist-growth. It would be better to make the waistband a little wider, though.

The four new old-friends ate a delicious meal spiced not only with garlic and oregano, but also lightly seasoned with their rekindled affection for each other. Even Ruth's affection for Carlos somehow managed to find a way around his arrogance.

At some point during the meal, Ruth started to hear the discussion—looping between the present, the past, and the future, from the facts of their daily lives and their hopes for the future to their children, their jobs, and their parents and siblings—only in the way people "hear" Muzak in an elevator. She used only enough of her brain to give the illusion she was involved, not enough to take away from an idea that had just come to her out of the blue. She was turning it around and around, right there in front of them, startled to realize it combined Carlos's fantasy, Vivian's talent, her own entrepreneurial-but-good-works drive, and David's upcoming availability.

Something about Carlos's tone of voice pulled her back. "No, no, that's not the way it is. It's never been that way. The government has always been about conserving its own power, not about working for the people."

"But what about . . . let's say . . . social security? Or unemployment insurance? Isn't that about helping the people?"

"David, you are so naïve. Listen up, let me explain how it really is."

David brushed away Carlos's implied superiority with a good-natured jibe of his own. Ruth thought he seemed immune to the kind of barb that she herself felt allergic to. With her, it went straight to her heart, whereas with him it only stayed on the surface for a nanosecond.

So much for her idea.

18
Focus

THE OPS MEETING CONSISTED OF FURIOUS ATTENTION to detail, intermittent chaos and occasional conflict. Caps and cartons and pumps, chemicals and frills, colors and scents, dollars and cents. Late vendors, schedules, Packaging versus Marketing, budgets, bottles, blahblahblah. Same-old, same-old. She didn't necessarily have to attend these meetings, but, politically, it was good to have a presence, not to be an invisible dragonfly. Oh well.

It was harder than usual to appear interested because she kept thinking about the new round of concept-testing focus groups and, in particular, the one she'd be observing this afternoon. She was using McKay & Cohen, the expensive but top-of-the-line market research firm she only brought in when there was a reason worth busting the budget for. She'd included Pat in the meetings to develop a strategy for these groups, thinking inclusion would prevent defensiveness and that she'd also learn something useful.

McKay & Cohen had free rein to tinker with everything in coming up with their approach. And so they did: participants would be cosmetics-users and non-users together. The venue would vary; some groups would be at their offices, some in homes, some over the telephone one at a time. They'd have follow-up sessions to make sure women didn't have second thoughts that remained uncommunicated. They'd also use projective techniques that encouraged contrarian thought and interaction.

After the meeting, she stopped in at Terry's office to pick up some data for her weekly report. When Terry asked about Lipsticks & Scarves, Ruth filled her in, complete with Jeremy's peeking over her shoulder for hand-dirtying purposes. But she assured Terry that Violins & Wine—she was still attached to that name and hoped Jeremy would come around to it—would make Lipsticks & Scarves yesterday's news.

"Have a seat. Let's talk," Terry said.

"Yes, ma'am."

"I was talking to Pat this morning about demographic breakdowns by age and zip code, and she did a funny thing. She referred to something Jeremy had said to her … " Terry picked up a stack of papers and made sure their edges were lined up, then stapled them together.

"So?"

Terry put down the papers and readied another. "… at lunch."

"At *lunch*? Pat's eating lunch with Jeremy?"

"That's what I thought, too." She set down her papers and put her elbows on the desk, leaning forward. "I called her on it. She backtracked fast and furious. Something about how she was eating by herself and Jeremy happened to walk in and there were no other tables so she thought she had to invite him to join her and on and on and on."

"You buy it?"

"Why do you think I'm telling you all this?"

"Me neither," Ruth said.

ON THE THRESHOLD of the beautifully-restored Art Deco building that housed McKay & Cohen, she had a little talk with herself.

They'd been very careful about screening for the composition of this group. No one who would be likely to sway the others' opinion—in either direction. No one who was too-too beautiful. A good range, both in terms of age, income, profession, geography—the usual criteria—but also psychological factors like family size and birth order.

Then again, maybe the whole idea really was wacky, maybe women really did want to pretend to be younger than they were. Maybe she should change the name of the line, if it ever ran, to "Denial."

It's a business idea and a business decision. I'll have given it my all. I'll go with the results. It's not a religion, it's a product. Roger that. Right.

Pat was already waiting in the reception area and greeted Ruth on the cordial side of formal. Ruth noted the photographs taken by Sandy McKay on her travels around the world. Since the last time Ruth had been here, she'd obviously been to a desert country—the camels' shadows on the dunes were as long and delicate as Japanese brush strokes—and a tropical rainforest with a riot of greenery and blossoms. Sandy's travel photography was always very dramatic. Kind of like Sandy.

"Hey, Ruth, long time no see," the receptionist said as she hung up. "How've you been?"

"I'm good, crazy busy but good. How about you? How's night school?"

"See these bags under my eyes? If I ever meet the person who invented statistics, I'll have to … Let's just say it's not my favorite."

"Good luck," Ruth said, thinking of youthful energy and trying to remember when she had it.

"What's with your visit? Not that I'm not happy to see you, of course. But usually, the client doesn't come for the groups themselves, just for the planning."

"I just couldn't keep away. This is my own personal baby we're testing. So, what room is everyone in today?"

"They're in Room C, and I think everyone's there already."

Ruth and Pat entered Room C's "Observation Annex," the area from which clients can watch the focus groups they're paying for. The main attraction—the window/mirror—had a trompe l'oeil golden picture frame painted on the wall around it. Unlike the minimalist one-way-mirror rooms she'd seen on police TV shows, this one was set up for clients' comfort. The plush chairs swiveled, their ochre color matching the oriental rug perfectly no matter which way they were facing.

"Hey there," Sandy McKay said. As she jumped up to greet Ruth, she removed her reading glasses and let the chain holding them blend with her golden necklaces and pendants. She pressed her lips together to make sure her lipstick was even, and gave Ruth an air-kiss on each cheek, an affectation from her travels.

She shook Pat's hand and said "Good to see you, too."

The moderator adjusted his tie and extended his cuffs below his suit sleeves, brushed off his shoulders, and did some relaxation exercises with his face, neck and shoulder muscles. He started for the door that led to the other side of the one-way mirror, "through the looking glass," as Sandy called it. Just before he opened it, he looked over at Ruth. "Showtime."

"Okay, while you get everyone settled and distribute the goody-bags, I'm going to run to the women's room," Ruth said.

When she got there, she was immediately joined by Sandy, who asked her why Miss Muffet hadn't taken Smiling 101 yet.

Ruth said, "Pat? Long story. How about something more interesting, like the latest installment in the saga of the middle-aged woman and her young lover? And for comic relief I'll tell you about the middle-aged woman whose husband wants to retire."

"Retire? Are you kidding? David? He wants to retire? Really? Let's have lunch next week. Meanwhile I'll try to come up with something that's sexy enough to talk about."

Ruth and Sandy re-entered the Observation Annex silently.

Chuck Cohen walked in behind them. Everyone got settled. Ruth made a mental note to talk to Sandy about Chuck's comb-over.

Ruth admired the moderator's relaxed air when he opened the session. He talked to the group in a way that managed to be intimate, yet respectful, getting them to talk about themselves as if they were talking to life-long friends. Ruth knew that comfortable participants can be as misleading as uncomfortable ones, but it was a good beginning.

He told them a little bit about focus groups in general and emphasized how the most valuable contribution they could make would be complete honesty. Many people, he explained, unconsciously tried to say what they thought the client wanted to hear or what they thought would be least likely to hurt the client's feelings. After all, these people reasoned, the client was paying them, so they should be "nice." He told a few stories of previous groups who were inappropriately "nice" and the trouble it created for the clients who went on to launch a doomed marketing campaign.

His appearance was particularly well-suited to his profession, being all things to all people. Not so tall as to be intimidating, nor so short as to appear weak. A bland face conveyed friendliness and dignity at the same time. His mouth looked like it was smiling even when it was neutral, so when he actually did smile, everyone felt doubly rewarded. He could pass for twenty-five or forty-five, but Ruth knew he was forty, had been married and divorced, and that he doted on his field-hockey-playing twelve-year-old daughter, whom he didn't get to see as much as he wanted.

He could shade his routine, being flirtatious or macho or even nervous, according to the group. Today he seemed to be shooting for "the favorite nephew."

One of the reasons Ruth loved observing focus groups, instead of just reading the reports, was that it was like being a tourist in the real world, to hear from people who weren't in the business. These were regular people with fresh opinions and no particular axe to grind.

What looked like an ordinary group of women always turned out to be a collection of the most diverse life experiences. The variations of how-to-live-a-life reminded her of those tiny cars in the circus. Once you open them up, there's no telling what will pop out. Ruth particularly loved it when the truth belied her initial impression.

Like the blonde woman with the tiny straw hat and the ditzy daisy-patterned dress. She looked as if the last thought in her head packed up and left five years before when she met her sugar-daddy and bought a life-time subscription to Soap Opera Nuggets.

It turned out she was a live-in nurse for an elderly man, working sixteen-hour shifts seven days a week for three weeks straight, then having a week off. The single mother of an infant son, she traveled to exotic locations on her week off. "I didn't really have a life in my twenties, but I'm saving most of what I make now and when I inherit Mr. Burns's house, I'll be set and can make up for the deprivation."

Soap Opera Nuggets, indeed.

The soft-spoken woman with gray hair and a puffy face, whose dowdy clothes made Ruth think her greatest interest in life might be baking chocolate chip cookies for her grandchildren, turned out to be a photojournalist who'd spent much of her adult life in some of the most dangerous spots in the world.

So far, no one seemed to be deferential to anyone else, no one seemed to be dominating. She knew the moderator was watching for that dynamic, too, and would pre-empt it if necessary.

Pat's face was a cipher, though her hair was somehow different. More serious? Shorter? Darker? Less puffy? And her earrings were singing a different tune, too. Less constipated—if earrings can be constipated—and more expansive.

The mock-debate activity started. Respondents chose their points of view from a hat—"Middle-aged women are beautiful," "I want to look young no matter how much trouble it is," etc.—and met with their assigned teams to strategize, then presented their arguments. What was interesting to Ruth was trying to figure out which ones were saying things they really believed and which ones were performing.

After they debated, they discussed the degree to which their arguments had reinforced or changed their actual points of view. That's when the good stuff came out.

The prim-looking woman who looked like a suburban housewife and was, in fact, a suburban housewife, said, "I used to think that it was crazy to want to look your age and given the choice, anyone would rather look younger. I would probably have said that the choice between looking good for a woman my age or looking good like a young woman was, as my grandchildren say, 'Duh!!!' Now I'm not so sure."

Then there was the one with four-inch gray roots in dark hair, who'd just moved to New York from Kansas, was recently divorced with grown children, and was not only terrified about trying to enter the work force after a twenty-five-year absence, but was also terrified by the other women. She said, "I can't help it, I still think it's not just about the media or about being brainwashed. Young is healthy. Healthy is good. Looking young means looking healthy. And if you look young and healthy, people treat you different than if you look old. They treat you better. I want that. Doesn't everyone?" She looked around at the others as if she were begging for money for food.

"That's ridiculous," said the mousy woman with stringy red hair who, it turned out, had published three collections of poetry and was running for the council of her town. "It's just because you've been trained to think that we're all supposed to look like Miss America. We get the idea that it's normal to be gorgeous and young and skinny. But it's *not* normal, not at all. Normal people look like us."

"I never thought about it that way, but maybe you're right. I guess I'm one of those people who just got swept up into thinking we were supposed to look a certain way. I've always been too busy." This woman, with frizzy blondish hair and large glasses, wearing a bright red turtleneck, had caused a few rolled eyeballs during the introductions during her long list of her accomplishments—PhD in Brahms, French horn player, orchestra conductor—until she got to the part about losing her husband to cancer. "But I think I'm starting to see things differently. When you get right down to it, it's not fair that we feel ashamed of what we look like."

"But it would be a lot easier to be honest about ourselves if everyone else was, too," the poet-politican said. "Like the dream about being the only naked person in a group."

Yeah, yeah, yeah, go for it, said Ruth's insides, while "Interesting, very interesting" is what came out of her mouth.

After about thirty minutes of a spirited conversation, it seemed to Ruth that the ground under the "young is good" partisans was shifting over to the "middle-aged is okay" ground. Everyone agreed, though, that it would be easier to look authentically middle-aged if everyone did it.

The moderator summed up and brought the session to a close by focusing the group's attention on the name of the product line. He presented six options, asked everyone to rank order them with six points for their first choice, five for their second choice, etc. He tallied the results on a large piece of posterboard:

37: Passion: Loving Who You Really Are
44: Violins & Wine: For the Woman Who Keeps Getting Better
46: About Face
12: Beauty's Rewards: Getting the Best from Life
10: Peak: The Best is Yet to Come
33: Always: Let the Good Times Last
7: Vintage: The Great Years

It was over. Ruth, Pat, Sandy, and the moderator gathered to compare their immediate reactions. They all, including Pat, agreed that if there *had* been a tide-turning, it was definitely in the direction they wanted. Sandy was anxious to look at the videotape to compare body-language with verbal language, and to check the transcripts for further clues, as well as to verify that the moderator hadn't unwittingly steered the conversation.

Ruth was pretty sure she'd gotten what she wanted. Riding down in the elevator, she asked Pat for her reaction. "It was interesting," she said. "I see what you mean about the difference between regular focus groups and other approaches."

"Good," Ruth said. "Surprising," is what she thought. On the spot, she hatched an idea. "But even so, I'm thinking the handwriting is on the wall. I think this idea—no matter what we call it—might be dead."

"What do you mean?"

They stepped out of the elevator and talked in the lobby.

"I've been thinking that Jeremy really doesn't like this idea and he is the boss, you know. He comes from another industry, it's true, but we've been bought. Life is different. Besides, he might know better than me. I suppose if the results of this new round of groups were a slam dunk, hundred and ten percent positive, which I doubt, I might change my mind, but … well, I doubt it."

19
One Hundred Ten Percent

"COLLEEN, CAN YOU DO ME A FAVOR?" Ruth stage-whispered as she leaned out of her office towards Colleen's desk.

Taking in the detritus of photographs, plants, file folders, figurines, and assorted dime-store accoutrements, she marveled that this seeming chaos was, in fact, more orderly than it used to be.

Very shortly after Jeremy had arrived, he'd looked askance at Colleen's desk. Ruth had been surprised at the level of detail to which he devoted his attention, but she'd laid down the desk-law, hoping it would pre-empt the need to lay down the clothes-law. Ruth knew that Colleen might look swamped by her desk material, but she always got things done fast and well. It was strictly a question of appearances. She told her she needed to keep a minimum number of square inches open so it resembled what the rest of the world considered businesslike. "Better to pick your battles," she'd advised Colleen, "and your desktop is not a battle worth fighting. Certainly not with Jeremy. You'll definitely lose."

At first the difference had been dramatic, but the desk had started to re-sprout. Ruth made a mental note to lay the law down a little lower.

Colleen put down her Charlie Brown mug and looked up. "You betcha. That's what they pay me for."

As Colleen bounced into the office, Ruth shut the door behind her. "Shutting the door? Cool! What's up?"

Ruth motioned for Colleen to take one of the chairs facing the desk. "I need your help. But," she enunciated each word separately, "It. Has. To. Be. Strictly. Confidential."

Under their garish-purple lids fringed with thick black lashes, Colleen's eyes widened. She leaned forward in her chair and tried to pull her mauve leather skirt down a millimeter closer to her knees.

"Sure. Anything. You know that. But are you okay?"

"I'm fine. But I need someone I can trust to help me figure something out."

"Really? Me?"

"You're smart and I know you're on my side. And also you don't take shit from anyone. Not your boyfriend, not your parents, and not from the folks around here. Well, I guess you do take a little from me, which is as it should be. But not from most people. This is good."

Colleen uncrossed her legs and hooked her hair behind her ears, revealing her purple-starburst earrings, as she smiled and said, "Really? Me? Wow, that's great. Cool. Thanks a lot. What do you want me to do? Is this like a secret mission kind of thing?"

"Exactly. Very secret. The only problem is I'm not sure exactly what the mission is." She put her elbows on the desk and folded her hands as if she were a first-grader as she explained how she knew there was something going on, she just didn't know what yet. It could just be takeover nerves and people wondering who was in and who was out. People were forming alliances with various Big Daddies, but she was biding her time.

"But what can I do?"

"I know a lot about a lot, but you talk to the other secretaries and hear other things. So just keep your eyes and ears open, that's all. Who knows, maybe I'm just being paranoid. Or maybe I'm being careful."

"Sure thing. Easy. I'm on the case. Gossips R Us."

"And be discreet."

"Discreet's my middle name. Absolutely. Discreet. What does it mean, again?" Ruth looked up, eyes wide, frowning.

"I'm kidding. Gotcha!"

Ruth went back to the second round of sketches and storyboards she'd received from the ad agency. This version had a chorus of spokeswomen, mostly non-famous, instead of a single middle-aged celebrity who implied everyone could be as beautiful as she if they used this-or-that product.

She stared at the faces and tried to imagine their lives. Some, no doubt, lived pampered lives, with massages, facials, plastic surgery, and servants. Maybe that accounted for some of their enduring beauty. But, surely, most had led lives filled with work, family, pain, joy, with loss, aging, worry, vacations, disappointments, promotions, enlightenment, pride. The tapestry of human experience. It was remarkable how attractive they all were, in different ways. Different expressions of female beauty. Like her African masks.

Jeremy called and asked her to come right up to his office. She'd been half expecting it. She was ready for him to tell her he'd decided to pull the plug on her project. She'd show him how much money had already been spent, so he might as well let her carry through with the concept-testing phase of the project. It was a big gamble, but she had to do it.

But that wasn't it. As soon as she walked into his office, he said he'd been re-thinking his opinion of the old lady idea. He just wanted her to know that he still wouldn't call himself "enthusiastic," but he acknowledged he came from another industry and might not know as much about cosmetics as she. Yet. He reassured her that she shouldn't hold the new round of focus groups to unrealistic standards.

"They don't need to be a hundred and ten percent positive or anything like that. Just regular standards will be fine."

Was that a smile? Or just the shadow of one? But she heard what he said, loud and clear. 110% positive. Exactly what she'd said to Pat. She didn't imagine it. Two snakes, not one.

Now she needed to find out exactly what kind of cahoots Pat and Jeremy were in. What, exactly, were they cooking up? She had her first hot flash of the day. ninety seconds long. Not the longest, not the shortest.

Ruth went to the women's room to clear her mind, a habit she developed in childhood, when the single bathroom in her family's apartment provided the only privacy. Sometimes she even went to a different floor to avoid running into anyone who might want to dilute her escapism by talking shop.

She spent a minute in the carpeted anteroom, in front of the mirror. Hearing what might be sniffling, she clicked her blush-on compact shut as noisily as she could, then blew her nose and coughed. A toilet flushed, then no more sniffling. Hand-washing, then the noisy hot-air hand dryer.

Ruth kept her attention on her face in the mirror, darkening her eyebrows with brushed eye-shadow and fussing with her hair. Pat emerged from the porcelain-and-steel inner sanctum, her face neither red nor puffy. Upon seeing Ruth, Pat immediately ordered her features to assume their ready position. Without the sniffling, Ruth wouldn't have detected anything.

"These allergies are driving me nuts," Pat said as she looked away.

"I know what you mean, David has them too. Have you tried vitamin C? He's had good success with that."

"Good idea."

Pat was about to leave when she turned back to Ruth and said, "I'm still dissatisfied with the cobalt blue bottle we're using for the 'April in Paris' bubble bath. The color's good, but the cloudy glass is pitted and the clear glass is just somehow not right."

"Find a viable alternative, on budget and in time, and I'll consider it. Get Tom to help you if you want."

Ruth turned back to her reflection, adjusting a pin on her suit jacket so it hung at a slightly more acute angle. Pat was still standing at the door.

"I'll be out in a minute if you want to talk about something else."

"No, not necessary. I'll let you know about the bottle."

In her office, the phone was beckoning. "Hi Roger. I hope this is a good-news call."

"Not quite. I'm not sure what kind of news it is."

"Meaning…?"

"I'm here with the R&D team, working on the middle-aged woman thing, trying to nail down what we'll present to you and Jeremy on the tenth. And we've come up against something. Not a problem, exactly. More like a dilemma, I guess you'd say."

"Dilemma? Details, please."

"It's just that these here products aren't really different from our regular products. They're fine products, they're good. But the thing of it is, is that they're fine for everyone, not just your old ladies—"

"Roger!"

"Yeah, yeah, mature women. So we're a little stymied. Plus there's other stuff, too. Could you come up here to talk about it?"

She put down the phone and waited for the day's second hot flash to subside.

By the time the elevator got from the eighteenth floor to the twenty-sixth, she'd run through the primary-color emotions. Anger, as usual, was first. It lasted until about the twenty-first floor, though the target shifted around. First was David, whose impending retirement plan was making her feel this project had to be good enough to be her last.

Then there was Jeremy. His main flaw was not being Dean, the best boss in the world, and his slightly-less-major ones were too numerous for this ride. Carlos's sin was the superiority with which she imagined he would regard her present situation.

Pat was a minor irritant, mostly because of her derision for the "women's libbers," without whom she wouldn't be where she was today. She'd be home with her trust fund. Or being an underpaid and undervalued museum docent in her tasteful clothes. Is this why we struggled so hard? Actually, thought Ruth, it probably was. So a woman could be as successful—and, inevitably sometimes, as much of a jerk—as a man.

The main target, as usual, was herself, for caring about it all so much.

As the elevator made the transition from the headiness of rapid climb to gradual deceleration and, finally, to a practically imperceptible stop on twenty-six, she worked her way up to her version of acceptance. She was who she was. If this current maelstrom didn't work out, maybe retiring wouldn't be so terrible. It was a teeth-gritting admission, but it was the best she could do.

Roger's office—indeed, all of Research & Development—was an enclave of testosterone in a sea of frippery. It was brown in all its guises: tan walls, deep walnut desk, black-and-white photos, paintings of boats and landscapes in browns and greys, and carpeting that would be called "taupe" by anyone but its occupant. The flowers were white, the plants huge and vertical. No curves or arcs.

When Ruth walked in, she sensed from the silence that they'd been talking about her. Applauding, denigrating, or gossiping?

"You guys look like you've been here all night," she said. "Is it really as bad as all that? Thank God there's no smoking in this building or I have a feeling I'd be choking on 'Essence of Cigar.'"

"Yeah, yeah, yeah," John MacDonald said. "Welcome to our world, missy. Glad to have you aboard." He pointed to the seat next to him, as the two placid sausages that were his lips became a claymation smile, a moving picture frame for his big misshapen teeth. He could be a sweet old guy out of the office, Ruth knew from the few times he'd come to her benefits, but was a tough bird at work. His jacket was off, tie loosened, sleeves rolled up.

"You know all the guys, don't you?" Roger asked. She looked around. Besides Roger and John, there was Samuel Francis, Mr. Stick-Up-His-Behind. He was the only one still in his jacket and tie and his "hello" was an infinitesimal nod of his carefully-coiffed head.

On the far side of the table was a new guy, Danny Jones. His round brown face with short curly black and gray hair fringing his male-pattern baldness seemed friendly. Or, at least, not guarded. Or maybe it was just the gap between his two front teeth.

"Is the party over? Can we get down to business?" John looked at his watch.

They recapped the morning's discussion for Ruth. Except for a few out-of-the-box ideas that were unworkable, most of the possibilities for the new line boiled down to lighter makeup, not the heavy stuff that tended to crack and cake on older women's thinner, dryer skin. They might instinctively go for the heavier stuff, but they were better off with less. Plain and simple.

Fine, thought Ruth. Good and honest and true. In a sense, they were exactly the kind of products Ruth had envisioned all along, products that said, "Don't hide yourself, let your beauty show. Better to look good as a fifty-year-old than foolish as a fifty-year-old who's trying to look twenty-five."

Samuel cleared his throat and looked at his delicate hands in front of his face as he rolled a pencil in the fingers of both hands as if he were rolling a joint. He said that all the products existed in other lines.

"And?" Ruth asked. "What's the problem?" They didn't have to say they were new products, they could just say they were pulling together things that are great for mature women. And it would mean no R&D, no extended product launch pipeline. A much quicker time to market. "Isn't this good? What doom-and-gloom are you all seeing that I'm not?"

"What you're not seeing is that Jeremy doesn't think it's good," Samuel said.

Roger's shaggy brows came alive as he explained that Jeremy had dropped by unexpectedly about an hour before. They'd filled him in.

"He was not a happy camper. He kept using the word 'cannibalize,' as in 'cannibalizing our other lines and our customer base.'"

Ruth slammed her fist on the table. This was not true; Jeremy was wrong. The important part is the people they'd pull away from the competition.

John agreed. Jeremy's opposition took him by surprise, too.

"Exactly what did he say?"

"He talked a little about how you've got such a good idea, it deserves more creativity, not just a tired old rehash of existing stuff. Things like that." John shook his head slowly.

That didn't make any sense. It must be some kind of cover story. She looked around at the faces staring at her. "I'll talk to him."

As she returned to her office, she didn't bother with any subtly-shaded emotions as she went right to the main event, bewilderment. She was waiting for the Polaroid picture of this situation to begin to come into focus.

20
Off the Wall

"I KNOW THERE'S A GIANT POSSIBILITY YOU'RE GOING TO THINK I'm totally crazy. Especially you, Carlos. I do, too. But do me a favor and don't say anything about it yet. Really, I just want you to hear me out and think about what I say. Then, maybe in a day or two, you can tell me what you think." The sound of her own wobbly voice reminded her of Purchasing-guy talking about intangibles to Jeremy.

"And when we do eventually talk about it," Ruth continued, "you might wind up thinking it's interesting or you might think it's off the wall, or who knows what? So you'll just tell me. And, Carlos, go easy."

"*Si, senora.*"

When she began, she looked at the purple-haired young woman at the bar, then checked out the two young men who looked too Wall Street to be in such a down-home TexMex place, and at the bartender polishing glasses just like they do on TV.

"I've been thinking and thinking about this idea ever since that day at lunch when we talked about our fantasy jobs. I tried to ignore it, but it just moved into my brain uninvited, like a squatter."

When she'd finally told David about it, he urged her to go public with Vivian and Carlos, even if they did think she was nuts. It was the only way to evict it from her brain. So she'd decided to risk humiliation as an antidote to obsession.

As if to prepare her, she'd had a dream in which she was cleaning up some of her own vomit. Afterwards, she was sitting on an unknown man's lap. Both she and he were wearing business clothes. She looked down to realize she'd left some vomit on his leg. He saw it, too, though he didn't recognize what it was. Ruth was tortured by the anticipation of her shame when he realized the terrible truth.

When she woke up, the dream felt negative. It must be telling her to abandon her nauseating idea. Halfway through the day, though, she remembered that she and her shrink had concluded, years ago, all her dreams about vomiting or "bathroom matters" were usually about creativity. Letting what was inside her come out for everyone to see made her feel exposed and frightened.

"Okay, I'm ready," Vivian said. I won't say anything until you tell me I can. This is asking a lot but, for you, I'll be silent, at least I'll try to be silent, no I really will be silent." Vivian pointed her long-neck beer at Carlos, saying, "And you, too, Carlos, right?"

"If Vivian can hold it in, I guess I can."

"When I'm finished talking, we'll just change the subject. We'll talk about … how about if we talk about our kids? So there won't be that horrible awkward moment when we all look at each other and don't know what to say next."

Carlos dipped a corn chip into the hotter-than-hot salsa and threw it in his mouth. "Kids. Good idea."

Ruth's eyes were searchlights, first aiming towards the ceiling, then down at Carlos and over to Vivian, also noticing over their shoulders the couple at the next table who were necking as if they were the only ones in the place. When she realized what she was doing, she decided to focus on Vivian.

"You know what I'm doing at work these days? That I'm all involved with women our age?"

And she was off. She asked them to put their less-than-enthusiastic feelings about make-up aside for a minute. She spoke of the huge numbers of women their age who weren't like their mothers, weren't willing to fit themselves into shapes never intended for them. But they still wanted to look good.

"I know you don't wear makeup, Viv, but you do choose stuff like clothes and barrettes and shoes based on what looks good. Right?"

Everyone looked at Ruth but no one said anything. "Hey guys, you *can* say something if I ask a question."

Vivian agreed that people like to look good. They clearly have different definitions of what looks good, as well as different thresholds of acceptable sacrifice for their appearance. "Like, for me, face lifts are a no-no but face exercises are okay. But looking good is good."

"Really?" Carlos was genuinely surprised. "Even you, babe?"

"Yeah, even me, babe."

Ruth reminded Vivian of their shopping trip and of their discussion about the mis-fit of women's pants to middle-aged bodies. And crotches and waistlines and fabrics.

"I do remember. That was actually fun, which is a word I never thought I'd say in the same sentence with shopping. I mean, there we were in the dressing room with all the naked ladies. It was a great education in underwear."

"Everyone I know who's our age feels that way, not just you and me. But no one knows what to do about it. Except Vivian."

"Vivian?" Carlos asked.

"Earth to Carlos? Haven't you noticed that I sew all my own clothes?"

"To save money."

"Saving money is good. But also because nothing in the store fits me right. And if it does fit right, it looks awful. Those clothing guys just aren't interested in ample bodies like mine, at least not middle-aged ample bodies, and certainly not moderately-hippie middle-aged ample bodies."

"Too many adjectives, I guess."

"Very funny, Carlos," Vivian said.

Ruth continued. While she couldn't make clothing, there *was* something she was good at. After an appropriately dramatic silence, she spoke of her talent for selling things to people who needed those things.

"Yeah, and … ?" Carlos said, with a rising voice that Ruth thought could mean curiosity or impatience or dread. Or even "I dare you."

"Suppose for just a minute that Vivian designed a line of clothing that was perfect for middle-aged women, so they could look good but also fit and even be comfortable. And suppose those clothes were manufactured. And then suppose she marketed the whole line of clothing to stores that would sell it."

"Is this a question I can answer?" Carlos said.

"No."

"Just so's I understand. You're talking about our going into … business … together? Making clothes and selling them?"

"But it gets better."

"I can't imagine how," Carlos said.

Vivian glared at him.

Ruth outlined the part of her vision she hadn't even told David about. What if the venture were a means to raise money for worthwhile causes? What if they gave a certain percentage of their profits to charity? Like Ben and Jerry's Ice Cream did?"

"Are you done? Can I talk now?" Carlos said.

"No," Vivian said. "Ruth asked us to hold our peace. So hold it, buster. Rules are rules."

He rolled his eyeballs and pulled at his beard. But he was silent.

Everyone chewed carefully and swallowed slowly, being sure to get all the morsels of food out from between their teeth. The jukebox was playing "I'm Proud to be an Okie from Muskogee," some people at the bar were singing along, and there were even a few who were dancing, making swirls and piles of the sawdust on the floor. The waiter, as if on cue, appeared at their table to clear it. The restaurant had filled up while they ate, and the laughter, singing and conversation were becoming boisterous, accentuating the silence at their table.

"How's Ida doing? Did the concert go okay? How was your date with the potential in-laws? Was the dress good? Did you get along? Did you offend them with your politics right away or did you wait a little bit?"

David patted her thigh under the table. Sure enough, Vivian and Carlos were like everyone else, they liked talking about their kid. They told the story of the evening they'd spent with Ida, her boyfriend, and his straight-as-a-gate parents.

Everyone had been polite and well-behaved. When they all went for coffee after the concert, the artificial politeness continued, everyone doing what they thought would make their kids happy. They made small talk about work and neighborhoods as if there were no elephant-sized subtext in the room.

"What a scene: we work for a Battered Woman's Shelter and a Prisoners' Foundation," Vivian said, "and they work for an investment bank and a Park Avenue law firm. And we live in Brooklyn and they live in Scarsdale. But we just mentioned all those things as if we were at a tea-party or something. You know, like 'Oh, I grew up in Brooklyn' or 'Scarsdale has such wonderful schools, I hear.' It was surreal."

Carlos, putting his elbows on the table, said, "But it turns out that the guy went to some executive junket a year ago and, while he was there, since his doctor had told him he had to learn to relax, he went to a Tai-Chi class, grumbling all the way. And he got hooked. And I'm into Tai-Chi, too, 'cause of my arthritis. So we talked about postures and routines and stuff. There we were, in some fancy place across from Lincoln Center, standing in the aisles and demonstrating 'Grasp Sparrow's Tail' and 'Needle at Sea Bottom' to each other. It was so, so cool."

"And my dress was perfect. And the scarf, too. Thank you, thank you. Now tell us about Josh. What's new with him? How's teaching? And the girlfriend?"

As Ruth and David walked to their car, she said, "Did you notice nobody said anything about the clothing business when we all said good-bye to each other? Did you think that was kind of weird?"

"Ruthie, you *told* them not to say anything! You can't complain that they did what you asked."

"I know, I know, but I just thought they'd say something like, 'We'll get back to you about the idea in a few days' or something like that."

"They did say they'd get back to us, didn't they?" David asked.

"Not exactly. They said they had a good time and then 'Speak to you soon.' Do you think it's because the idea was so ridiculous they were embarrassed and just didn't know what to say?"

"No, Ruthie. I think if Carlos thought it was ridiculous, no matter what your rules were, he would have let you know. They were doing exactly what you said you wanted, and you can't blame them for not knowing that you didn't mean what you said. You're just making yourself nuts."

"Okay, okay. You're right."

Just the same, though, she couldn't help feeling ashamed, as if she'd vomited in front of everyone.

21
Suffocation by Stuff

"I JUST DON'T UNDERSTAND EXACTLY WHEN this happened," Ruth said softly, as if to herself, the next day when she and David were finally cleaning out their garage. They had talked about doing it for months, but never managed to get around to it until the Community Center asked for contributions to their annual rummage sale, forcing them to put a "clean out garage" date on their calendars. Lucky for David, there was a Yankee game on the radio. They'd been at it for about an hour when Ruth started running out of steam.

"When what happened?" David was on the other side of the garage, facing the dusty wall of shelves crowded with sports equipment. He turned to look at Ruth as he blew on a ski boot he'd uncovered. "Whose is this, and does that person only have one leg?" He threw it on the "discard" pile.

"This," she said, pointing with both hands to the stuff in the garage as she made a 360-degree turn.

"No big deal, just stuff we picked up along the way. We'll get rid of it easy enough. I'm actually having fun going through it all. I forgot about most of this stuff. Like this wooden tennis racket. Wow, what a relic, complete with this old press you'd use to keep it from warping, remember? Boy, I remember how excited Josh was when we gave it to him. Can you imagine if someone had told us then how obsolete it would be?" He threw it on the pile of things to go to the Community Center.

After a few minutes of working silently with baseball as background, David said, "I can't believe we still have this camping lantern. I wonder if it works. What do you think, we ever going camping again?" he asked.

"Not a chance."

He put it on the Community Center pile, then brushed off his hands. "Remember that time we went camping with Caryl and David? And we took the dog? And he wandered over to the next campsite and ate their dope? And we had to hold him all night long, imagining we were going to have to take him to a doggie ER and explain that he'd OD-ed? Was that Rufus or Nero?"

"Rufus. See, that's what I mean."

"*What's* what you mean?"

She considered every word. "We have so much … past."

"Huh?"

"Everything around us, the stuff in the garage, like that camping lantern, the furniture in the house, even the bushes and flowers, every single thing here has a whole story attached to it. Nothing's neutral. Nothing's just what it is, it's all part of what's already happened. In the past. It's drowning me. Like, look at this."

"What is that?"

"It's the cast I had on my leg after my skiing accident. I was about sixteen or seventeen. I can't believe I've saved it all this time."

"Me neither."

She saw the word "Release" on the heel of the cast, scrawled by her sister Marge. It meant that, when Ruth had started to lose control on the slope, she'd have been better off releasing the pressure and letting herself fall than trying to right herself by digging in her left ski. Nice of Marge to rub it in on her cast.

"Get rid of it. Fast."

"OK. But cleaning out the *stuff* is okay. It doesn't clean out the memories, though."

"You want to clean out the memories? Hey, we'll lose our memories soon enough, don't rush it." He laughed at his joke as he dropped a darkly-stained wooden box onto the pile of discards. It was handmade, with their names burnished on the front, and a brass-colored latched cover. It had been made and filled with 144 handmade candles, given to them by Seth the candle-maker as a wedding present.

"I wonder what ever happened to Seth," he mused.

"Are you getting rid of that? It's a perfectly good box."

"I thought you wanted to get rid of stuff. We can give it to the center instead of throwing it out, if you'd rather."

"But it has our name on it. Can't we keep it?"

"No one will mind the name."

"Okay I guess. But anyway it doesn't really matter if I do or I don't," Ruth said. She stopped cleaning off the cross-country ski in her hands, dropping the cleaning rag and looking through the open garage door into the distance.

"Do or don't what?"

Slowly, emphasizing each word, as if she'd explained this a hundred times to a student who wasn't paying attention, she said, "Do or don't want to get rid of stuff. It isn't the stuff that's the problem."

Rubbing one of the many bicycle water bottles to see which charity ride it had come from, he asked Ruth to tell him what was really bugging her.

She sat down on a half barrel of sand, folding and refolding a stack of tablecloths with varying stains. "It's just that our past is so much bigger than our future. It's been a great past, but maybe that's part of the problem."

"The problem?"

"Everyplace I look around here I see something that pulls me back into the past. You just have to walk around a little bit and you see it."

She pointed towards one corner of the garage. "Outside that corner is the tree we planted when Josh came home from 1st grade on Arbor Day with something that looked like a twig." She turned a little to the left. "Right around there is the magnolia we got when you got out of the hospital." She kept turning in place, arm outstretched, finger pointed, and stopped to enumerate at various points. "The dogwood Mary and Jim gave us as a housewarming present and then we got the second one to match it but we couldn't find the same color. The sculpture we got with the money my folks gave us for a video recorder. The spirit house we brought back from Thailand. See what I mean? And that's just outside the house. Inside is worse. Doesn't it all ever make you feel … I don't know … complacent? Stuck?"

"No. All this stuff seems good to me."

"I used to feel like being surrounded by all my stuff was like being hugged by my life, by our life together. Now maybe it's a little too much of a bear-hug."

"You'd feel better if everything was new and had no associations?"

Was he actually *trying* not to understand? She stamped her foot in frustration and tried not to weep as she explained that she was mourning the fact that so much of her life had gone by, that she was coasting on her old memories and not creating new ones. "I feel like I'm starting to stop living."

The baseball announcer's voice rose with an urgency fit for the outbreak of war, as if specifically to annoy Ruth. It hijacked David's attention, and Ruth knew better than to try to interrupt. She'd lose. Who could be as interesting as a double down the right field line?

As soon as there was a commercial, he said, "You want to know what I think?"

"I'm not sure. Does it have to do with the Yankees?"

"I think it may feel right now like this bad feeling is about something real. But maybe all this stuff, the feeling old and all, is … you know … about the whole hormonal thing? You know?"

"I hate that, David. I really hate it. It's like saying 'Oh, she's hysterical, she must be premenstrual.' Jeez, how patronizing can you be?"

"I thought it would be reassuring to think it might be chemical because chemistry can be fixed."

"No, it is not reassuring. How about taking me seriously, just this once?"

He slammed the screwdriver kit down on the workbench, and the fourteen different-sized ends he'd been arranging spilled out of the broken box. "I take you plenty seriously, Ruthie. But while we're on the subject, did you remember that I said I wanted to retire when you invented a whole new business for me to be part of? Or did you just not take it seriously?"

Ruth was fingering a long dry snakeskin that Josh's pet snake had left as a souvenir before he escaped. She put it down gingerly in the "Things to Keep" pile, balancing it on top of a bike rack. "I heard it. Loud and clear."

"But chose not to believe it?"

"Not exactly. Maybe I thought you just wanted to retire from being a math teacher but wouldn't mind doing something else."

"I told you, Ruthie. No more jobs. Retirement with a capital G-O-L-F."

"Okay, okay, you're right and I'm sorry. I guess I got swept up in being excited about my idea."

The UPS truck pulled up with two cartons, a large one from Land's End and a smaller one from Josh with the stuff, mostly books, he'd asked if he could store at the house. "Just what we need," David said as he signed for them. "More things to get rid of some day. Which reminds me, we really should go through all the books in the house and get rid of the ones we've already read or are never going to read. We can give them to the Community Center."

"I don't know if they want books."

"Well, then, the library."

They looked at each other. Ruth suspected David was just listening to the baseball game but willed herself to believe it was a moment of mutual understanding. She knew that when David was roused to annoyance, he got over it instantly, so "forgiveness" was too strong a word. But she liked to think it was mutual *something*.

"Want to take a break?" he asked.

Ruth brewed coffee and decided to grab some of the butter cookies they only ate when their sense of virtue or neediness outweighed their concerns about cholesterol. They sipped quietly until David asked, "Ruthie, don't jump down my throat, but … is something going on?"

"What do you mean?"

David told her that, while he believed everything she'd just said about the past and the present, he also had the feeling that there was something else bothering her.

"I guess you're right. There is something else."

"Is it work? Or me? If I did something, I'm sorry. Whatever it is."

"It's not you."

When he urged her to spill her gripes, she made him promise not to use it as ammunition for why she should retire.

"You think I'd do that?"

She licked her finger and picked up a few crumbs from her plate, then ate them absentmindedly. "No doubt about it."

David promised not to mention the R-word and asked if Colleen had found something out. She told him that Colleen had, in fact, unearthed a few affairs, but that wasn't the interesting part. Just as she finished the story of the '110%-positive' communication path between Pat and Jeremy and Jeremy's unexpected reaction to her cleverly-planted fake information, the phone rang.

David said over his shoulder as he walked away, "How could she do that? After all you've done for her? Time to give up on smoothing Pat's edges? Maybe a farewell chat with her? Or a heart-to-heart with Jeremy?"

"On the calendar. Monday morning. With Pat. Not farewell, though. Not yet, anyway. Something more useful, I hope."

She lingered over her coffee while he chatted. On their way back to the musty-smelling garage, he said, "You'll never guess who that was. On the phone." He opened the large door to let some air in. "It was Carlos." He grinned, though she could tell he was trying not to.

"Carlos? Carlos called, not Vivian?" She put down the beer mugs from St. Lucia.

"He wants to get together. So we made a date for Monday night, after work. I checked your calendar to make sure it's okay."

"Monday? What's the rush?" She flipped through the pages of some half-finished coloring books. "It's not about the clothing business thing already, is it? What do you think?"

"I think it's about the clothing business thing. Actually, I know it."

"How do you know?"

"He said so."

"Come on David, stop being so cute. What did he say? Exactly. Was it 'That's the looniest idea I ever heard, are you out of your skull?' or did Vivian make him say it nicer than that?"

"He said they've been thinking about it and they want to talk about it, and he wants you to know that this doesn't mean they're going to do it, they just want to chat—"

"Chat? Carlos said 'chat'?"

"Well, no, actually, he said 'rap.' They want to rap and ask some questions. But he said to tell you not to get excited. It's just to talk about it a little more. So don't get excited."

"Fat chance. I think I'm gonna puke."

22
Filling Ruth's Sneakers

MONDAY MORNING, WHEN PAT CAME INTO RUTH'S OFFICE, she had her usual chip in residence on her shoulder, carefully balanced by her ramrod-straight posture. She doesn't suspect a thing, Ruth thought. I'm sure of it. Naïve or smug, take your pick.

"Hi, Ruth. What did you want to see me about?"

So much for the niceties, thought Ruth. Not that I'm dying to tell her how my weekend was, but she should know she's supposed to ask. "Have a seat, Pat. How are you? Did you have a nice weekend?"

"Yes, thanks."

"We need to talk."

"Okay." Pat's single word sounded like a question. She shifted her position in her seat but didn't bother to straighten the resulting wrinkles in her skirt.

What a gutsy little pipsqueak, Ruth thought. She's like the 14-year old who's cleaning her room under duress. Trying to prove to herself, or maybe to her mother, she can succeed at something and not just be a trust fund kid. Funny, in her own way that makes her sort of a rebel, which I'm actually sympathetic to.

Ruth gave Pat the opportunity to confess, straight off, that she'd been doing something she shouldn't have been doing. Pat's face betrayed a moment of fear, then went back to her previous impassivity, like the kid's drawing tablet with a film that, when lifted, erases the drawing. Peekaboo—now you see her, now you don't.

"I don't know what you're talking about."

"Trish." Ruth put down her cup and leaned forward. She spoke softly. "Let's cut the performance and get to the matter at hand. What's going on with you and Jeremy on the new line?" She folded her arms and hardened her stare.

Pat was startled into silence for a moment, looking down at the cup of tea she held between her hands in her lap. When she raised her eyes, it wasn't to look at Ruth, but to the window behind Ruth.

"How did you know about that?"

Bingo. "Did you really think you could go behind my back and not have it get back to me? Even with the boss."

"It was only to—"

"Even if you don't like the project—and you've made no secret about that, which, by the way, is a political error—you're obliged to work for the good of the department and the company. Or at least *appear* to be doing so. Are you trying to further *your* career or sabotage *mine*?" Stop, Ruth. Don't overdo it.

Pat's jaw tensed and her fist clenched. "I *am* working for the good of the company. And anyway, I can't believe you're talking to me about undermining and sabotaging."

Ruth leaned back in her chair. "Huh?"

"You and your generation spout all that women's lib stuff about women helping each other along in their careers, but you've resented me from the beginning."

This was interesting. Ruth wasn't crazy about the tone of voice but was glad they were unearthing some truth. Maybe beating "mommy" at work is better than beating mommy at home.

"I don't know what you mean, Pat. And I really want to," Ruth said with as much sincerity as she could muster.

"It sometimes appears you believe there's room for only one intelligent and powerful woman around here. Judy doesn't count because she does that puppy-dog routine, as it were. But my mind is focused right where it belongs, on the bottom line." Pat shook her head as if she were brushing hair out of her eyes, though her hair was far from her eyes and far from loose enough to fall anywhere. "You said you wanted to understand, so understand this: I think you feel threatened."

"I honestly don't know if this will be good or bad news for you, but I don't really think about you enough to be threatened by you. Really, Pat, I'm not saying that to be spiteful."

And out it came. Not venom, exactly. Wounded and striking back. Pat resented having been passed over for a promotion to another department the year before. Someone she considered less qualified had gotten it, even though it would have been a natural career step for her.

"And I would have gotten it, too, if you hadn't blocked it. You talk about developing your staff and helping us with our careers, but when the time came, you just couldn't abide seeing me succeed. Because I'm not your clone, I'm different from you."

"You think I'm the one who blocked your promotion?"

"Oh, Ruth, please don't condescend. It was obvious. Everyone knew. I always knew it, but then when Jeremy confirmed it—"

"Jeremy wasn't even here then."

"But he talked to people and found out. I always knew, but he just made it official."

Poor Pat. Pat the puppet. Ruth realized she should have told her long ago that it had been Dean who'd vetoed her big move. Ruth would have okayed it, even though she wasn't 100% sure Pat was ready, but Dean was adamant.

There had never been any doubt about Pat's technical skills. The concern was about her ability to manage people. People are much harder to manage than paper, projects, or fragrances. She reminded Pat that they'd discussed those weaknesses at her performance reviews. Dean thought it was too big a deficit for such a big leap.

"If I'd known how much you held it against me, I certainly would have told you. You could have asked."

Pat slouched a bit. Ruth could practically see the chip on her shoulder start to tumble. "Dean did it?"

"Would you like to see the paperwork?"

"Then why did Jeremy tell me it was you?"

"Now *that's* a very interesting question."

Ruth led the dance of revelation. She'd ask a question; Pat would answer, then back off. Ruth would come at it from a different angle, and Pat would answer again before backing off. Ruth didn't mind being patient, because she didn't think Pat was backing away from the truth out of crankiness or antagonism. It was humiliation. That was different.

During the conversation, she saw a physical transformation, too. Pat's face became older, more tired. Her hair would not be considered messy for anyone else, but for Pat it qualified. Instead of a center part from which two rigidly-defined sections of hair framed her face, there were actually strands hanging over her eyes in a way that would be sexy on another woman. And her eyes were changed somehow. They weren't darting, but they also weren't steady. It was as if they were unmasked, as if she'd previously had a cataract—a cataract of pretense—which was gone.

Something inside her dissolved, too, something that had been holding everything together for presentation to the outside world. The clothes managed without the internal support, but the body and face collapsed.

They eventually stitched the whole story together. In retrospect, it became clear that Jeremy had started manipulating Pat shortly after he arrived. He may have fooled people into thinking he didn't understand emotion by not displaying his own, but he had clearly seen the tension between Pat and Ruth. He even encouraged it, telling Pat he agreed that Ruth was a corporate misfit, and calling her charity benefits an unprofessional diversion. He ultimately stoked resentment into fury by telling Pat that Ruth was behind her non-promotion.

It was a baby step from there to enlisting Pat to keep him apprised of developments on About Face. He didn't want anything about the project to come as a surprise to him. "No detail is too small," he'd said.

Pat had assumed Jeremy thought, as she did, that About Face was a dumb idea and that he wanted to be ready for the 'go/no-go' decision. The point of all this cloak-and-dagger stuff, or so she thought, was that Jeremy wanted to have an iron-clad reason to get rid of Ruth. He was new, she was well-respected, it would have been too big a battle to fire her otherwise. She didn't share his corporate values, as Pat herself did. If it appeared Ruth was losing her edge, though, getting rid of her would be easier.

When the discouraging results of the first series of focus groups came in, she expected him to pull the project. She even rehearsed her reaction. She decided not to be overly surprised or overly sympathetic, because everyone knew she didn't much like the idea. But a little surprised, a little sympathetic.

Then, last Friday, when she told him Ruth was thinking of ending it herself, she thought he'd be so happy and tell her the project was dead. But no. He said he was going to let the project run. She couldn't believe it.

"Not hard to understand. Pretty clever, actually," Ruth said. "If About Face succeeded, fine. The company would make a lot of money under his watch. If it failed, that wouldn't be so bad either. In a different way."

"And then he sent down…." She took her pile of papers off Ruth's desk, peeled off a green sticky note, and showed it to Ruth. It had a drawing of a pair of sneakers.

At least she had the good grace to blush when explaining that it was a joking reference to her filling Ruth's shoes someday.

Pat took a strand of hair and began absent-mindedly twirling it. "I know, realistically speaking, some people might think I'm a bit young to hope for that. But I thought I'd do a good job. And it would be poetic justice, after you gave that promotion to Isabel instead of me. Or so I thought."

"I can see how you might think that."

Pat looked straight at Ruth. "Are you making fun?"

"No. You thought I'd unfairly slowed your career, which means a lot to you, so it didn't seem unreasonable to you to unfairly slow mine."

"Not many people around here understand that my career is important to me. They all think that because I don't need the money…."

Ruth waited. Pat wasn't going to get away with retreating into her turtle-shell of pretense.

"… it doesn't matter to me one way or the other. But it does. It's not about money, it's about, well, about … competence, about independence, so to speak. And other matters and issues."

"I see."

"In my defense, though, as it were, I never thought he was going to let the project proceed. I never thought he'd actually let the company lose money on a new product, merely for reasons of his own ambition. That really surprised me. And confused me."

"It *is* surprising."

"But by then I was sort of … well, committed to helping him. Do you think that he really was planning to give me the job? After he let the project run and it failed and you … well, you … you left. Or do you think he was leading me on, lying to me?"

"Pat, if you believe nothing else I tell you, believe this: There's no way he would have given you my job. And he probably wouldn't even have let you keep your job. Because you'd know too much."

"Perhaps you're right. That would make him—"

"A bastard?"

Pat's face woke up. "Yes, a bastard. A stinking bastard."

"Who else knows about all this?"

"Nobody. Nobody at work, at any rate."

"Have you kept notes about what's gone on? To document it? For self-protection in case it should all backfire?"

"Jeremy instructed me not to commit anything in writing. Sometimes we'd email each other, but I didn't save any of them. E-mail's too public."

"I need to think for a minute."

"I need to use the rest room."

Ruth paced as her brain raced. It all made sense. Jeremy wanted her out, Pat wanted her out, they joined forces. If she was responsible for an expensive failure, they'd both get their way. But Jeremy was using Pat. Too bad she hadn't looked to me as a mentor instead of Jeremy. Oh well, that's her problem.

When Pat returned a few minutes later, she looked more like her old self. Amazing what complete disclosure plus a little makeup does for her, thought Ruth. I wonder if there's a New Product in that idea? A mirror to tell the truth to, plus some products? Or a tape recorder? Maybe a diary?

"Okay, here's the plan. It's simple. You just continue to give Jeremy information about About Face. I'll even make it easy for you, I'll hand-feed it to you. All I want you to do for me is not tell him you and I had this talk."

"That's it?"

"That's it. Of course, if he tells you anything that you think would help me out, I'd appreciate your telling me. You never know, you might actually want me on your side someday. But all I'm asking you to do is not tell him we've spoken."

"But what will happen? With Violins & Wine?"

"First of all, it's now About Face, not Violins & Wine. It's a good project, it always has been, and it's going to get even better. Now, as to what you've done behind my back. For now, I don't plan to bust you. Perhaps I should. Most people would. But I'm trying to focus on your loyalty to Mimosa's bottom line instead of your ambition. Keep in mind, though, that a few minutes ago—somewhere back around puppy dogs and clones—you were very close to being out of here. Consider that you have used up eight of your nine lives. And that you owe me."

"Thank you," Pat said, only slightly above a whisper.

"That didn't hurt, did it?"

"What?"

"So, are we agreed?"

"I won't say anything. And also, I offer my apology for the trouble I've caused. I certainly wish I'd been privy to the information about Dean and the promotion all along. But you can count on me from now on."

"Good. And one more thing. I don't want you to tell anyone about this, not Judy or Tom or Colleen or anyone else. It's really better for you not to, and it's better for me too."

"Fine."

They shook hands. They smiled mechanically. Ruth considered Pat's half-hearted apology a start, and she was firm in her resolve about what to do. And so very glad at the possibility that the hard part was over.

23
The Cost of Failure

RUTH FORCED HERSELF TO CONCENTRATE on a mountain of memos and reports, trying not to see everything through the distorting prism of her battle with Jeremy. After reducing the stack by half, she allowed herself to replay the mental videotape of her confrontation with Pat, but only twice, and concluded that it had gone reasonably well with no major gaffes. She'd been firm and clear, and it had worked. Firm and clear were good. She hadn't always been so firm and clear.

"SHOULD I TAKE 100% COTTON T-SHIRTS or cotton-poly blends, mom? The packing list says cotton is better, but you know how wrinkled they'll get. Do people care about wrinkles in Africa? What do you think?"

"Whatever you want, Ruthie darling. You obviously can make up your own mind about things."

"Mo–om, if you're not going to help me, I wish you wouldn't stand there watching me pack every single thing. She picked four pure cotton shirts and two blends, folded them neatly and put them in a corner of her duffel bag. Then she grabbed one more cotton-poly blend and shoved it in.

"Doris's son thought he'd join the Peace Corps too, but he changed his mind at the last minute and—"

"I'm not changing my mind, mom." Only five pairs of underpants on the packing list? She rolled up six, put them in the duffel, and put the other two back in her drawer.

"Why is this happening to me? Between your sister's hitchhiking around god-only-knows-where and your being in Africa, I won't sleep for a single night. Can't you change your mind? Just this once? Do it for me?"

Ruth tried to count to ten before answering. She only got up to four, but at least she didn't stamp her foot. "Stop this, I'm going."

"I'm just trying to help by looking out for your best interests. Someday you'll thank me. You'll find a good husband and start a career. Your father agrees with me, even though he doesn't say so to you. Maybe men don't talk like that."

"Or maybe because he's actually proud of me, as in, 'Ask not what your country can do for you, ask what you can do for your country.' I thought you believed that."

"I'm sure there's a way to do something for your country that's not so dangerous. Africa, for goodness sake. Look at all those shots for all those diseases. And there are wild animals and .... You can help out at the American Cancer Society or the Friends of the Library or even be a candystriper if you want to volunteer."

Candystriper? Thank goodness her mother was saying something ridiculous enough to make the decision easier. "I'm going, Mom, and I'm really excited about it. A week from tomorrow." She zipped up the duffel bag to see how much room there was left, then unzipped it. She didn't know what else to say; this kind of discussion was new territory.

"So, do you think I should take the blue jeans that are already worn in or new ones? I think maybe the new ones, so they'll last longer, because probably they'll—"

"Whatever you think. I'm sure either one would be fine." Helen silently left the room, which was just as well, because, as soon as Ruth's hands stopped shaking and she caught her breath, she would have to penetrate the dresser drawer where she hid her cigarettes under her jeans.

A KNOCK BROUGHT HER BACK to the present, where Judy was peeking around Ruth's partly-open door. Receiving her invitation, she entered and closed the door behind her.

In the chair facing Ruth she rubbed her hands together, then wrung them out.

"Something wrong?" Ruth asked.

"No. I don't think so. Well, I don't really know."

Judy told Ruth that when she'd been up on the twentieth floor, speaking to someone about the packaging for the two-tone lipsticks so she could work on the pricing parameters, she noticed Pat on the phone at Sue's desk.

"Sue who's on maternity leave?"

"Yeah, and I thought it was weird. So I ... well, I ... You know, Pat's been so mean to me lately, so I did something I maybe shouldn't have done ... not *shouldn't* have, exactly, but—

"Tell me."

Judy took a roundabout way to the elevator so she could listen invisibly. Pat was talking to Bunny, the friend who had come to the office to take her out for a birthday lunch about a month before. A little older than Pat, she was obviously in command of the friendship, a mentor of some sort. She'd avoided eye contact with Ruth and extended the limpest hand possible when it became impossible to avoid shaking.

Judy heard Pat say she thought maybe Bunny's advice hadn't been so good after all. That things hadn't turned out the way they'd both thought. And that she was going to do the right thing.

"She said that? The right thing?"

"I think she might have cried a little. I'm not sure." She picked a piece of lint off her black skirt and looked up at Ruth with a smile that advertised mischief. "Then came the best part."

Ruth pushed back from her desk slightly, folded one leg under her, and propped her chin on her hand with her elbow on the arm of her chair. "You're just full of surprises, aren't you?"

"Pat said something like, 'Bunny that's not true. You're wrong. I'm not such a silly fool and. . . ." Judy closed her mouth and bit her lips.

"And?"

"And Ruth's not such a bitch."

"Really? 'Ruth's not such a bitch.'"

"That part I'm sure of. Then she listened for awhile and even held the phone away from her ear. And that's when I left. So, do you know what this is all about?"

"I think so."

"What?"

"I can't tell you until it's over. But then I will."

Just as Judy left, Danny Jones entered. It was his first time in her office, and as she welcomed him, she could see his eyes taking in the artwork.

They made small talk. Very small talk. He asked about her artwork, especially the African photos. She told him about her Peace Corps past. He told her about his family, proud that his wife was a doctor and that his kids were taking music lessons. Ruth let him guide the route of the conversation, knowing he had something on his mind—no one had free time to drop in to chat about artwork and families. But if he didn't get to the reason for his visit soon, she'd have to take over.

Eventually, he asked about the new line, especially about how she'd convinced Jeremy that using existing products would be ethical as well as marketable.

"It was easier than I'd thought it would be. And now we're doing media planning and that really is the fun part for me."

Danny said he'd thought the meeting with Roger was—he searched for the word—unusual. Especially the weird things Jeremy had said.

"The weird things. Right. And which weird things would those be?"

"Roger didn't tell you?"

Danny said that Jeremy had been adamant: If they were going to proceed with About Face, he wanted to do it "for real." And that meant brand new products, developed from scratch, with R&D going full steam ahead. He told them to go back to the drawing board for new products. And if they were just a little new, maybe a tweak here or there, so they wouldn't require extensive testing and could get to the market fast, so much the better. He'd consider re-packaging existing products, but only as a last resort.

"'A little tweaking,' he said? Really?" Ruth asked. Jeremy obviously thought cosmetics were like financial services, things you can rush out to the market.

"Verbatim. 'Expense is less of a concern than timing.'" Danny imitated Jeremy's fast-forward smile perfectly.

It's true, thought Ruth. He's after a quick expensive failure. That's why Roger wants to have lunch when he gets back from vacation. To clue me in.

"Danny, I appreciate your stopping by to chat. A lot."

His real smile displayed a deep dimple on his right cheek. "Terry told me you're one of the good guys and I should trust you."

"Terry? You know Terry that well?"

"Didn't you know? She's dating my brother. In Chicago. They met at some conference."

"The devil! She never told me."

As Danny got up to go, Ruth said she had nothing of equal value to trade for his valuable information, but in the meantime it might come in handy for him to know that Roger's secretary Joan really liked chocolate. The darker the better. "And you definitely want to be Joan's friend."

It was funny, actually, that Mr. Corporate Man, Mr. By-the-Numbers, was trying to make the company lose money so he could get rid of her. For ambition? For some kind of personal anti-feminist-hippy thing?

In a certain way, he was right about her. She *was* a kind of misfit. He knew she was different from him, in terms of values and goals and general attitude toward life. And he couldn't stand that she was successful anyway. It made a mockery of his devotion to corporate life. That was understandable.

And here she was, Ms. Ambivalent-About-Corporations, the one who was honestly trying to make the company money. Yes, fulfill some ambition, too. And also do a "good thing."

It was all so distorted, like funny-mirrors in a carnival.

24
Picnic Rapping

AFTER WORK, SHE WALKED TO CENTRAL PARK, where David and Carlos had arranged a picnic dinner. The weather report had been promising, Vivian had a meeting in Manhattan that afternoon, and David could drive in after school. Ruth had asked David to act as if he really intended to participate in the hypothetical clothing business, at least until they started making real plans. If they ever did. Which they wouldn't.

"That way, it will be more symmetrical. And I won't have to deal with Carlos on my own."

"Only if you don't harbor any secret fantasies that I'll really get sucked in. Because I won't."

"Deal."

The men had planned the menu and divided the responsibilities. And she didn't have to do anything. Except obsess about her soap opera of a day.

So far, based on her session with Pat and what she'd heard from Judy and then from Danny, the larger outlines of the plan she was formulating for handling Jeremy seemed sound. Now she was heading for the soap opera playing on a different channel: Hippies and Ex-Hippies Talk About a Business.

She slowed down as she approached the southwest corner of the park, savoring the moment of being at the border of two worlds. A jazz quartet was playing old favorites. She returned the pony-tailed vibraphone player's smile. A bunch of green-sweatshirted roller-bladers noisily assembled before they entered the park for their workout. Frail elderly people sat on the benches, listening to the music and eating sandwiches they'd brought from home. The few religious nuts didn't seem to be bothering anyone, diluted as their rantings were by the music and athleticism.

As soon as she entered the park itself, all thoughts of Pat and Jeremy, of cosmetics and advertising, of the unpredictability of human behavior, became bubbles and drifted upward. As they floated away, she noticed all the colors around her seemed more intense than usual. Have there always been so many different kinds of green, she wondered?

"Hey, honey, over here." She was glad David was there before the others. She joined him on a wooden bench with a missing slat. After a perfunctory kiss, she leaned her head on his shoulder and they sat in birdsong-saturated silence for a minute.

"Don't you want to know how it went with Pat today?" Ruth asked after a while.

"Of course. I was just about to ask."

"It went okay, I think. I'll tell you all the gory details when I can bear to think about it again."

"But the short version?"

"The short version is that Jeremy's really been using her. Wants About Face to fail so he can get rid of me. Promised her my job. Made fun of my sneakers."

"No!" The one syllable had enough force to jostle her head from its resting place.

"HI YOU TWO. HOPE WE'RE NOT INTERRUPTING." Carlos reached over to give Ruth a kiss. Then he and David shook hands.

A kiss? Did Vivian tell him to do that?

Like a defendant trying to read the jury when they return to the courtroom with a verdict, Ruth wondered whether this unusual show of affection was a sign of openness to her idea or Carlos's idea of a consolation prize, a sympathy kiss.

At a nearby picnic table, Carlos and David unpacked their various backpacks and shopping bags, putting the containers of food at one end and the dinner-ware at the other.

"Hummus. Pita bread. Olives. Stuffed grape leaves. Organic salad." Carlos set his contributions out on the table.

"Sandwiches for everyone," David said. "Here's the vegetarian section, here's for vegans, and carnivores can select from here."

"How many people are we expecting?" Vivian asked.

"I take sandwiches to school for lunch every day. Leftovers today mean less work for me tomorrow. And the next day. And the next. So eat as much as you want, but don't worry about left-overs."

"And here are some drinks," continued Carlos. "All soft. Except for this one over here that looks like iced tea but isn't. Open container laws—such a crock."

For five minutes, there was joyful, if chaotic, passing back and forth of food, drinks, salt and pepper, salad dressing, serving spoons, napkins. Then, as if on cue, all requests to pass a certain dish or bowl stopped at the same moment and the sounds of contented chewing were accompanied by the birds and roller-bladers inside the park and the car horns outside. A robin landed on the table and stared at them.

"Mmmm, nice moment," David said.

"Damn straight," Carlos said. The robin flew off. A squirrel took his place.

After a few more chews, Vivian said, "Someone has to go first, and I volunteer and the first thing I want to say is how brilliant it was to tell us not to react right away because you were right that if we had reacted right away, it would probably have been along the lines of 'No thanks it's not our kind of thing and by the way are you out of your mind.' But now that we've had some time to let it all sink in and settle down, it's …

different. I mean, we're still not ready to sign on the dotted line or anything—"

"I know, David told me you said you just wanted to ask some stuff and talk it over. That's okay."

So far so good, thought Ruth. She'd prepared herself for skepticism if not direct challenges. She'd vowed not to be drawn into an argument with Carlos, not to become defensive in any way, to separate what he said from how he said it. She told herself it was like bargaining, that it really didn't matter that much, they could still be friends after the picnic even if they didn't want to do the business.

"This has been kind of a trip," Carlos said. He looked up at Ruth. "You are definitely full of surprises, chica."

"You think so, boychik?"

At first, Carlos had thought the idea of a business was loco. But after awhile, the idea of giving money away was too seductive to ignore.

"It's my fantasy job. As you know. Sneaky girl."

He wanted to know how much they'd be giving away, saying he wouldn't be as interested in giving away $100 as $100,000.

Ruth outlined a few ways they could structure the charitable giving. They could give a certain amount of money for each garment sold. Or they could give a certain percentage of the profits—"

"Or all the profits," Carlos said."

"Right, or all the profits. Any way you look at it, though, the more we made, the more we'd give. If you want, I can draw up a few charts of 'if we made this much, we could give away this much' and show different possibilities."

"Cool."

Carlos certainly was in a good mood. The idea of giving money away seemed to be like candy.

"This sure is different from anything we've ever thought about before," Vivian said. "I know I like designing my own clothes and I like it that you like them so much too. But for strangers? How would

I know what colors? And how many in the different sizes? I don't understand the business part at all. How do you know what to make and how many and what sizes and how do you sell it to the stores and how do you know how much to charge and stuff like that?"

"That's what I bring to the party," Ruth said. "And what I don't know already, I can learn. We can all learn."

They talked for hours, jumping from how the business might work to how long it would take them to get started to how they could finance the start-up to colors and fabrics and styles.

David brought up the subject of money and, in particular, salaries. He volunteered to go first. "Teacher's salaries are public records, so we don't have much trouble talking about it."

"We don't have trouble with it either, man," Carlos said. "Maybe because our identities aren't linked to our salaries."

No one was surprised that Carlos earned the least and Ruth the most. Vivian and Carlos were kind enough not to react to Ruth's salary with grumblings about people starving in Mississippi or Cuba or any other place. It was easy to agree that in their alleged business they'd each earn the same amount, and that it would be less than Ruth made and more than Carlos made.

Ruth asked the question that had been on her mind since Carlos had first called: why were they interested in this? She knew about Carlos's fantasy of giving money away, of course, but his interest, or pre-interest, still surprised her.

"Believe me, I'm more surprised than you. But it's giving money away. That's all. And maybe there's some stuff at work that's hard to take."

"There always has been," Vivian said.

"It just feels worse lately."

"We've seen lots of people get burned out, but we just thought it wouldn't happen to us. Or rather, Carlos thought it wouldn't happen to him. He's the saint in the family." Vivian stroked his cheek.

"Don't you feel the same way, babe?"

She did, but without being surprised about it. She also liked the idea of a new outlet for her creativity. And she also thought it would be fun and she was attracted to the fun. Especially if it generated money for worthy projects. And she also liked the idea of having enough money to help Ida pay off her student loans.

Ruth advocated for the devil by cautioning Vivian that starting a business was a very iffy venture. She might give up her salary at BSW but not make anything at the clothing business. Plus they wouldn't have anything to give to charity.

"There's no guarantee." The idea of a working relationship with Carlos was making Ruth start to backpedal.

Carlos said, "Not a big problem. In our world, there's always a need for people who know what they're doing and are willing to work hard to make a difference for not very much money. There aren't that many of us. We're in demand."

"It's pretty wonderful to be able to say that about yourselves," David said.

"Yeah, it's nice," Vivian said. "In a perfect world, though, we'd also have been able to put Ida through school."

"In a really perfect world," Carlos said, "all kids could go to school for free."

Two nuns walked past them. The older one was talking in soft, solemn tones. While the younger one listened, she fixed a strand of hair that had escaped her head-piece.

"Good evening," the nuns said.

"Good evening," they all replied.

Darkness and the temperature had fallen when they weren't paying attention. "When it's dark enough that you can hardly see two nuns ten feet away, it must be time to call it a night," David said. "Don't you think?"

They packed up their picnic paraphernalia and headed toward the park exit, reassuring each other one more time they weren't committed to anything, just intrigued enough to keep thinking about it and talking about it. That's all.

After they separated, Carlos and Vivian heading west toward the subway, Ruth and David south toward their car, David said, "I guess we have a lot to talk about."

"We sure do, honey. Don't know if I can stay awake in the car long enough to get through it all, though."

A transvestite hooker passed them, resplendent in a silver-sequined dress with a slit up to mid-thigh and a bright-blue boa, wearing a small sign saying "Please help me save up for sex change." He looked David up and down ostentatiously.

"Poor guy," David said, when they'd passed.

Ruth said, "I don't know, in a crazy sort of way, I envy her."

"Is it the boa?"

"Very funny. No, it's because ... this guy feels like he's a woman trapped in a man's body, and she knows the inside and the outside don't match, and she also knows exactly what the mis-match is all about. And how to fix it."

"And?"

"It's just that old feeling that my insides and outsides don't match. In a different way from her, of course. But I'm not exactly sure which part needs to change. Or how. Does everyone feel that way?"

"You've had a long day, Ruthie. Sleep in the car. You'll feel better tomorrow."

25
Ads Sell Stuff

A WEEK LATER, ON THE BUS TO WORK, Ruth became entranced by a tall, willowy African-American woman with impossibly short hair, bright red lipstick, and huge hoop earrings, whose spike heels and calf-length sheath skirt made her look like she was walking down a fashion-show runway instead of the aisle of the bus. In the middle of her stampeding fantasy about the glamorous life the woman led and her self-confidence about her face and body, she remembered something Maria had said at last night's meeting of The Brain Trust.

The long-postponed topic had been envy, any kind of envy. There was so much to choose from: looks, career, creativity, money, intelligence, marriage and children, courage, spirituality. Even alleged penis envy.

Maria had seemed to fold in on herself as she said that she envied complete strangers, like people in her flower shop or on the street. She closed her dark eyes, accentuating the unlikely freckles on her pale face, as she told how she invented lives for these people and then envied the invented lives.

"Mostly I always think they look like they're so comfortable with who they are. They could be nerdy guys with pants above their ankles. Or grannies who take a half hour choosing a brand of toilet paper, but in my mind they're supremely centered."

Fantasy-and-envy. Like Maria. She reminded herself that the tall beautiful woman might have problems of her own. She looked around at the other bus passengers. The woman in front of her was frantically flipping through typewritten pages that were dimpled with red handwritten editorial comments. The man across the aisle was asleep, mouth open, head inclining toward his neighbor, who seemed to be trying to distance her shoulder from his head. These were all just regular people, as was the woman who'd just been the subject of her fantasies. Regular people; remember that.

At her office, she cleared her desk of routine correspondence before concentrating on the email she'd been looking forward to writing since her confrontation with Pat ten days before. She'd been feeding Jeremy slightly discouraging news about the progress of About Face. She told him about advertising problems and product-coloration glitches, things she would normally have kept from him. Nothing too dire; she didn't want to give him an attack of scruples. Just a negative shading of the truth, enough to get up his hopes about a big fat flop. It was almost sexual, trying to keep his excitement stoked but not erupting.

A few days before, she'd demonstrated some of the products they were considering for the line. She used tubes, brushes and bottles on a mannequin in his office, explaining to him the thinner and dryer skin of middle-aged faces.

"Right over here by the eyes, it tends to be dark and cast a shadow. Do you see? Lightweight and light-colored make-up is an optical illusion. It doesn't look like a big glob of makeup plastered on, but it does eliminate the shadow."

"And here's another common problem: graying and thinning eyebrows. It's much better to fill them in with eye-shadow and a little brush than with an eyebrow pencil. Don't you think those darker eyebrows make a big difference?"

She'd known Jeremy would squirm. It took men a little while at the company to become inured to talk of this or that cosmetic on this or that facial flaw, and he hadn't been there long enough. She enjoyed every squirm.

In the end, he gave the most minimal kind of support he could muster.

"I guess you must know what you're doing. I guess." Sigh. "Because you have such a great track record here." Sigh. "It seems kind of iffy to me, but I'm going to try to ignore my skeptical inner voice. Sure, let's go with it. Go with it for now."

If it hadn't been for her session with Pat, and then her corroboration from Danny, she'd have spent a lot of time trying to interpret his exaggerated tolerance. But she knew the hammed-up sighing was fake, a sigh-fi tale to make sure Ruth was impressed with his reluctance.

Meanwhile, Pat had been cooperative and, if not exactly friendly, a little less stiff. No smiles, but not so many frowns and silences. No abrupt turning-on-the-heel in a huff. Progress.

She wanted to get the tone of this email exactly right. Appreciative but no kow-towing. Professional, not girlish. She wanted him to think he'd won.

> To: Jeremy Crater
> From: Ruth Talbot
> Re: About Face
>
> Jeremy, I just wanted to thank you for the confidence you expressed at our meeting last week. I know you have reservations about the About Face line, but I appreciate that you heard me out and agreed to let it proceed.
>
> I also heard what you said, that you're not 100% enthusiastic about it, that you think the focus groups results haven't been as strong as you like. That's why it's so gratifying that you allowed my experience and track record to persuade you.
>
> I want you to know I am prepared to take full responsibility for what happens to this line.
>
> Thanks again.

As she wrote, she tried to visualize Jeremy's glee when he read the part about full responsibility. He'd think that, when About Face cost the company money and prestige, she'd take the fall.

Sure enough, he replied immediately with "Thanks." Ruth thought he must be planning to use it later when she fell flat on her middle-aged women's libber face. Now she knew what was meant by that Shakespearean quote about someone "hoist on his own petard." That's what she was helping Jeremy to do. Petard-hoisting. It felt wicked. She almost cackled.

She printed out the emails and filed them.

Then she went to Terry's office to pick her up for lunch. Ruth was taking her out for her last day as a data-nerd at Mimosa. By mutual agreement, they were going to blow their low-carb diets to smithereens with lemon-sauced linguine and stuffed zucchini blossoms at the new Trattoria in the neighborhood.

She tried to be unobtrusive about examining Terry while they ordered and waited for their food. The contrast between who she *appeared* to be and who Ruth knew her to be was always delightful. While some at Mimosa dressed as if they were the brightly-colored flowers posing against the white walls, Terry was a devout member of the dress-to-blend-in congregation, all part of her deceptively calm appearance. Quietly attractive, in her late-30's, she had mid-length light brown hair and a pale face that was unremarkable, the kind witnesses would have trouble describing to the police.

Practically before the plate had hit the table, Terry lifted a zucchini blossom, tipped her head back, and gently inserted it in her open mouth. Removing her napkin from her neckline, she meticulously wiped the three fingers she'd just used to deliver the zucchini blossom to its target, then tucked the napkin back in.

"I'm going to miss you," Ruth said. "It's been great having a fellow bullshit-detector, even though you have everyone else fooled with your pastel-colored suits and your soft voice. Everyone but Danny Jones, that is."

"Don't worry, I was going to tell you about Ron. Besides, the move isn't about him. Not entirely, anyway."

Terry had reached the end of her rope at Mimosa. It wasn't the work, it was the people. Jeremy had made a Big Daddy named Norman her counterpart in Communications, instead of Harriet, whom everyone had expected to get the job. Now Harriet had to report to Norman-the-moron and she, Terry, had to work with Harriet, whose reaction to it all was to become a monster.

"Everything's changed. I didn't mind my work, I liked it, even. Liked making things add up and fit together." She signaled to the waiter to fill her water glass and was silent as he did so.

As soon as the waiter left, Ruth said, "Don't get too gooey about numbers or you'll sound like Jeremy."

"Don't get me started. I like numbers because they're kind of … poetic. They have their own beauty. Truth and beauty. He likes them because they're predictable. Because he can control them. It's different."

She took a sip of water and looked around. "I figure sooner or later Jeremy's going to try to get rid of me."

Ruth invoked the Talbot-family story about the Peace Corps volunteer who, at his exit interview, when asked what was the most valuable lesson he'd learned in his two years, said, "There are jerks all over the world."

"Don't you think there will be jerks where you're going, too?"

"Maybe new jerks will take awhile to be intolerable."

Terry detailed the research she'd done about jobs, cities, salaries, while Ruth envied her ability to be so analytic about figuring out what she wanted and then getting it. She was busy scolding herself for her shortcomings in that department and resolving to be more like Terry. Then she realized that, not two days before, she'd commented to David on Vivian's wonderful ability to leap, open-armed, from one idea or experience to another, with no planning, no expectations, and accept whatever she found.

At least she wasn't the only one who experienced this kind of equal-opportunity envy. At last night's Brain Trust meeting, Charlie had described the same kind of fickle envy.

"Let's say I meet someone who's really sophisticated—you know, they travel and know about wine, can talk about musical theory, stuff like that—so I feel envious of all that, I wish I were so educated and suave instead of so ordinary and dumb. And then the next day, I meet someone who's the opposite—they never go anywhere, don't know a damned thing about wine, they're working class, have a zillion kids and are really devoted to their family, go to all the Little League games and have hot dogs for dinner every night. Damned if I'm not envious of them, too, wishing I were genuine and authentic and really connected to what life was all about instead of being a pretender. It makes me nuts."

"Do you think the Little League lady and the Sophisticate envy each other?" Sarah asked.

"You might be interested to know that I envy you, Charlie," Ruth said. "The way you're such a talented weaver. Artist, really. And have the courage to show your work to the world at large and have other people look at it and pay money for it."

Charlie brightened, but only briefly, like a light bulb going on and off. "Thanks. That's nice. But I'd still love to stop torturing myself." She picked a loose thread off her vest, another of her creations, this time with an impressionistic scene of blazing autumn trees.

"Since we're confessing to our crazies—sorry, Charlie, but you said it—let me add mine. With me," Jane said, "envy shows its ugly face right after admiration. It actually makes me not want to meet people I might admire. 'Cause the envy that comes afterwards is painful. Crazy."

"I think it's getting worse as I get older," Charlie said. "Now regret is mixed in with envy. What a mess."

"Here's what I think," offered Blanche. "It's not like you think Ms. Sophisticate is the way to be. Or Ms. Little League. It's that you see them as something with a definition, like a label. It's the lack of ambivalence that's so appealing."

"When I was a kid, I outlined everything in the coloring book with a black line before I filled in the inside part with a color," Sarah said. "It's like that. It's like the black line that holds everything in. Don't you think?"

"Here's a good one," Maria said. "I read it somewhere, I think in one of those trashy women's magazines that you only admit to reading in a doctor's office. But I really don't remember."

"You're lucky you even remember *what* you read, let alone where you read it," Sarah said.

"It was about comparing *our* insides to *their* outsides. You just can't win that way. It's worse than apples and oranges. It's apples and … umbrellas. Insides and outsides. Can't compare."

"Ooooh, it's simple and clear and pithy. Like a good product slogan," Ruth said. "I like it. Insides and outsides."

And here she was, comparing her undefined insides to Terry's black-outlined outsides. She just had to stop doing that.

After lunch, Ruth went to the advertising agency. The receptionist, her hair a working definition of anarchy in what must have been a trend, led Ruth down the long corridor to the conference room.

"Would you like some coffee or tea, Ruth?"

"No thanks, I'm fine."

"A soft drink maybe?"

"Nope. I just came from lunch. I don't need anything."

"Temperature okay?"

Ruth was enjoying the royal treatment reserved for clients.

"No, really, I'm fine. Listen, I hope you don't mind my mentioning something to you. But I figure you'd want to know."

"Do I have something green in my teeth?"

"It's your sweater. It's pretty and everything but it's inside-out. You must have put it on in a rush. That happens to me sometimes, so I know—"

"Oh Ruth, you're a stitch. But you got me nervous there for a second."

She thinks I'm kidding? She did it on purpose? It's a style? How did I miss this?

"I'll let the gang know you're here." Gloria was still laughing as she left.

Ruth's rep Marty announced his entry with the staccato of his cowboy boots. At least he's not wearing his Stetson, Ruth thought. He brought along two young assistants who conformed to the same nonconformist ethic as the receptionist. These kids are really sticking it to their parents.

Marty put his feet up on the table as if to model his boots for everyone. His assistants sat on either side of him but kept their feet on the floor.

"Howdy, partner," Ruth said. "Looks like you guys have been busy." She pointed at the huge posters around the room. There were ads for travel companies and vacuum cleaners, stock brokers and autos. She particularly liked the one with the photograph of a smiling middle-aged woman in a cap and gown, captioned, "It's never too late to be what you want to be when you grow up."

Marty said, "Very busy. Including your campaign. We think you'll like it. You gave us good direction. Half the battle. We liked old-and-young photos of the same person. Very visual. Speaks for itself. Let's look at a few ways to go." He spoke to the ceiling, "Let's roll it."

The lights dimmed and the screen descended. Two stark pictures of Tina Turner greeted them. On the left, she was in her twenties, unmistakably young, pretty, and seductive. On the right, she was clearly older. She exuded power and energy. Her beauty was less "pretty girl, good girl," and more "I'm me and I like it and if you don't, it's your problem."

The caption, filling the bottom half of the screen, read "What's Age Got to Do with It?"

"This caption is obviously just for Tina. God love her. Of course, we'd have to get her permission. Who knows if she'd give it. Next."

Then came similarly-matched photos of Sophia Loren ("Sorry all you 20-somethings, you'll have to wait awhile to look this good"), Catherine Deneuve ("She looks great for her age," with the last three words crossed out), and Lauren Hutton ("A real 50, not a fake 25").

Finally, before and after shots of an unfamous woman who was pretty when young, beautiful when middle aged. It was captioned, "Like fine wines and violins, women get better and better." The lights went on. Marty took his feet off the table. "What do you think? Which ones grabbed you? We can come up with others, too. If you want."

"I was just thinking," she said. "These slides were great, exactly what I'd asked you to do."

"But…?" Marty asked.

First she told him they'd changed the name. She loved it that they were reluctant to see Violins & Wine go, and not just because they'd already used the slogan in one of their slides. But she was sure. "The customers have spoken."

Then she said she was troubled by the fact that, even though they were saying you don't have to look young to look beautiful, they were only showing middle-aged women who were extremely youthful and gorgeous. She was starting to think it didn't add up. Maybe they still hadn't nailed the message?

"Wait a second. Isn't gorgeous the point?" said the sidekick with the shaved-and-tattoed head, tapping his pencil.

"Yes. And no. Like I said, I'm struggling to nail the message."

"Are you saying we should use faces that aren't so beautiful so 'regular' women, as you put it, will feel like they have a chance?"

The other sidekick, with striped hair and dressed in many shades of black, was only partially able to hide her disdain. "That's like using a beat-up old Volkswagen to sell a spiffy new BMW. Or something like that."

Had Ruth and all her friends just been called beat-up Volkswagens by this pipsqueak who knew nothing? "You better watch out or I'll tell your mother what you just said about her."

"What? You know my mother? But how—"

"Never mind. It was a joke."

"Oh, I get it. But what you're saying isn't what advertising is all about. Advertising isn't supposed to say, 'You're fine the way you are.' No, advertising gives people hope, it gives them an aspiration to be better. And it shows them *how* to be better."

"Well, thanks for the lesson, and I hate to disillusion you, but what advertising is really about is selling stuff. Like toilet bowl cleaners and lipstick and cars and clothes and food. Hope and aspiration? No, it's about selling. And I have to figure out how I want to do that."

Ruth turned to Marty and explained that, perhaps for this campaign more than any other, it was very important for the message to be crystal-clear. So she needed to take some time to figure it out.

"And we're here to help you," he said with emphasis, as much to his sidekicks as to Ruth. He walked over to the white board and drew a square in the middle of it. She'd never noticed how tall and thin he was. Ruth wondered if his heart, lungs, liver and kidneys were similarly elongated. Did he have a chest X-ray in his family photo album?

He wrote "female beauty" inside the square. "This is what we're talking about, right?"

Everyone nodded.

"There's internal beauty—you know, being a good person, doing good works—and there's external beauty, the Catherine Deneuve type," Ruth said.

Marty wrote "internal" and "external" on opposite sides of the white board with arrows from each to the central square. "Since we're in the cosmetics business, I assume we're talking about the external type?" He started to draw a check-mark above the word "external."

"Not so fast," Ruth said. She suggested they try to think outside of Marty's box. She asked if they didn't agree that, sometimes, when you admire the kinds of things someone *does*, you also think they're beautiful.

"Example?" Marty asked.

Ruth looked at all the photos around the room. She thought of the women she admired. Finally, she said, "How about Christiane Amanpour? She wouldn't necessarily win a beauty contest, but you perceive her as beautiful because you know how great she is."

"Who's she?" the pipsqueaks asked simultaneously.

"Well, never mind. How about Coretta Scott King? Or Sandra Day O'Connor who, now that I think about it, looks a little like Lauren Hutton."

"You think Sandra Day O'Connor's beautiful?" bald-boy asked.

"Well, maybe not beautiful like Brigitte Bardot—"

"Who?" hair-of-many-colors asked.

"In a Brittany Spears kind of way, then. Maybe she looks good enough that she doesn't need to worry about being beautiful. What you see when you look at her is who she is, not just how she looks."

"I still don't get how this sells cosmetics," she said, but minus the truculence. "You want to tell people they don't need to worry about what they look like as long as they're good people? To sell make-up?"

"You've got a point," Ruth said. "Let's back up. The original idea for About Face was that middle-aged women don't need to try to look young to look good."

A chorus of agreement.

"Question," Marty said. "Are we saying that middle-aged beauty and youthful beauty are two different things? Just as good as each other? Or that middle-aged beauty is actually better?"

"Or," Ruth said softly, "are we saying that beauty isn't so important when you get older? I keep coming back to that. Even though you're right, kids, that it doesn't exactly seem to be the way to sell cosmetics."

Everyone was silent for a moment. Then Ruth shook her head and said, "No, no, that's not it, I'm not saying beauty isn't important when you get older. I do want to sell cosmetics. But I *am* saying middle-aged beauty is different. It's not about winning beauty contests, it's about something else. It's why you see Christiane Amanpour's face as beautiful—and by the way, guys, you see her face on CNN—even though it's not a beauty-contest kind of beauty."

Marty erased what was on the white board and said, "Try this. Take a paper and write the names of women who are middle-aged and beautiful. No, not necessarily beautiful, but attractive. No matter if we know the people. Just so *you* know who you find attractive. Then we'll look for conclusions."

The five made their lists silently. Then they discussed them, sometimes arguing over people they knew in common, and whether they really were attractive or not. They described members of their personal lists so that, by the time they were done, everyone felt they knew bald-boy's Aunt Frances and striped-head's piano teacher Mrs. Russell, as well as Marty's wife and Ruth's sister.

After feeling lost in the murk of indefinable qualities, a sense of direction eventually began to emerge. They thought they knew why, for example, bald-boy's Aunt Frances was more attractive than his Aunt Simone. And why the piano teacher was attractive but the French tutor wasn't.

They concluded that, besides objectively-beautiful types like Sophia Loren, the middle-aged women they considered attractive fell into two groups. First were those who were loved, or at least respected, by the judges. The love colored the perception, created open arms, saw beauty whether it was there or not. The piano teacher and Ruth's sister fell into this group.

But there were also people whom the nominator thought beautiful even though he or she didn't particularly love them. After awhile, the group decided these people—like Aunt Frances—were those whose bearing suggested they considered themselves attractive. Their own opinion helped form others'.

"With young people, then," Marty said, "attractiveness is a stand-alone kind of quality. Later, it's more connected to your 'you-ness.' Complicated. Interesting."

"I like this," Ruth said.

And the assistants, in their own way, echoed her sentiments.

"Cool."

"Way cool."

26
Two Ruths

A WEEK LATER, THINGS WERE MOVING right along. The decision to use existing products meant a vastly compressed process of getting to market: no research, no lab testing, just packaging the elements into a line with its own identity.

The new focus groups were providing the results she'd hoped for and expected, and Packaging was sending samples daily. The ad agency, too, had jumped on the new idea for a campaign.

She was looking at the head-shot photos the agency had sent for her evaluation. They were just what she'd wanted: young and old versions of the same women, ordinary women. Of the few who were celebrities, most were famous for their work, not their beauty. The effect was perfect: these older women were warm and inviting and radiantly beautiful, not Barbie-doll beautiful. Showing was definitely better than telling.

She spread the photos out on her desk in different formats, like a deck of cards. First all the young ones. Then all the older ones. Then the young ones paired with their older selves. Arranged and rearranged.

The shuffling reminded Ruth of a photo-juxtaposition that came out of a trip she and David had taken back to their volunteer villages in Africa, their tenth anniversary gift to themselves. It would be a perfect time, they thought, to introduce six-year-old Josh to a part of the world where not everyone watches Sesame Street and eats

Cheerios and has bunk beds so their friends can come for a sleepover. It was a photo of a young Ruth and a not-so-young Ruth.

The trip had been great timing for Ruth, because she'd just made the move from the Human Resources Department of Mimosa to Marketing. Transitions were always tough, but this one was especially so. Just as wrenching as when she'd moved, some seven years before, from the publishing industry to cosmetics.

She'd tormented herself with the thought that Human Resources was about helping people but Marketing was "only" about selling stuff. Friends tried to help her by pointing out that Human Resources was all about administrivia, while in Marketing she'd have the opportunity to be creative. The new job carried a big raise, and that was the deciding factor, as they were just starting their college fund for Josh. Creative, not trivial.

A trip back to her Peace Corps past seemed just the thing to help her over the hump.

THEY SPENT A FEW DAYS in the capital first, hoping to acclimate Josh gradually. They couldn't bring themselves to stay in the fanciest hotel, but they did indulge in a place with a swimming pool and a TV in the room ("for Josh's sake," they told themselves).

Things in the capital seemed exactly the same—same statuesque women gliding along with baskets on their heads, same beggars, same smell of wood smoke, same heat, same flies. While the lack of change was a comfortable nostalgia for them, they knew it wasn't a particularly good sign for the country itself.

After visiting their old haunts, including a courtesy call on the Peace Corps office, they rented a car and drove southeast, most of the way to David's remote village. They stayed overnight in a hotel that had neither swimming pool nor TV, but it was clean and it had hot water and beds with mosquito nets. The next day, they got to the village and parked just outside the entrance, hoping to walk in quietly with no fuss.

A tall young man, about twenty years old, spotted them within seconds. He took one look at David and said, "Day-day?"

"Papp-Gaye?"

"Daddy, did you just say PopGuy?"

"Sort of." Laughter, hand-shaking, hugging and back-slapping, joyful tears and shouts followed, with various villagers coming over to join them. As soon as there was a sufficient lull, David explained to Josh and Ruth that Papp-Gaye had been about six—Josh's present age—when David had last seen him, and had always said his name as Dayday.

They spent the morning walking around. The village kids were curious about these rare visitors, white people no less, and followed them around in a gaggle as they stopped to greet people and drink tea.

After awhile, David asked Papp-Gaye about his father, who'd just started to bake bread when David lived there. Hearing that he was now the baker for the hotel they'd stayed at the previous night, David confessed that, when he was just learning to bake and Papp-Gaye himself would deliver three loaves to David each morning, he'd eat one right away while it was still edible, then secretly bury the others so no one would know he'd discarded them.

"We knew of the burying of the bread loaves. Thinking it being a white man's custom. From your country."

As they walked, David noticed that several of the wells he'd built with his own hands, some fourteen or fifteen years before, were still functioning.

"Imagine that," he said to Josh. "I came here, helped to build some wells, and people are still drinking the water they provide. Without these wells, they'd have to walk for miles to get what they need."

"With buckets on their head, dad?"

"Heavy buckets."

"Are you a hero, dad?"

"I don't know if I'd go that far."

"Yes, yes, a hero. Can I Show and Tell you when I get back to school?"

"I would love to be Show-and-Telled."

After a few hours, they headed back to the car, along the way distributing the pencils and crayons they'd brought for the village children. They took along lots of home-made bread, oranges and bottled water, and bought shish-kebabs of well-done mystery-meat from vendors on the side of the road.

Towards the end of the afternoon, they got to Ruth's village. The family compounds were where they'd always been, each with a cooking hut in the middle of the ring of sleeping huts. There were more compounds now, established around the periphery of the others, testifying to the growth of the village. The hut Ruth had shared with Vivian on the dunes was gone, as was the vegetable garden, but the ocean, of course, was right where she'd left it. A Club Med had even sprouted down the beach, a few kilometers from where she'd lived.

When the people in the village saw the toubabs, they immediately ran for the Peace Corps Volunteer currently living there, thinking they'd know each other. The volunteer gave the Talbots a grand tour of the village, explaining where the various families Ruth remembered were now living.

Ruth had brought along a picture of her twenty-two-year-old self in front of her hut, thinking it might come in handy if no one recognized her. She referred to it as a picture of "Baby Ruth," but she'd never needed to show it. She'd also brought presents: for the adults, framed photos from her time in the village along with zip-lock baggies; for the kids, crayons and pencils and notebooks.

The volunteer explained that there was no longer a vegetable garden because the village had grown sufficiently for there to be a nearby market where vegetables were sold. The villagers used the money they got from selling their rice and fish to buy vegetables at the market.

"So they're eating vegetables?" Ruth asked.

"Of course. Why wouldn't they?"

Before leaving, they took hundreds of pictures. There was the village and the villagers. There were the Talbots in the village and with the villagers. And there was the photo of Ruth holding her "Baby Ruth" photo.

LOOKING AT THE AGENCY'S SPREAD, Ruth-the-Marketing-Executive conjured up that photo of "Married Ruth Holding Baby Ruth." She remembered when she'd first seen it, all she saw was how she'd aged. She wondered if she'd be kinder to herself now, after having learned to appreciate an older woman's kind of beauty from the agency's photos. Or would she still hate the photo, maybe even more than when she'd first seen it?

She called the agency and told them she loved the spread and specified which pictures she liked best. Then she went to the Packaging Department to talk about some of their recent samples of bottles, pumps, and cartons. Back in her office, she started constructing a flow chart of the process: packaging, advertising, media selection, retail outlets, the whole enchilada.

She left work at four-thirty, the earliest she'd left in a long time.

27
It Is About Me

DAVID WAS READING THE PAPER when she got home, with a glass of red wine next to him and Bach's cello suites on the CD player. "Hey, you're home early. Nice surprise."

"I have to find something." She ran upstairs to their main storage closet. Locating the suitcase where they kept all the photos that didn't make it into the albums or onto the wall, she lugged it downstairs, set it on the table and opened it.

Explaining to David what she was looking for, he joined her and they started sifting through it. After a few distractions, all of which started with "Remember this one, when we ... ?" Ruth found it and took a long hard look.

"Why did this picture get buried in the suitcase? It's a great picture. I love this picture. Married Me holding Baby Me. It's great."

"You didn't think it was so great at the time, as I recall. Looking older, etcetera etcetera."

"I was so wrong, David."

Still holding the photo, she went downstairs and over to the couch, folded her knees and let gravity take her down. David sat next to her with the newspaper. She took off her shoes and extended her feet into his lap, wiggling her toes and crumpling the paper.

"Okay, okay, I get it." As he rubbed her feet, she told him about her day at work and he told her about his.

Ruth asked him what he thought about the ad campaign.

"It's good."

"Good-plus or good-minus?"

"You're being pretty demanding, especially for someone who's getting a foot rub."

"You're right. I'll shut up if you keep rubbing."

"It's actually kind of perfect."

"Perfect, you say?"

"It's not the end of the world to get older. Badda bing, badda bam."

With all her research and analysis, that's what he reduced it to? "Isn't that a little simplistic?"

"Simple, maybe, but not simplistic. A lot of wisdom is simple. Look at 'You can't always get what you want.' Or 'E=mc squared.' Or 'It's the economy, stupid.'"

"It's just that—ow, be careful with that big toe on my right foot—it's just that it's also about demographic segments and societal influences and … you know, stuff like that."

"I'm just boiling it down is all."

"Whatever you say. Just keep rubbing and I'll be your best friend."

After a while, the rubbing became softer, less concerned with relieving tired muscles than with tracing outlines. Ruth understood David's unspoken invitation and sent her RSVP; instead of brusque movements pushing her foot into David's hands and indicating "Continue the foot rub please," her gentle reciprocity said "yes."

David threw the cushions from the back of the couch on the floor and they lay down together, facing each other. They kissed slowly, and she gave her full attention to David's lower lip. It was full and expressive, soft, and she explored it with her tongue. He gave himself over to her exploration until, inevitably, the kissing accelerated.

David took the lead in undressing, first himself, quickly. Then her, not so quickly.

"Wish I'd known to wear my nice underwear," Ruth said.

"I'd just have to be a little more careful about taking it off," he said as he slowly slid her white cotton panties down to her knees. He stood up very slowly and took her legs out of their white cotton handcuffs, kissing the inside of each ankle as he did so. He drew the curtains and retrieved his wine glass. He took a sip, then got back down and offered it to Ruth. He removed Ruth's remaining article of clothing, her watch.

Later, David cooked dinner while Ruth took a bath. After dinner, they watched a movie on TV, then read for awhile, she a woman's magazine in which she saw three photos of inside-out sweaters, he the ever-present stack of papers to grade.

When they went to bed, Ruth expected to be able to fall asleep quickly, what with feeling loved, with her belly full of food and wine and her body smelling of lavender bath-oil. But, instead, her mind returned to the end of last night's Brain Trust meeting, after the discussion of envy. Blanche had asked for the group's wisdom about a problem employee, whom everyone agreed she should fire even though they knew that was the answer Blanche was hoping to avoid.

Then Ruth had asked for a sounding board. "I'm not looking for an answer, just some help thinking something through."

"Of course. That's what we do. That's why we're called women," Sarah said.

"Besides, it will be a relief to talk about your problems instead of mine," Blanche said.

"Is it the middle-aged makeup thing?"

"Sort of. The project itself is going along fine. More politics than usual, and that part's horrible, but that's not really the problem. I don't think."

"What's the problem?"

The problem, as she explained it, was her inability to get excited about the project. She'd thought she would be on fire and, instead, was lukewarm. When she wasn't having a hot flash.

"I can't help seeing the way I feel about my work now and comparing it to the way I felt when I was a Peace Corps Volunteer. Back then I just felt so very alive."

"So young?" Jane said.

"It *was* great to be young. Although, of course, I never realized it. But it was more than that. I thought I was doing something worthwhile. Looking back, I don't know if my work there really was worthwhile. But I felt like I was making a difference, whether I was or not."

"Ruth, you've been working at Mimosa for a long time. Why is this such a crisis?"

"I don't know. Is it part of some clichéd middle-aged angst? Or is it just part of getting older that you don't feel passionate about stuff anymore?"

There was no answer. Was that her answer?

Then Ruth told them about the new business she was thinking of leaving Mimosa to start. On the one hand, she thought maybe it was stupid to throw away a good career for an idea that might be half-baked. On the other, she thought if she stayed she might regret it later on.

Blanche volunteered to tell her how difficult it was to run a small business. It was a coin-toss whether it was worse dealing with employees or customers.

Sarah's voice let everyone know to get out of her way, when she said, "What I see is a talented, healthy, affluent woman trying to decide between safety and excitement. I think you're damned lucky to have those two choices and you should just choose one. You've been talking about leaving for years now. Frankly, I never really thought you meant it, thought you were just playing with yourself. Now you sound like maybe you do mean it. So enough about self-actualization and authenticity and passion in middle age and doing something worthwhile. You're stuck and you're floundering and the only way to get unstuck is to just pick one or the other. I say this with only the greatest of love and respect, you understand."

No one spoke. Some looked at Sarah, some at Ruth.

Sarah continued. "Look, there's no one right answer. Life is not a Chapter Quiz, trying to get it just right. Just do one or the other. So you're not frozen anymore."

"You know, Sarah," Jane said, "we can't all be—"

"No, it's okay, really," Ruth said. "I asked. I'm listening."

"It's late and we should wrap up soon," Blanche said, "so I'll be brief. I think you should stay at Mimosa. Because you might find that you wouldn't be excited by the new venture just like you weren't excited by About Face. And then you'd regret having left. And also because running a small business is, in my opinion, anything but exciting."

"Not me," Jane said. "I think you should jump ship. If the new business doesn't work out, like Blanche says, you'll be in a different place and something else will present itself."

"Well, I remember that Ruth said she's not really looking for us to solve her problem for her," Maria said, "so I won't vote. But I will say that I sort of agree with Sarah, that either one is fine. It's the not-deciding that's making you miserable. Flip a coin. Do plusses and minuses. Consult a psychic."

DAVID WAS UP and drinking his second cup of coffee by the time Ruth got out of bed and went down to the kitchen. She gave him the look that said, "Don't-even-think-about-talking-to-me-before-I've-had-some-coffee," grabbed a steaming mug with a pinch of sugar and a splash of milk, and shuffled into the living room in her own isolation bubble.

She flipped through the local paper. The floats for the Memorial Day parade were proceeding. Larry's was having a sale. Taxes were going up. The photo of the little league team on page three caught her attention. The smiles on the kids' faces were irresistible. She especially liked one little girl in the second row who had clearly been visited by the tooth fairy recently. More than once. Adorable.

The leaves on the maple tree behind the kids were filling out, becoming round and protective. The kids fit under it perfectly, as if the tree were cradling them. And she realized she'd dreamed about the autumn tree on the vest Charlie had been wearing at The Brain Trust's meeting. The tree had been like a jigsaw puzzle, a big one, 1,000 pieces or so, with lots of straight edges that made it difficult to assemble. But when the pieces were put together, the tree wasn't a jigsaw puzzle any more, nor Charlie's vest, it was a real tree.

What was it about that tree? It was colorful and beautiful and somehow a jigsaw puzzle and a vest and a real tree all at once. Wait, that was it: It had virtually all its brilliant leaves, making it a fanfare of color, but it also had mounds of dry leaves around it, as if they'd fallen a few weeks before. They were raked into piles, smelling crisp and earthy, the kind of piles you'd want to jump into.

She stretched, leaned back, and looked out the window while she tried to think how this dream-fragment might relate to her life. The sky was a soft dusty blue, outdone by the intensely red leaves of the cherry tree in their yard. Without warning, a nest-building bird flew right into the window with a loud smash, then plopped to the ground.

David came in from the kitchen, mug in hand. "What was that? Are you okay?"

"It was a bird," Ruth managed to whisper. "It just flew right at me. Like it was aiming."

He went outside, took a quick look, and came back. "It's dead, honey. Broken neck, I think."

"Let's wait and see if it comes back to life?" she suggested.

With previous bird-crashes, the victims sometimes only imitated death, stunned and still for a few minutes before flying away. But not this time. A minute ago, that bird was building a nest. Now it was dead.

It was like a speeded-up stop-action version of her mother's dying, five years before, with little warning. But the bird episode, so compressed in time, was starker.

Ruth's sobs were as unexpected as they were uncontrollable. David held her gently until the grief passed. As soon as it did, she looked at David with her mouth open, her brow wrinkled tightly, as if she were going to ask a question, and said "Ohmygod, I got it."

"What?"

"The bird. The dream. And the campaign. And what you said. I got it. It's been staring me in the face all along."

"Look, maybe you—"

"It's about me. I know, I know, not everything is about me, but this is. Not a demographic slice of the country. Not society and its pressures. Me. Like you said. Imagine that. Where has my brain been?"

"Like I said?" He offered a dry sleeve.

"You said it was about it being okay to get older. And it was myself I was talking to."

Her parents' deaths, her uncooperative body with its hot flashes, its aches, and the emerging road map on her face, her fear of an aimless retirement, it was all weighing her down. She no longer had an infinite number of possibilities for the future. There would be fewer new chapters and more chapters closing. It had all snuck up on her when she wasn't paying attention. She'd been struggling mightily against it, like trying to hold back the waves at the beach.

The dream-tree, too. Even though the tree's cycle was nearing its end, with dead leaves at the base, it was at its most beautiful. Of course.

That's what it was, her very own struggle with decay and death. She was simultaneously glad to have finally realized this and sheepish that it took her so long.

"How come I never realized this before? Did you know?"

"Kind of. Well, I suspected. But I didn't exactly know."

"Why didn't you say so?"

"I thought I did."

PART V

28
Lying Outside the Box

IT TOOK A LOT OF HARD WORK OVER THE SUMMER and all her relationship skills—not to mention the IOUs she'd built up over the years—but Ruth was able to mobilize the troops to get About Face up and running for the September launches. September had been her target. It always felt like a beginning: New school year, crisp air, new books, new clothes. New product line. New way of looking at middle aged women. At herself. And this year, a new life for David.

The preliminary sales figures were so good it was a little unnerving and she cautioned herself not to project them into the future. Preliminary results didn't always tell the whole story, people could be excited about something new but then lose interest.

She remembered reciting this same party line to Jeremy, but in the opposite direction, when she'd told him not to project the "perfectly decent" Lipsticks & Scarves results into the future, explaining that they could get much better. Of course, if she'd known how he was going to tinker with that campaign—so much for "looking over her shoulder"—she might have joined him in his pessimism. She'd tried to advise him that the advertising was condescending and the price was too high for the size of the product, considering herself a saint for doing so.

"Jeremy, marketing cosmetics to women is different from the kinds of marketing that went on at B&D. Those were different kinds of products with different kinds of appeals. Also, the demographic—"

"I know what I'm doing. I've studied the numbers. It will be fine."

As it turned out, the product did all right. Not as well as it would have done, she was sure, if she'd made the decisions. But, she had to admit, not as poorly as she'd have predicted. Perhaps they both learned a little? Nah, probably not.

Meanwhile, even though she managed not to broad-jump to grandiose conclusions based on About Face's preliminary sales figures, it was hard to ignore the growing word-of-mouth. Buzz was even better than sales, at least at first. It seemed to be one of those ideas that captured the right idea at the right time, and people were talking about it. And not just middle-aged people. That was the best part.

Yes, AARP loved it, and so did the late-night TV shows watched only by insomniacs. But mainstream media were also paying attention to About Face, and to Mimosa, now seen as a forward-thinking, progressive-minded, avant-garde kind of company. It was getting a little heady, never mind the pun. She was keeping a low profile for now, and was gracious whenever one of her colleagues congratulated her. "It's a team effort," she'd say. Or "You win some, you lose some." All the while, she knew her moment in the sun was coming.

It was the kind of beautiful day that autumn brings. David had his Thursday evening golf dinner. She'd planned to have dinner with Josh, but he'd cancelled in favor of taking care of a sick girlfriend. On the spur of the moment, she decided to go to the meeting of the Cosmetics Association of America. Maybe she just wanted to be with other people who did the same kind of work she did so she could feel good about her successes. Maybe she was expecting a few pats on the back. And the program didn't look too-too boring.

She called Jeremy to see if he was going and to let him know she was finally going to be a good corporate citizen. She'd also tell him that if he was going only to show the Mimosa flag, he didn't need to because she'd show it. She hoped, when she didn't get through, it didn't mean she was going to have to hang out with him at the meeting.

Two buses later, she entered the meeting a few minutes late and realized almost immediately she'd been crazy to think this meeting wouldn't be boring. Now she remembered why she never went. Thank goodness she got a seat near the back and could slip out easily. She'd miss the post-speech networking, but it was worth it.

"Folks, I'd like to take a very short departure from our program," the moderator said, "and just bring up to the stage for a quick hello the man behind some of the current cosmetics marketing headlines—hahaha—the product line people are starting to talk about. And buy for their mothers."

Laughter.

"Jeremy, come on up here."

Applause.

"Let's all give a hand to Jeremy Crater, the man who took over at Mimosa and very quickly put middle-aged women on the map with About Face."

So much for the meeting being boring. Was she really hearing this? The man who put middle-aged women on the map?

"Thanks, Stan. I appreciate the kind words. But, you know, it wasn't *me* who put middle-aged women on the map."

Good boy, she thought. Give credit to the folks behind you, under you, around you. Not only is it truer-than-true, and the right thing to do, being humble looks good.

"No, they've been there all along. I just made them a little prettier."

Were people really laughing at this stuff?

"No, actually, even *that's* not true." And with a serious, sanctimonious voice, he continued. "They've actually been pretty all along; I just helped people understand the way in which they're pretty. If you know what I mean."

Ooohs and aaahhs.

He's got to say something about the team behind him. Everyone does. Doesn't he know that?

"So, Jeremy, tell us. What does it feel like to have nudged an existing paradigm aside a little bit to make room for another one? The Holy Grail of any consumer product."

"I just want to tell you all that, when things are … are revolutionary and … when they're the result of thinking outside the box, if you will, like … like wheels on luggage—now didn't *that* change everything?—or like About Face … there are always nay-sayers. Yes, nay-sayers all over. About every detail. Even the name of the product. But you need to stick to your guns if you know you're right, like I did. And you'll get here too. Thank you."

Ruth needed air. She snuck out, knowing there was an advantage to knowing what Jeremy had said without his knowing she knew. She didn't know yet how she'd be able to use the advantage, but she knew she surely was going to use it somehow. The gloves were now officially off.

Next morning, she got to the office early so she could work on the article she'd long since promised the editor of "Mimosa's Faces," the company organ. Projects of more urgency or interest had kept her from doing more than an outline and very rough draft, but now she knew exactly the way to revise it. It would use About Face as a case study of the evolution of a new product line, culminating in its marketing challenges. At 9:10 she called Phoebe.

"Ruth, I haven't seen you for ages. And congratulations on About Face, by the way. Don't tell me you're calling to say you won't write that article after all, are you?"

"Thanks for the congratulations, I have a great team behind me. And no, not at all. I'm going to ask a favor. A different kind of favor."

Ruth asked if Phoebe could run the article sooner than the date they'd agreed upon, some three weeks away. Phoebe said she'd have done it anyway but, as it turned out, she was ecstatic because,

"Someone didn't make their deadline. I won't mention names, but the initials are Joan Robinson. I know, it happens all the time. But it's aggravating all the time."

"I'll bring it right up."

"You mean *now*?"

"Now."

"Ruth, you are an angel."

"So are you."

"Whatever you say."

Next, she called Artie Conover, David's childhood friend. As one of the editors of the weekly trade publication The American Cosmetics Journal, he'd always been after something interesting from Ruth—though she understood that something juicy would be even better. She told him she'd written a piece for her company newsletter on the subject of About Face—how the idea arose, how it was developed, and the marketing challenges it presented. She wondered if he'd be interested in it? He asked her to send it right over. But he made no promises.

Then she gathered her papers with her article and called Jeremy to say she'd be stopping by in about twenty minutes. He wanted to know how much time she'd need. When she said she wasn't sure, it could be anywhere from ten minutes to an hour, he asked her to speak to his secretary to "put herself on his calendar."

"This time, Jeremy, it needs to be now. Do you think you'll be there in twenty minutes?"

"It's not a question of whether I will or won't be here. I'm in the middle of something important. I can't possibly—"

"I'm sorry to break into your day this way. And I know it's not the way you usually do things, and ordinarily I'd be happy to oblige, but, believe me, you'll want to make an exception in this case."

Twenty minutes later, as promised, she walked into his office with every one of her sixty-two inches at its stretching point.

"Hi, Jeremy, sorry about the interruption." Not really, she thought.

He barely looked up. "Yes. What's so important?"

"About Face is doing well, so far, don't you think? I know we can't project sales figures so early, but so far, so good."

"Yes, yes. So far so good. Surely that's not why you came up here?"

She asked if he remembered the memo she'd written him a few months ago.

"What memo?"

She'd hoped he'd say that. She reminded him it was the one where she'd promised to take responsibility if it were a flop. The one where she appreciated his confidence in her judgment.

She didn't wait for an invitation to sit.

"No, I don't. But what's this got to do with anything?"

"I heard your gracious speech at the CAA meeting last night."

"Oh, that. You were there? I didn't see you. I thought you didn't go to those things."

"I saw you. And I heard you."

"Is that what this is all about?" He smiled, and this time it lasted more than a millisecond, probably because it was a smile for himself, not for an audience.

She was surprised he'd taken credit the way he did. She was about to explain all the reasons the world at large should think of Mimosa as an integrated team, when his condescending smile did its disappearing act.

"What?"

"I especially loved the part about the nay-sayers. And the paradigm. Like wheels on luggage. I wouldn't have expected you to give me credit by name, but there is the part about, 'I had a whole team behind me, some very talented people, blahblahblah.' You forgot that part of the speech."

She knew scolding a CEO who already didn't much care for her was dicey. Maybe it was that smile-imitation that tipped her over.

He folded his hands like a principal addressing a naughty

child. Being CEO, he explained, meant he was the public face of the company. It's not important who gets credit for things. It wasn't important at B&D and it isn't here. It's all for the company. That's what being a team means.

"Now, no more hysterics, no more temper tantrums. It's not personal, it's business. I'd have thought you'd know the difference by now."

"Maybe it was different at B&D, but here at Mimosa, the personal and the business are on speaking terms with each other. This is a very different culture."

"Things are much more complicated than that. It may not be evident to you, but I can assure you, this is one of those complex situations where there's a lot going on under the surface and behind the scenes."

"No, things aren't always so complicated. This one's simple. Give credit to the team. It's good for them. It's good for you. And it's true. Believe me."

Didn't he know it was his turn to speak? Was he trying to figure out what to say? And did it have to do with firing her? Let him just try.

"Besides," she continued, everyone here knows About Face is my baby."

"Fine. So you do get the credit you want."

"Jeremy, you're forgetting that memo."

"Ruth, my dear. Anyone with half a brain can write a memo and back-date it. Take my advice and forget this whole thing. And I will try to forget this interchange, though I can't be sure I'll be able to."

"Funny how things work. In a funny quirk of timing, next week's newsletter has an article about us. It's all about the process of developing the idea behind About Face."

Jeremy's phone rang. He picked it up before the first ring had finished. "Yes."

A few tongue-darts while he listened.

"I'll call him back. I know, but tell him I'll call in the next hour or so."

He wrote something down on a green sticky note, then looked up, semi-vacantly. When his eyes came back into focus, he said "Right, the newsletter. Right. Well, you're right. Everyone here knows what an important role you played. And anyway, people here are not the point. It's people out there"—he gestured stiffly outside his window—"who count."

"You'd be surprised." She got up to leave. When she got near the door, she hesitated, then turned back and added, "Did I ever tell you the editor of The American Cosmetics Journal is a friend? Not a professional friend, a personal friend. The article that appears in the newsletter will be lengthened, lots of quotes from all the members of my team—Tom, Judy, even Pat who originally didn't like the project so much but seems to have come around these days—and photos, and it will be in The American Cosmetics Journal. In the next week or two."

He asked Ruth to come back in. He asked her to take a deep breath, demonstrating how.

"Maybe I *should* have mentioned you last night. My wife tells me.... Well, anyway, let's just say we're clear. We understand each other. I didn't realize you were so sensitive about getting credit for things." Tongue-dart, right on schedule.

She hated how the word "sensitive" was always used by a man about a woman. When the woman was criticizing him for something. Something he deserved to be criticized for. To belittle her anger. This is how he was calming her down? Try again, Jeremy.

"*I* come up with a great idea, *I* champion it, *I* overcome your objections, *I* put myself out on a limb, then *you* say you did it all. How did you put it again? You thought outside the box and held onto your convictions? In spite of all those nay-sayers? And when I call you on it, you call that being sensitive?"

"Nonetheless, I don't think The American Cosmetics Journal is a good idea. The house newsletter, well, all right if you really … if you really want to, but … Ruth, I insist that you not publish that article."

Oh really? she thought. Insist? She was starting to enjoy herself.

"Maybe there's something I can do for you in return?" he said.

"For starters, I'd like to have 100% of Colleen back."

"Oh that. I'd already decided to—"

"And I'll think about what else." She thought maybe she'd gone too far, but when he didn't answer, she knew she hadn't. She turned on her heel and strode out, straightening one of the pictures on the wall on her way.

All she had to do now was make sure Artie ran the piece. On its own merits or as a favor to her, she didn't care which. He just had to run it.

29

The Personal is Professional

"AFTER ALL THESE YEARS, YOU STILL EXPECT ME to be on time?" A red-faced Vivian approached the steps of the Metropolitan Museum, where Ruth had been enjoying the people-watching while she waited.

"I don't know that I actually expect it. Hope, maybe?" She looked at her wrist only to realize she'd been in such a rush she'd forgotten to put her watch on after her shower. "But even if I knew you'd be late, what would I do, be intentionally late? It would make me crazy having to figure out how late is really late and how late is okay-late?"

"Your brain is very complicated, isn't it?"

"What time is it anyway?"

"Ten-fifteen," Vivian said. "I think. I'm actually not sure because the other day I thought my watch was running fast so I re-set it but now I think it might have been on time after all, it was just that my assistant at work was even later than me, so I—"

"Only fifteen minutes. Not bad. So here we both are. Wanna start again?"

"Hi Ruthie. Nice outfit."

"Hi Viv. Thanks. You too."

They were both wearing a black sweater with black slacks for their Saturday girls' outing, though Vivian's pants had a gusset that provided comfort as well as flattering an ample body. She also wore a turquoise-and-silver necklace and wildly colorful shoes, while Ruth had on a blue-and-green scarf and black flats.

"Let's go in." Vivian hooked her arm in Ruth's as they started in.

Vivian asked Ruth where she wanted to go first. Arts of Africa/Oceania/Americas? For old times' sake? Or the Eygyptian Art, except that's what she'd done the last time she visited. She narrowed her choices down to European Paintings, Greek and Roman Art, or Modern Art. Or maybe Islamic Art. She asked Ruth to choose.

Ruth reached into the outer compartment of her purse for an article she'd clipped years ago and located the day before, "The Highlights of the Metropolitan Museum of Art in Only an Hour."

"A cheat sheet? You want to use a cheat sheet? To go to the museum and look at art? Are you serious? Ruthie, a museum is for pleasure, to look at beautiful things, or maybe they're not beautiful, they're just intellectually stimulating, or maybe they're beautiful *and* intellectually stimulating, but anyway they're supposed to be something you *want* to do, not something you *have* to do, not something you want to get through as fast and as efficiently as possible, like reading a summary of War and Peace before the test."

Ruth's defense—she didn't get to come to the museum very often, she wanted to make the most of her visit, and if someone else had evaluated it for her ahead of time, so much the better—was logical, she knew, but she also knew logic wasn't all there was to it. She felt every molecule inside her start to shrink away from her skin, into a ball.

Vivian didn't get to the museum very often, either, but figured that whatever she got to see would just be what she got to see. If she didn't see every single work of art that someone else had previously decided was important, it didn't bother her.

"Part of the fun is the unpredictability. Otherwise I'd feel like I was back in school."

"I once did this at the Louvre and—"

"Don't sulk, Ruthie, please. I just can't do it that way. Maybe it is a good idea, after all, and I shouldn't have jumped down your throat. I'm sorry for that. But I just can't do it that way. Can we please do it my way? Less planned? Think of it as a spontaneity exercise. Wait, I wasn't making fun. I'm asking. Okay? Please?"

"Okay, but you know what this means." Ruth lowered her voice, both in pitch and volume, as she intentionally furrowed her brow.

"What?"

"It means I'm going to have to come back another day with my article to see the things we missed."

"Ruthie, I don't really think you—"

"I'm kidding." She cackled. "Lighten up, will you?"

Vivian did a Jeremy-type smile, then whirled her index finger in the air and brought it down on her museum map with her eyes closed. She looked at her finger's location and said, "How about if we go to European Paintings?"

Wending their way through the art proved easier than choosing their approach to the wending process. They wanted to spend the same amount of time in front of each painting. And they liked about the same amount of discussion. They even wanted lunch at the same time.

They found a Chinese restaurant; it was cheap, it was fast, it had a table available. As they sat down, Vivian said, "Remember the last time we had lunch in a Chinese restaurant?"

Guess she does remember after all, thought Ruth. But she's laughing about it. Laughing?

"I think so. It was when we had that fight, right? Well, actually, it wasn't really a fight. A fight is where two people argue. You just got mad at me and stormed out." Her voice betrayed her.

Vivian had been fiddling with her chopsticks, trying to get just the right fingers in just the right position. She looked up. Her laugh faded and she blinked a few times. "Don't tell me you're still mad at that. You sound like you're mad. No, you couldn't still be mad." She frowned. "Nobody could be mad this long. Could they?"

"It just always felt like you threw away our friendship more easily than I would have. As if it were a spur of the moment idea and didn't really matter to you all that much."

A waitress deposited a pot of tea on the table. In her high-pitched voice, she asked, "I take order, ladies?"

"Just about ready," Vivian said. "I'll have the Szechuan Chicken, and no MSG please."

"Very good, miss."

"Me too," Ruth said. "The same."

"Now that you say it, I guess I can see how it would look that way. But it's just where we were at, at the time. We were in different places."

"I don't want to fight about it again, but—"

"It's like looking at art. All those paintings we just looked at, don't people evaluate them in their historical context? 'Cause otherwise, if it's about the composition or the color or the draftsmanship, then if someone painted the Mona Lisa today, would it be just as famous? You know what I mean? It's just that what I'm trying to say is that the other stuff going on in our lives when we fought is important."

"You didn't seem to think that at the time. It was more like 'I'm right, you're wrong, get out of my life.'"

"Maybe I wasn't so nice about it, but I didn't think it through ahead of time. And, anyway, would it have hurt less if I'd broken up with you all rational and polite?"

Ruth had never thought about it that way. Was it the break up itself or the anger, the lack of respect?

"I'm sorry I hurt your feelings, Ruthie. I knew at the time I had, but it's just the the way it was. And…."

"Yes?"

"And I'm glad we've made up."

"Me too."

They waited for the waitress to arrange the food.

"While we're on the subject of working things out, I need to talk about some clothing business stuff," Ruth said.

"Good. Shoot."

Ruth told Vivian that she was continuing to think about it, doing some figuring and planning and conceptualizing. She wanted to go over some of the numbers she'd come up with. But mostly she wanted to talk about some as-yet-undiscussed issues.

Vivian kept eating and nodding during Ruth's little speech. But as soon as Ruth was done, she said she never really understood *why* Ruth was thinking about starting this business. With all the money she and David must have, and with Ruth having such fun with the old-lady makeup thing, she needed to know if this was just a passing fancy. Which would quickly pass?

"And, anyway, aren't we too old to be starting something new?"

Ruth moved her chair back a few inches. "I guess that's exactly the point. The age thing, I mean."

Ruth described her recent epiphany about her own aging and the forces that seemed to be closing in on her—menopause, David's retirement, her desire to do something more worthwhile than selling makeup. She wanted to find the way to accept aging without necessarily giving into it. And she thought that, for her, the clothing business was the fine line between acceptance and surrender.

She knew making clothes wouldn't be the same kind of "doing good" Vivian did at work, but it would do enough good for her, especially with the charitable giving.

"I've been thinking about it more and more, too," Vivian said.

"You have? A business thing? Capitalism and all that?"

"Are you making fun?"

"No, really, I swear."

"Don't make fun. This is hard enough as is. You have no idea how hard."

"What's hard?"

"I can't believe this is happening in a Chinese restaurant again but … "

"You and Carlos aren't splitting up?"

"It's not that bad. At least I don't think it's that bad, but we'll see what you think."

"My God, Vivian, what is it?"

"I need to clear up some issues, some personality issues, I guess you'd call them."

"I want to talk about that too." What a relief. Ruth had been worrying about broaching the topic of Carlos. Would she say he was volatile? Or prickly? No, too many puns with that one. How about strong-willed? Or provocative? No, she was going to have to go with the truth, that he was a pain in the ass. But Vivian was going to talk about it first. Hallelujah. Ruth didn't need to be so nervous after all.

"You do?" Vivian clipped her hair behind her neck, exposing sweaty armpits but not any self-consciousness about them.

"You're not surprised, are you? I mean, Carlos and I don't exactly get along like you'd think of business partners getting along. I'm sure Fisher and Price, or Pitney and Bowes, or, let's see, who else, Sears and Roebuck had a better—"

"Enough. You and Carlos?"

"Of course. Me and Carlos. Isn't that what you meant?"

"No, not at all. It's…."

Vivian's search for the right way to begin seemed to take an hour. Ruth didn't know if it was the silence or the unusual damming of Vivian's stream of consciousness that was more worrisome. Everyone else in the restaurant conspired to be particularly quiet at that moment; no voices, no glasses clinking, no plates clattering.

When Vivian finally launched into an opening with some traction, it was about David. She had a big problem with David's always being so unruffled, as if he were surfing above the emotional undertow. It was dishonest.

"It's not like I have anything against being rational, some of my best friends are even rational. But rational all the time is something else, something kinda abnormal. No one can really be so unconflicted, no one's glass can always be half full, it's just not natural, so I figure this Mr. Nice Guy stuff must be an act and I hate acts. You hate conflict, I hate acting because you just don't know what's real and what's part of the act, so you don't know what's what and that feels dangerous to me. And to Carlos."

"Dangerous? He's just an easy-going guy with an even keel. A very even keel. He's always been that way."

"I don't think anyone's keel is really quite so even."

"If this weren't so amazing to me, it would be funny," Ruth said.

"Ha-ha funny? Strange funny? What?"

"Well, both really."

Ruth told Vivian how she'd been dreading talking about her own misgivings at the idea of working with Carlos. And for the opposite reasons: you always knew what Carlos was thinking and feeling, and it was usually negative. Unless you agreed with him 100%. Ruth didn't think she could stand up to the bullying on an on-going basis.

"He's gotten a lot better. If you'd seen him—"

"I know. He's even gotten better since that brunch at your house. But better than terrible is still not so great."

They briefly toyed with the idea of the two women doing it by themselves. In the end, though, Vivian said she just couldn't do it that way. She looked at the ceiling, at the floor, at the walls—everywhere, in fact, but at Ruth—as she explained that if Carlos weren't involved, he'd make her life miserable for being in a business. Things were tricky enough between them without adding this additional strain to the mix.

Vivian suggested she and Ruth and Carlos do it without David, since he didn't seem to want to un-retire, anyway. Ruth refused, though she knew it just might work. For one thing, she knew he'd want to come to some of the business meetings, if only to hang out with friends. She was not, absolutely not, going to tell him he couldn't. She also knew, though she didn't say it, she needed David as a buffer between her and Carlos.

"What do we do now? Just forget the whole thing?" Ruth asked.

The waitress's sing-song voice came out of nowhere. "I can take plates, ladies? You finish?" She started gathering the dishes. "You want dessert? We got kumquats, we got ice cream, we got—"

"We're finished," Vivian said and got up to pay.

Ruth didn't know if Vivian was talking to the waitress or to her.

30
Working it Out

TEN DAYS LATER, THE AMERICAN COSMETICS JOURNAL printed an edited version of Ruth's piece, but with a twist. An editor had been at the ACA meeting when Jeremy took credit for developing About Face. Noticing the discrepancy between Jeremy's account and Ruth's article, he wrote a sidebar about the internal conflict that can accompany success. He'd called Ruth before running the sidebar to see if she could give him a reason to pull it, like an inaccuracy or point of view he hadn't considered, but "No comment," was what she'd said at first, then just, "Run the sidebar, it's fine."

After the article appeared, she was called to Mark Bloom's office. He was now the Group President of B&D's Personal Care Products Division and, by all accounts, was happy as a Big Daddy, even though Personal Care was a small division. And he was doing a good job. She would have been glad to see him if it weren't for the circumstances.

She got there a little early, having even remembered to change out of her sneakers first. While she waited, she chatted with Mark's secretary, who warned her something was going on in there that involved words like "honor" and "team" at high volume. Uh-oh.

Mark's door opened, Jeremy emerged and walked by her without a word, a glance, or a faux-smile.

She braced herself and refrained from asking Mark how he liked his new job or how his family was. He launched the topic immediately: he was not happy about the article calling attention to B&D's little bit of dirty linen.

It was clear to him, he said, after being at his new job for about fifteen minutes, that B&D's corporate culture was quite different from Mimosa's. He'd expected it to be different, as anyone would. Jeremy's credit-stealing ploy was right out of the B&D playbook, nothing but 'business as usual' in his old position, so it was understandable in that context. But it was disappointing that he hadn't yet learned things were different at Mimosa. It wasn't rocket science. And he would need to learn it if he wanted to be a good leader.

Mark went on to praise her for the sterling job she'd done with About Face, referring obliquely to her long-term career path. He told her he thought B&D was an interesting and intellectually challenging place to work, if she should ever be interested. Down the road, that is.

Once upon a time, she would have been walking on air for weeks over her political success and the praise from the big boss. Now, though, it seemed to complicate matters. Retire? Become an entrepreneur? Move up the corporate ladder? Yikes.

When she got back to Mimosa's headquarters and emerged from the elevator on the eighteenth floor to confront the contrived white landscape and smelled the floral "Toujours Mon Amour," it struck her. She was winning her battles, yes—things were going pretty well with About Face, with Pat, and she was even beating Jeremy out at office politics—but maybe winning wasn't so important if she was playing the wrong game. Validation, yes. Happiness, no.

She thought of the activist and the investment banker she'd met at a community awards presentation a year or so ago. The activist had said, "I don't have much money, but I sure have a lot of fun." The investment banker said wistfully, "Funny, with me it's exactly the opposite."

She went to her office and located the green "Clothing Business with V & C" folder, remembering and mourning the exciting fantasies it had unleashed. She flipped through the many "Plusses and Minuses" lists, trying to soothe herself by concentrating on the minuses.

And then she noticed a pattern. There were six plusses-and-minuses lists, each written about a week after the previous one. When she looked at them in order, she saw that each one had more plusses and fewer minuses than the last. From time to time, she'd broken down a "plus" item from one list into two smaller "plusses" on the next. That's how the plus list got longer.

"Doing Good" became: "Changing perceptions about how women are supposed to look," and "Helping women feel better about themselves." The latter became, in an iteration two weeks later, "Helping women feel comfortable in their skin" and "Giving women confidence to walk down the street and just be themselves," which later became further divided.

Likewise, she'd occasionally combined two details that were in the "Minus" column so that they were one, making that list shorter. "Financial risk" and "Long hours of entrepreneurship" became combined into "Life will change dramatically."

She'd always thought her Plus/Minus lists sprung entirely from her left brain, but this time something else had gone on. Like a Ouija board? Something inside her *knew* she wanted to do this business, knew she wanted the Plusses to outnumber the Minuses, and made it happen.

I don't know much about intuition but I know it when I see it, she thought. Now she knew why people made such a big deal about it.

That's why she was so unexcited when Jeremy gave the go-ahead for About Face. It was her intuition, overruling all the plusses and minuses, dampening false enthusiasm, begging to be heard. It just took her a little while to open her ears. Or whatever part of the body hears intuition.

She crumpled and discarded her lists, breathless with a cocktail of fear and excitement at the thought of leaving what had always grounded her so she could take a chance on soaring. Like those crazy hang-gliders she'd once seen step off a cliff at a restaurant in France.

Before she had a chance to think about it, she called Vivian at work.

"Viv, let's get together on Saturday. Or Sunday. Or Friday night. Or any night. Let's work it out. The personality thing. We can work it out, I know we can. I really want to do this. Don't you?

"Yes."

VIVIAN AND CARLOS OPENED the door together. They didn't say much, but their abundant marital eye contact was either conveying a secret message or enabling them to avoid eye contact with Ruth and David. Vivian wasn't struggling to get her words out fast enough to dump the contents of her speeding brain. Carlos's reticence, on the other hand, wasn't newsworthy but had a grumpy overlay.

When they were settled, Vivian said, "So you've come here today, or rather we're all here today, to talk about, well, about getting along is I guess what you could say is what we're here to talk about. I guess. And thanks for coming over." She lifted her frizzy hair off her neck, holding it with her left hand while she fanned her neck with her right. She put on some music by Dr. John.

Ruth said, "Maybe we can start by nailing down a little more precisely what we want to accomplish. Sometimes framing the question in the right way can help you come up with the answer?" She uncapped her pen and turned to a clean page on her legal pad.

"Very organized," Carlos said.

"Is that good or bad?" Ruth tried not to sound bitchy.

"It just feels kind of corporate. Like, man, do we need a flip chart? Should I change my clothes?"

Vivian said, "Give it a rest, Carlos. Don't you have meetings at work? Don't you decide what you want to talk about? Wake up. Get some caffeine in your system. Make an effort, here." She raised a mug to his mouth. He took it from her and drank with loud slurps.

Ruth tried again. "It's like Vivian said, that if we're going to think about working together, we need to know we can get along and make decisions together."

"Is getting along really the point? Anyway, I have an announcement." He got up in one motion from his cross-legged position on a pillow and turned up the volume of the music. He grabbed a wooden statuette, an African fertility symbol, and held it to his mouth like a microphone. Speaking in a public-announcement voice, he said, "I've decided I can't do this. Giving money away is very nice, muy bueno. But I can't be in a manufacturing business." He put the statue down and spoke in a normal voice to Vivian. "You want to do this, babe, fine, but count me out."

"Turn down the music. And no way it's gonna work for me to do it without you," Vivian said. "You'd come home from work and—"

"I can't believe you think—"

"I'm right, you know I'm right."

"Babe, you're just having one of your—"

"You're right, Carlos," Ruth said.

"About…?" Carlos said.

"About the business. But not the music. Turn it down, please." He did.

"You can't be involved in a manufacturing business. I know that. I've known it all along, really."

"You do surprise me, Ruthie. Mucho."

"Right. But you can be involved in a foundation, right?"

He didn't need to be involved in the business, she explained. In fact, it would be better if he weren't. She and Vivian would do that.

He'd have nothing to do with the design or manufacture or marketing of the clothes. He'd only be involved with the business's foundation.

"Why didn't I think of that?" Carlos crossed the room and resumed his cushioned cross-legged position. "This could work. Maybe. So maybe we don't have to talk about relationships?"

"Yes we do," Ruth and Vivian said simultaneously.

"It seems only right that I go first." David walked over to a newly-hung photo of the four of them in Africa and stared at it as if he were speaking to it, not them, as he told Vivian he knew what she'd said to Ruth about him. And it didn't bother him. He turned around and looked at her. "My feelings don't get hurt very easily."

Vivian shot back that his unhurt feelings were exactly what she was talking about. Some people might be relieved that he never got mad, but she thought it was more like he never got engaged with what was going on. Like he was above it all, looking down. Like he was hiding something. She went over to where he was standing, as if she were going to confront him nose-to-nose. Instead, she just took the photo from the wall and held it in her lap.

"If I am, then I'm hiding it from myself, too," David said. "Which, I admit, is a possibility. But not one I can do...."

"It's like Vivian says, man. You think you're above it all. Condescending."

"Maybe if I sat down and you stood up? Then I wouldn't be above it all? Sorry, not funny."

"Condescending? Carlos, you are the Emperor of Condescending," Ruth said. "Interesting that you don't like being condescended to. Neither do I."

"I have strong opinions, that's all. It's not condescending. You're just being adolescent about this."

"You don't think it's condescending to let everyone know that you're better and smarter and more moral than them? And holier, too. That's the *definition* of condescending." Her doodling got darker and more emphatic. More spirals, less geometric patterns.

He folded his arms. "Maybe I do think that what I'm saying is better. Everyone does. Or they wouldn't say it. I may not always be right, but I can't help it if I *think* I'm right. And, besides, I *am* right a lot of the time."

"This is good, guys, really good." Vivian filled everyone's coffee cup, then returned the photo to its spot on the wall.

"Well, babe, other than cheering us on as we argue, what do *you* think? I've never known you to be at a loss for words."

Vivian agreed that Carlos was condescending when he made like he was better than everyone. And David was condescending when he made like he was above it all. The two sides of the condescension coin: one doesn't get involved and the other gets too involved.

"I don't much like it either way, but when I don't like it, I don't sulk like you do, Ruthie, I push back." She punched the sofa pillow.

"I know, believe me I know."

"It's better to push back." Another punch for the pillow.

"It's not my way."

"You can force yourself." Carlos's tone was softer. "Like sticking your finger down your throat when you feel sick. Even if you don't want to, it feels better after."

"I don't think so. I am what I am."

Carlos stared at his empty mug as he said, "I know I'm sometimes argumentative. And other things." He put down the mug and caressed his bracelet. "But it's like what you just said. I am what I am. I'm here to give money away, punto. If we fight, we fight. We'll get over it."

"That doesn't work for me," Ruth said.

No one spoke for a moment.

"For example, Carlos," Ruth said softly, "I'm not completely okay about the little disagreement we had last time we were here."

"What disagreement?"

"About my being a capitalist on the backs of labor. That one."

"Really? But we made up," Carlos said.

"I guess we did. Partly. On the *what* part, but not the *how* part. When you say things in that way you have—like calling me adolescent a minute ago—it interferes with my hearing what you say. You may feel all made up. I don't. Punto, punto, the end."

Carlos cleared his throat and looked around. He said that until very recently, he would have said that was stupid. "'Black is black and white is white whether you say it with a smile or a temper tantrum' is what I would have said."

"But now…?" Ruth asked.

A few days before, he'd been confronted with the same "stupid"—finger-quotes let everyone know he was actually being self-aware—point of view at work. During a team-building role play exercise, he and his colleagues tried to reach consensus about a complicated decision. There, too, he'd antagonized the others so much they refused to listen to his opinions, which turned out to be largely correct. Even worse, some of their opinions, which he'd derided, were also correct.

"So all your wisdom was wasted," Ruth said.

Carlos turned towards her with his previous softness replaced by flint. "You mockin' me?"

"Hey, man, Ruth was just saying—"

"Don't do that. Ruthie fights her own battles pretty good. You want to fight, fight your own. Oh, but I forgot, you don't do that."

"I wasn't mocking you, Carlos. Just saying what I think you were saying, that you knew a lot but they didn't hear you," Ruth said. She wrote something on her pad.

Carlos offered to apologize to Ruth again for last time, if it would help. But he said, the softness once again in his voice and his face, he knew he might not have all the answers, but he was pretty much what he was. He wanted to give money away. He wasn't up for a personality transplant.

"You need to know I'm never going to be a Mr. Play By The Rules, a Mr. Reasonable Tone of Voice kind of guy like David."

She bit off the thumbnail it had taken three weeks of willpower to grow. Damn, she thought. She couldn't even muster an "Oh well."

"The truth is," David said. "I hate conflict. I even hate talking about conflict. But I guess I'd agree that if we're going to have it—"

"And we are," Ruth said.

"—then I'd want for it to come into the open, we deal with it, and it goes away. Quickly. And maybe …" He looked at Vivian. "Maybe I could be more open, too, more negative, if that's what being open turns out to be, if there were a way to pop the pimple, clean up the mess, and move on."

"I have an idea," Vivian said. "It's actually a great idea. It's your idea, Carlos, and it's brilliant."

"Why do I think I'm not going to like this, babe?"

Vivian explained that it wasn't the team-building role play exercise that had enlightened Carlos as much as the conversation afterwards. With the help of the facilitator, everyone had to talk about their experience during the role play, the good, the bad and the ugly. Not the content, the process. And everyone else had to listen to them. Not say anything, just listen. They called this kind of conversation an "exploration."

"The cool part was that when someone said I pissed her off, I didn't have to apologize. And people get pissed off for the stupidest reasons."

"But you had to listen," Vivian said.

"Sounds like conflict to me," David said.

"But you also got to find out about the stuff you do that people like," Vivian said in her chirpiest voice.

The women wanted to try an exploration-conversation, the men didn't. The women prevailed. They assured Carlos he wasn't being asked to change, they appealed to his sense of fairness and courage, and they reminded him it was all about giving money away. David had his own pimple-popping metaphor thrown back at him, with their confidence that this would do that.

Even though they were tired, they grabbed sandwiches and forced themselves to "explore" the meeting they'd just had while they ate, including hurts and annoyance and pride and all the other emotions in between. If one of them forgot the rules and started defending, another was quick with a reminder.

Carlos said he was beginning to understand what Ruth and others got so upset about, that she needed to be heard and understood, even if not agreed with. And Ruth understood that Carlos was the opposite, not caring about being understood or agreed with, as long as he got his say if not his way. They even rehashed the fight they'd had about their world views. Ruth was finally able to let go of it. David admitted to some misgivings about the things that had been said to him, which everyone took to be progress.

And they thought the "Exploration" format worked. Ruth liked having a mechanism that not only allowed her to express herself, it *mandated* it. David could stand dealing with the inevitable clashes, even some involving him, because it was quick and therapeutic. Carlos liked having his say and was willing to listen to others to get it.

Vivian said, "This feels like an emotional enema, guys. Sort of like going to the dentist, you know what I mean? Something that you know is good for you and you know you'll feel better once it's over, glad you did it and all, but still not something you particularly want to do."

"Way to mix your metaphors, babe."

31
Changing Patterns

SHORTLY AFTER THEIR EXPLORATION-CONVERSATION, RUTH announced to David and the Suarez's that, for her, the discussion was no longer hypothetical. The momentum shifted, as if everyone had been waiting for someone else to go first. The subtle change from "We *would* do this and that" to "We *will* do this and that" signaled more than a change from the conditional to the future tense.

From that point on, Ruth lived parallel lives, one planning an exciting future for the new business—"Changing Patterns" was the working name—and another going through the motions of a successful product line at Mimosa.

David still had no interest in working with a capital "W." It had nothing to do with the interpersonal issues. He was glad they'd worked it out, but he wanted to retire, period. "I want to be part of the group, go to meetings so you can't talk about me behind my back, I just don't want to work very hard." And Carlos, as evaluator of grant requests for charitable giving, would only work part-time.

It was official: Vivian and Ruth were the full-time honchos of Changing Patterns: Clothing that Fits and Flatters.

They were careful with money, but generous with capital letters: Vivian was the Vice President in Charge of Design and Production, in the Department of Making Clothes. Ruth was the Vice President of Marketing and Sales, in the Department of Making Money.

Carlos was the Vice President of the Department of Giving Money Away. They had no President.

"The 'giving money away' part will help me get over the 'Vice President' part. Me, a Vice President. Carramba."

"Get over yourself," Ruth said. "It doesn't make you a bad person. Or a good person, either, for that matter."

Ruth and Vivian would earn the same, Carlos would make one third of that, and an equal amount would go to the charities he proposed and all four decided upon. Whatever David did or didn't contribute would be free.

For the Talbots, Ruth's Changing Patterns salary plus David's pension would add up to about sixty percent of their previous income. They'd start drawing some investment income to boost it and make up the difference by cutting back on some expenses, especially their contributions to their retirement accounts. They were sure the decrease in money would be more than offset by the boost in zest.

Carlos would negotiate a four-day-a-week salary at the Prisoner's Rights Foundation. Adding his Changing Patterns salary to that meant he was getting a raise. Between the two Suarez's, the family income was now about the same as the Talbots', and was about 130% of what it had been.

David and Ruth decided to refinance their house for a start-up loan to Changing Patterns. The Small Business Administration also fast-tracked a loan, probably because the application came from two women, one with a Spanish name.

The BSW gave them space in their building in exchange for employing some of the residents. "They didn't realize we would have done that anyway," Vivian said. "So I didn't mention it. They're happy, we're happy."

The VP of Design and Production and the VP of Marketing and Sales spent a weekend assembling fabrics. Natural fabrics only, they decided immediately.

"It's true they wrinkle faster, but then they're wrinkled and you don't have to worry about whether they're going to wrinkle," Vivian said.

"Kind of like us."

With the cottons, linens, tencels, and wools they assembled—solids, prints, tapestries, even some African Kente cloth for old times' sake—they'd put together a few samples with elastic waists, hidden crotch-patches, pleats, raised waistlines, gores over the abdomen, strategically placed darts, a bit of forgiving spandex. Ruth had appointments with buyers from two major department stores. Two loans, two possible buyers, free rent. Changing Patterns was about to be off and running.

After choosing the business structure and clothing structure, the four met to discuss the as-yet-unearned money they'd be giving away. They unanimously decided to focus on women, though not just middle-aged women. They'd only give to projects they could visit in a day or less. "No overnight expenses for our puny budget," Carlos said. "That way, there's more to give."

"And this way we can all visit if we don't have to worry about hotels and plane fares," added Ruth.

Then they turned their attention to the mechanics of soliciting and evaluating grant proposals. Carlos knew a lot about this and managed to explain it without infuriating his friends. He spoke for about fifteen minutes, answered the occasional question, made more eye contact with everyone, didn't speak much Spanish. Even he recognized how much progress he'd made since the team-building exercise at work.

"So, are we done? Can we have lunch?" Vivian looked at her watch and stretched her arms above her head, then got up and bent over from the waist. She started to gather mugs and glasses, and the men started to help her, but Ruth stayed where she was.

"Not exactly. Don't we need to do our exploration?"

"Oh, that stuff is so complicated," David said. Maybe we can skip it this time. We're all okay about what happened, aren't we? It went well, didn't it?"

Ruth sat still. "Not complicated. Simple. What you liked, what pissed you off. Who wants to go first?"

RUTH AND JEREMY HAD NEVER discussed their separate-and-unequal meetings with Mark Smith, but his demeanor towards her was changed. Still no sense of humor, but neither was there any sarcasm. And just a smidgen of something that was either respect or arms-distance. Or maybe it was just that he knew he was stuck with her now.

She, in return, neither crowed nor made him eat crow, didn't play any trump cards when they disagreed about something. Equilibrium.

Shortly after the start of the New Year, Ruth took the elevator up to his office to deliver her news, dressed for the occasion in the silk jeans Vivian had made for her and her spiky, come-get-me heels. She was surprised she wasn't nervous and wanted to look over her shoulder for the missing second-guessing. As if reading a familiar bedtime story to a child to lull her to trust and let go, she thought through the events of the last few months.

About Face had been more successful than she'd dared hope. Good sales, great word-of-mouth—the kind of "this is the latest thing" attention that no amount of money can buy. It was as if they'd invented middle age. Or liberated all the middle-aged women who were imprisoned and ready to be sprung into being cool.

Ruth had been on a couple of talk shows, as had Jeremy. She'd given countless demonstrations, and given products away at well-publicized events to worthy charities. She'd even been on panels with psychologists to discuss the effects of aging on women. Most people at Mimosa were happy for her, though a few were too jealous for enthusiasm, but all were grateful for the profits and publicity she brought to the company.

The elevator dinged. Ruth heard it as a trumpet fanfare, announcing the soprano entering the stage to the wild applause of the audience. And part of the audience was the women of The Brain Trust who had, in fact, applauded her decision to start the business and leave Mimosa.

"So unlike you," they'd said.

"So bold."

"Go for it."

"Don't forget the free samples for us little people."

"Well, I guess we're not as little as we used to be. So we need you to do this."

"Congratulations."

Feeling every syllable of their encouragement, she told a tired and battle-weary Jeremy she was leaving. His surprise was hardly distinguishable from delight. Whenever he started to break into a smile, he'd widen his mouth to make his expression appear to be one of amazement instead of joy. Or fake a yawn. Ruth gave him credit for at least pretending.

He moved from the desk to the couch and invited her to sit on the preferred seat facing the window. He made some tea and asked her the kinds of questions a person would ask if they cared about you, like why she was leaving, what she'd be doing and where she'd be going. Since she wasn't telling anyone about Changing Patterns just yet, she was vague, mentioning that she had a few possibilities but would take some time off to reflect.

"That's a good idea," he said, patting her arm.

He told her about the time he'd left his first job after college and sensed he was at a huge fork in the road. Now that he looked back on it, he saw how many different ways there were to have a satisfying life, but at the time he'd thought there was only one "right answer." He'd always tried to impart that lesson to his boys but suspected his opinion of what they really should do came through without his intending it to. Quick smile.

It was the first time he'd ever spoken of his personal life. She knew she'd made his day and didn't even mind his pleasure or his transformation.

About Face's success would serve Changing Patterns very well, she was sure, creating a huge market for products for middle-aged women. In addition to the trendiness of maturity, her near-celebrity status would help with loans and publicity. Her name was on everyone's middle-aged lips and now she'd just move it down to their hips. She didn't feel triumphant, as she'd expected to, nor even vengeful. She just felt whole, like all the pieces of her disparate self were finding each other, shaking hands, and working together.

She and Jeremy briefly discussed who would succeed her. She liked to think he'd need to account for the way he'd allowed her to "slip through his fingers." One of the ways he'd try to redeem himself, she imagined, would be to try to attract a superstar from his previous company. She suspected Pat would hope for Ruth's job as soon as she heard about her resignation, even though she was hugely under-qualified. Thank goodness she wouldn't have to deal with Pat's disappointment and incomprehension at being passed over.

As Ruth left Jeremy's office, she found herself wishing she'd done this a lot sooner. The interchange was one of her favorite mental images, one she returned to from time to time as if looking at a photo in her hallway.

Oh well, she thought, and then realized that from the second she'd gotten up that morning and donned her inappropriate outfit until that very moment, it was her first "Oh well." She hummed her way down in the elevator, through the rest of her day and the next two weeks. On her last day at Mimosa, she wanted to burn her color-coded organizer, but settled for throwing it in the wastebasket.

32
Joy

IT HAD BEEN TEN MONTHS SINCE SHE'D LEFT Mimosa and they were working on Changing Patterns' second fall line. The first one had been small, because they'd had to rush, but it had been slightly more successful than their conservative projections for it. The Spring line was all designed and in the hands of the manufacturers, with every indication that it would do well enough to fund their first charitable contributions. For this second Fall line, they'd added cloth purses to their skirts, pants, and tops.

"Let's be the ones to finally invent the perfect purse," Ruth said, "big on the inside and small on the outside."

Even better than their moderate financial success was that, every time Ruth dared peer inside herself on a search-and-destroy mission for regret or anguish about the move from corporate executive to entrepreneur, she was relieved to find none. She'd left just the way she'd always wanted, on a high. In fact, leaving had been relatively easy once she'd done the hard part, *deciding* to leave.

As Ruth looked up from the laptop on which she was creating the Marketing Plan for the new line, she thought she saw a bowl of fish and rice in the middle of the table, just like the ones she used to have once a week in Senegal.

IBRAHIM N'DIAYE CAME TO PICK Ruth and Vivian up for their regular Thursday lunch at his house in the next town. About six months before, on one of his weekly trips to Djembering to sell bottled water, tomato paste and other staples to the kiosk that passed for a grocery store, he'd invited them for the first time. They never knew if it was courtesy, curiosity, or just to boost his prestige with his friends and neighbors. During that first lunch, he'd invited them for the next week, and, at some point, they'd agreed to swap English lessons for lunch. It meant Ibrahim had to make an extra round trip to Djembering to pick them up and then take them home again, but time was not a precious commodity and English was.

Like many Senegalese men, he was tall and thin, loose-limbed and athletic at the same time. He wore old blue jeans and a green tee shirt that was less faded than most. He looked completely natural in Western clothes, with no hint of how exotic he looked in his traditional powder blue full-length robe with dark blue embroidery.

He arrived in his "new" car, also his delivery truck, with a smile that would have taken over his face if he didn't try to rein it in. "Welcome into my automobile, my American friend ladies," he said as he opened the door for them. When the two girls got in, they saw that every dashboard button was missing, leaving the allotted spaces looking like empty eyeball sockets. The handles in the back doors had long ago been replaced with pieces of twine, themselves now on their last legs, and the seats were cracked and belching foam. Red dust covered every horizontal surface. None of these defects, though, seemed to detract from Ibrahim's pride in being the commander of this vehicle. Ruth and Vivian looked at each other and raised their eyebrows.

During the ten-kilometer trip over back roads that were little more than ruts in the sand, he swerved or slowed down at every hole, rock, and slow-moving herd, eager to extend whatever meager lifespan the car had remaining. The ride was bone-jarring nonetheless, even for 20-something bones. Ruth was finally getting the knack of releasing just enough of her hold on certain muscles so her body was flexible, absorbing some of the shock and making the bumps less violent. It had been a hard lesson to learn, that less control was softer in the long run. The trick was to find the balance point and not relax so much that she fell over.

The sky, a dusty blue with occasional wispy clouds, seemed bigger and more maternal than the sky at home. The landscape was in its muted dry-season palette. A pervasive brownness blanketed the faded colors of the sparse grasses and the scrawny goats and long-horned cattle. The exception to the brownness was the Senegalese women's clothing. Their exuberant splashes of color would have been brilliant anywhere, but against the subdued backdrop of the dry-season landscape, they were a riotous display. Their dresses and matching headscarves—blue, pink, fuchsia, yellow, green, and every other imaginable color—seemed to shout of a joy in color, indeed, in life. Ruth loved watching the women they passed on the road. They walked as gracefully and confidently as if they were on a models' runway, even with the loads they balanced on their heads.

At Ibrahim and Fatou's house, they walked past the pigeon coop on the left, under the laundry on the line, then picked their way between the chickens, roosters, and sheep. Fatou greeted them. Thin, with glasses too big for her face, she wore a red-orange cloth wrapped around the bottom half of her body, with a ruffled blouse of the same cloth. Like the cherry on the sundae, some of that cloth was also wrapped around her head.

Everyone greeted each other in the traditional way, beginning with "Nanga def?" Today's lunch crowd was smaller than usual, only Ibrahim and Fatou, their maid Aminata, and their three children—the two daughters, Ayisha and Maguette, and the son Abdou.

Aminata carried a wide shallow bowl, white with gaily painted flowers around the outside, covered by an inverted one just like it, like a giant white clam shell. In the middle of the yard, where two tall trees created an oasis of shade and gentle breezes, a large green and white woven mat had been laid on the ground. Aminata had a blue cloth under her arm, which Fatou removed and spread on top of the mat. Aminata set the bowl down.

Ruth, Vivian, and Ibrahim walked to the edge of the mat, took off their shoes, then joined Fatou and Aminata around the bowl. The children squeezed in wherever they could, on the mat or on a lap.

Fatou gave spoons to Ruth and Ibrahim, the only ones who wanted them, then uncovered the bowl of *thiebou dien*— fish and rice. To the Senegalese in this relatively prosperous village, it was just an ordinary lunch, something they had four or five times a week, but to Ruth and Vivian, it was a treat: a mound of rice cooked in a savory tomato-based sauce, topped by chunks of herb-stuffed fish. And there were vegetables on the mound, too: carrots, cabbage, even eggplant. The air in the circle was filled with smells of the food, the hair pomade used by the African women, the animals, and the children's sweetness. Julietta, a neighbor and friend, arrived just as they started eating. She offered and received an abbreviated greeting, took a spoon and sat down in the space everyone made for her in the circle.

Conversation became spirited, with elaborate teasing about whether it was better to be the first wife of the household, as Fatou was for Ibrahim, or a second wife, as Aminata was for her husband Babacar. Fatou and Aminata broke off pieces of the fish and vegetables with their right hand and distributed them around the edge of the bowl in front of each person. Those who ate with their hands took some rice, fish, and vegetables with their right hand, squeezed the liquid out, then stuck out their tongue as they brought their hand up to their mouth. They put the egg-shaped lump on their outstretched tongue, looking as if they were licking their hand. Fish bones and other rejected matter dropped unceremoniously from mouth to ground.

Three-year old Maguette got up from Aminata's lap, went outside the circle of eaters, removed her shoe, then threw it at the bowl, pleased with her feat. Her smile faded, though, at Julietta's reaction, a trumpet-blast of Wolof. Was the scolding for spoiling the food or the shoe? Maguette cried briefly, then looked around for another lap. Julietta went back to her lunch.

A little later, Abdou, the chubby two-year old, slapped his older sister Ayisha. At four years old, she was barely bigger than him, and returned the blow only half-heartedly before tearfully seeking shelter in her father's lap. Ibrahim comforted her absent-mindedly while talking to Julietta. No one reprimanded Abdou, nor cared who started the fight. The eating and talking continued, with everyone taking care of the kids as if they were their own, whether providing a lap, a handful of food, or a scolding. Anything except a breast, which Abdou knew exactly where to find. No one seemed particularly concerned about the fish-bones or the sand Ruth was horrified to see the kids occasionally scooping up and eating.

Many years later, when Ruth heard the expression "It takes a village to raise a child," she thought of lunches with Ibrahim, Fatou and the kids and the way everyone took care of all of them.

Abdou came over to Ruth tentatively, and, after much consideration, sat in her lap for the first time. He was the last hold-out of the kids, who had all been terrified of the white girls at first but eventually came around. He pulled on her earring and giggled. When he saw her smile, he tried the other earring. Another smile. He investigated the rest of her face, the tip of her nose, her lips, touching and pinching and stretching. Finally, he got bored and just sat in her lap peacefully. Ruth's Wolof wasn't quite as good as Vivian's, but she followed enough of the musical-sounding conversation around the lunch bowl to laugh at the right times and even contribute a thought now and then. She hugged Abdou and relaxed.

Unfurling the cramped leg she'd folded under her at the start of her extended daydream, she surveyed the scene in the Design and Sample Room of Changing Patterns' offices. Six women were sitting in a friendly circle around the oversized distressed-oak table in the middle of the high-ceilinged room. What she'd daydreamed into a bowl of fish and rice was a colorful jumble of fabrics, threads, ribbons, laces, buttons, and other assorted notions, mingled with colored papers, markers and tape. At various times, one or another of them would reach into the pile to get one of the items. She'd hold it up to her work and decide to use it. Or decide not to, and throw it back on the pile. Ordered chaos. Or was it chaotic order?

Along one wall, jutting into the central space like Rockettes' legs, sewing machines and ironing boards alternated. A woman was in each space between a sewing machine and an ironing board, turning from one to the other as she worked. The air was filled with conversations, Carole King singing "Tapestry," and the steady hum of needles penetrating fabric to create seams.

Ruth often preferred working here in the room they called the Student Union to her own office in one of the surrounding cubicles. Even though there was no carpeting or photographs of her family, there was a wall-size collage of the staff's photographs and there were child-painted murals of their products.

She realized it wasn't just the pile of notions in the center of the table that reminded her of the fish and rice. It was the fellowship. It was the community, the wholeness.

Vivian was cutting pieces of fabric she pulled from the middle of the table and gluing or stitching them, adding flourishes with ribbons and even markers, to design new garments, which the others were producing as samples for the new line to be sent to their manufacturing plant. The women at the sewing machines and irons were blocking the clothes together, while those at the table were adding the signature Changing Patterns embellishments, the flowers and birds that looked like embroidery and sometimes were.

Vivian and Ruth knew it was an unorthodox approach to clothing design, but it worked for this unusual village of entrepreneurs.

They were all working against a tight deadline, which they had to make because any delays in getting the samples to the factory cost money their tight budget could not afford. Everywhere was activity: cutting, stitching, embroidering, folding, wrapping, labeling.

"Jeannie, hand me that clump of greenish embroidery thread, would ya?" Martha asked. She was a heavy-set 40-ish woman with hair that had once been salt and pepper but whose salt, in an unfortunate henna accident, had been replaced by a garish orange so she now looked like an orange and brown tabby cat. A tabby cat whose orange roots were growing out white.

"Okay, but … green? On that pink denim? Are you sure that's what you want?" Jeannie asked.

"Hey, I'm having my own private little brainstorming session over here—"

"Is that sort of like playing with yourself?"

"Not so exciting." She frowned. "I'm just trying a little of this and a little of that. And then I'll see what works," Martha said.

"Okay, whatever." Jeannie threw the thread to the other end of the table. "But I thought Vivian was the designer."

"That's okay," Vivian said. "I design it the way I like it, and then if you can make it better, that's fine by me. As long as you make it better by…."

She looked up at the wall calendar above the row of sewing machines. "Hey, would someone please turn the page of the calendar so we're looking at this month?"

One of the sewers obliged. "That's better. As I was saying, you just need to do what you need to do by next Tuesday."

"I hear ya," Martha said.

A baby cried. Joan looked at her watch, then went over to the port-a-crib in the corner, saying "Milk and cookies time, right on schedule." She was a large woman, in her thirties, with an athlete's gait and a soothing voice. She picked up her five-month-old and brought her over to the table. She unbuttoned her polka dot blouse, put Celeste in nursing position, and continued working.

"Be careful you don't get breast milk on the clothes," Vivian said.

"Get off my back, boss—or, rather, my front. It just happened that once, anyway. Besides, you didn't mind that time we ran out of milk for the coffee and I became the resident cow."

"I still can't believe you did that. And I thought *I* was the nutty one."

"Hah. Move over, old lady. I'm gunning for your reputation."

Joy skipped into the room. She stopped just inside the door and looked around, then spotted her mother at one of the sewing machines. She skipped over to her.

"Guess what, mommy."

"What, Joy?" Ruth and Vivian said at the same time as Harriet, Joy's mother.

"I got 100 on the math test. I told you I would."

Harriet gave Joy a big hug. "That's great, sweetie. You're a genius."

"Hey, me too," Ruth said.

Joy skipped around the table and presented her cheek for Ruth's kiss. Then she walked over to Vivian and presented her cheek.

"You're gettin' pretty kissy, missy," Vivian said as she complied.

Joan said, "Just in time for a little baby-sitting, if you don't mind." She pulled Celeste away from her breast and handed her to Joy's eagerly outstretched arms.

"Wait a second," Ruth said. "What about her homework?"

"And her snack?" Jeannie asked. Turning to Joy and smiling flirtatiously, she said, "I brought those cookies you like so much. Don't you want one? Or two?"

"Yes, I do I do I do. I'll eat them while I play with Celeste. And then I'll do my homework after." She looked over at Harriet for approval.

"Hell-LOW, everyone," Vivian said in a sing-song voice. "We have a deadline, remember?"

Ruth lifted her head, reached under the braid her hair had gotten barely long enough to form, and reflexively massaged her neck. It was hot and sweaty. Is this a hot flash? she wondered. Don't know. It's Indian summer and it's hot in here so maybe it's not. Or maybe it is.

She absorbed the colors of the jumbled fabric, the motion and noises of the sewing, the smells of food and even people, simultaneously, also realizing how much she enjoyed what she was doing. Not for the possibility of success, nor even for the grandiose ideas about helping women feel better. She just enjoyed it. More than enjoyed it; she couldn't wait to get to work every day.

Here it is, she thought. The present moment I've always wanted to be in. I used to think I wanted closure, but this is better. Closure is really a little taste of death.

Colleen poked her head in the room. "Ruth, you have a phone call? And guess what? It's Ann, the buyer from Bloomingdale's. Can you take it?"

"Oh thank goodness she finally called back. I'll come back to my office to take it. Thanks."

She thought about how to sweet-talk the buyer as she went through the dark curved hallway to her office, enjoying the click of her high heels on the concrete floor. It turned out that no sweet-talk was necessary, and Ann put her on the calendar—a little sooner than Ruth would have wished, as it turned out.

Ruth called David at home and left a message on the machine. "Hi, hon, I know you're taking advantage of the weather to say hello to the golf course, but I wanted you to find this message waiting when you get back. Guess what! I'm on Ann's calendar for day after tomorrow. It was easy. Also, I spoke to Josh this morning and I haven't had a second to call until now. He's coming to dinner tonight. We're not doing anything, are we? I'll stop on the way home and get some fish. Would you make your wonderful risotto? The one with the wild mushrooms? And a salad? He's bringing dessert. And his new girlfriend. Maybe I'll see if Vivian and Carlos want to come, too. Okay? I love you. Oh, by the way, Joy got 100 on her math test. Isn't that great?"

As she hung up, she looked at the three-photo frame on her desk, a congratulations present from David. On the left was "Baby Ruth," the very picture of her twenty-two-year-old self she'd brought to the village when she went back at thirty-six. In the middle was "Married Ruth Holding Baby Ruth," the photo David had taken during their visit. And on the right was a photo taken last year, of her fifty-three-year old self—"Grown-Up Ruth"—holding the photo called "Married Ruth Holding Baby Ruth." Going around the frame was Rumi's advice to "Exist as you are or be as you look." A story within a story within a story.

She loved the way the triptych depicted the thread running from then to now. More than a thread, really. She was the same person. That was her *and* this was her. Maybe the outside had aged but the inside had grown.

She thought about how much she'd have to do to prepare for the meeting at Bloomingdale's, wondering how she'd manage to get it all done in time. She thought about Joy's math test, her pleasure magnified by Joy's own glee. The thought of Josh and his new girlfriend sent her mind galloping into the future, with warmth and its maternal companion, worry. And she also realized how much she craved David's risotto and wild mushrooms dish, redolent of the woods and the earth, at the same time she knew she'd been allowing herself caloric liberties lately because of the generous fit of her new Changing Patterns pants.

The emotional mix felt like a casserole, each ingredient heightening the others' impact. Like mixing spike heels with her hippy pants, or being an entrepreneur who does good for the world, like starting a business when it's time to retire.

She started back down the corridor to the nexus of light and activity in the Design and Sample Room. It felt like being in the subway, going around a curve between stations, and seeing the back car when you're in the front. Or maybe it was seeing the front when you're in the back. Something about time collapsing. "Well, well, well," she thought.

About the Author

CAROLE HOWARD has published short fiction, personal essays, a walking guide to Paris, and two novels. She has traveled extensively, visiting and/or volunteering in about fifty countries, including fifteen in Africa. Her African experiences inform both novels. Carole lives with her husband in New York's beautiful Mid-Hudson Valley.

www.ingramcontent.com/pod-product-compliance
Lightning Source LLC
LaVergne TN
LVHW010638110826
845149LV00014B/2882

* 9 7 8 0 9 8 5 2 9 4 8 5 4 *